THE MAKANA'S LEGACY

M. K. ALEJA

ISBN: 979-8-9900390-4-9

*For my parents, who taught me
faith and unconditional love.*

A Note to Readers

Throughout this novel, you will encounter phrases in the CHamoru language. To enhance your reading experience, I have provided a glossary of translations at the back of the book. Please refer to this glossary whenever you need to understand these phrases or learn how they are pronounced.

MAP OF GUAM

N
W E
S
Philippine Sea
Andersen Air Force Base
Yigo
Dededo
Tamuning
Hagatña
Guam Int'l Airport
Asan
Maite
Piti
Barrigada
Naval Base Guam
Sinajaña
Ordot
Mangilao
Chalan Pago
Pacific Ocean
Yona
Agat
Santa Rita
Talofofo
Umatac
Inarajan
Merizo
Cocos Island
Guam
(United States)
Capital
Road
Airport
0   5 Kilometers
0   5 Miles

Contents

Prologue

The soft wind blew across the island, carrying the smell of the ocean and the jungle with it. The waves gently lapped at the golden sand before pulling back into the deep, endless sea. The huge palm trees swayed with the breeze, and the sounds of the jungle were calm, blending into the quiet of the darkness. It was a peaceful night.

However, that peace would not last.

In a small village hidden in the heart of the jungle, there was movement. A young girl hurried up a ladder to her family's home, her heart racing as she slipped inside. Her mom quickly pulled her close, shushing her gently but firmly and hiding her beneath a pile of woven mats. The air was heavy with tension, and even the insects, usually loud at night, seemed to quiet down as if they knew something huge was coming.

Outside, an old man sat by his thatched hut. His skin was dark and weathered from long years of being under the constant rays of the sun, and his face marked with deep wrinkles, each telling a story of hardship, wisdom and responsibility. His name was Napo, and he was a *makåna,* one of the last of his kind. In front of him sat a small altar, where the skulls once belonging to his ancestors were carefully placed. These skulls had once been honored and respected, but now, fewer people believed in their power and that of the spirit world.

Napo knelt down and gently placed offerings of food and small tokens on the altar. His words were filled with sadness as he whispered in an ancient language, praying to the spirits of his ancestors. The connection between his people and the spirit world was growing weaker with each generation, and the Spanish invaders were to blame. The old ways, once central to their lives, were fading, and with them, the spirits were growing silent.

A sound came from the jungle - the rustling of leaves and snapping of branches. Napo lifted his head, eyes wide as his hands trembled. It wasn't the spirits answering his prayers. Instead, it was something far worse. Spanish soldiers burst through the trees, their armor glinting in the moonlight and faces unforgiving and hard with anger.

There was nowhere left to run, leaving Napo to stand his ground, though he knew what was coming. He was old, and he had seen many things in his life, but nothing like this. The Spanish had come to take his land, his people, and their way of life. They no longer allowed the old ways, calling them witchcraft and heathenism. To the Spanish, Napo was not a healer - he was an enemy of their new order.

The soldiers grabbed Napo and forced him to the ground, his body pressing hard into the dirt. They kicked, beat, and spat on him, his blood mixing with the earth. He could barely breathe, but what hurt him most was watching as they destroyed his altar. The skulls of his ancestors, so precious to him, were crushed beneath their boots.

The year was 1565, and Spain had claimed the island and outlawed the beliefs and practices of the CHamoru people. The *makåna*, who had once been respected as both protectors and healers, were now treated like criminals. The invisible thread that tied the people to their ancestors was being severed, strand by strand.

As Napo lay on the ground, weak and broken, he whispered his final prayer. It wasn't a plea for help. He knew there was no saving him now. Instead, it was a message to the spirits. He called out to them one last time, not for himself, but for the future of his people.

Even as his body gave out, the spirits heard him. Though their voices were faint, they were still there, watching from the shadows. Napo's time had come to an end, and the spirits of his ancestors stood ready to welcome him.

In the years that followed, the Spanish's grip tightened. Slowly the knowledge of the ancient healers was forgotten and dismissed as superstition. Fewer children were born with the gift, and fewer still were taught to recognize the signs. The *makåna*, once symbols of hope and wisdom, were nearly forgotten.

But even in the darkest time, there is always a spark of light. For as Napo's body grew cold in the dirt, the spirits were preparing for the birth of a new soul. One that would carry the traces of a lost legacy. They would walk the line between the living and the dead, between the old ways and the new.

The spirits waited patiently, knowing that their bond with the living could not be lost. As they made plans to restore that sacred connection, something dark and sinister lurked in the shadows, waiting for its moment to corrupt the bond and spread its own darkness.

Chapter 1

Troubled Youth

In her tiny living room, Annie Leon Guerrero sat with her fingers twisting the frayed beads of her rosary. The gentle ticking of the clock was the only sound that broke the afternoon silence. Like every single day, she prayed for strength, and because life hadn't been easy for her, she often found herself repeating the same words time and again, "God gives his toughest battles to his strongest soldiers." She had held onto those words throughout the years, especially after Pedro's death.

The one thing that had kept her grounded despite her grief had been her faith. First, she had lost her husband,

Pedro, and now, it felt like she was losing Joleen too, her only daughter. Even in the most challenging situations, Annie had always trusted that God had a purpose. Lately, however, she had been wondering how much more she could take. She prayed harder, asking for guidance, patience, and above all, Joleen's physical and emotional well-being.

Outside, the world went on as usual, the chatter of neighbors and distant hum of traffic providing a backdrop to Annie's solitude. Everything around her felt distant and blurred, as if she were watching life through frosted glass. Her thoughts returned to Joleen and the growing distance between them, trapping her in her own bubble of anxiety. She had always thought that a mother's love could protect her kids from the brutalities in the world, but she wasn't so sure anymore. Joleen had slipped out of her grasp, and no amount of faith seemed to bring her back.

Annie's home was modest, a small concrete house surrounded by a garden that she had tended for years. To her, the garden was a place where she could escape the worries of life for a few moments of peace. It was full of vibrant plants and flowers that flourished under her care. The air was always rich with the smell of damp earth and blooming flowers, giving the garden an almost sacred feel. The house itself sat at the edge of the village, not far from the main road, but tucked away enough to give her a sense of privacy.

Every morning, Annie would step out onto the small

porch with a cup of coffee, taking in the view of the garden before starting her daily chores. However, this daily ritual also reminded her of everything she had lost. On this particular Sunday morning, the sky was clear, and a soft breeze blew through the trees, rustling the leaves. Deciding to take a stroll through her yard, she tied her shoulder-length dark brown hair - a few strands of grey beginning to show - using a hair tie atop her head and got up from her couch. Stepping out through her front door, she walked slowly, taking in the beauty around her.

Her mango tree was starting to fill in with branches and leaves, a promising sign, but she knew it would still take a couple more years before it would bear fruit. She had almost a dozen banana trees in two varieties, but only a couple of bunches were visible and just beginning to grow. As she moved further along, Annie discovered some guava and a juicy papaya ripe for picking. She smiled at the thought of sharing her harvest with her coworkers. Her little papaya grove was filled with even more papayas, each one larger than a cantaloupe, soon to be ready for harvest. She also checked her hot pepper plants, known as *donne' ti'au*, which always seemed to have peppers ready to pick.

Annie and her late husband, Pedro, had loved that they could grow most of their favorite fruits and vegetables right in their own yard. It was one of the many joys of living on a lush, tropical island like Guam. The vibrant vegetation hid most of their single-story concrete home from view. Aside from their covered carport, what could be seen from the street was a well-manicured lawn, with healthy trees and plants surrounding them. But for the past couple of years, the stroll through her yard and the discovery of produce ready to harvest had held little joy for Annie. Each step felt heavier, each moment of solitude reminding her of the emptiness in her heart.

She had never imagined she would have to raise Joleen on her own. When she married Pedro, she thought they would grow old together, side by side, watching their daughter flourish. Pedro had been the love of her life; steady, hardworking, and full of warmth. He wasn't a man of many words, but his presence had been enough. His love for Annie and Joleen was always clear, even in the small gestures - like the way he would bring home fresh coconut for Joleen after a long day of work, or the way he would quietly fix things around the house without being asked.

Pedro worked as an electrician, a job that wasn't without risks but provided their family with stability. Thanks to his steady paycheck, Annie was able to save money, and they didn't have to worry about a mortgage. Life felt secure, and even though she still worked, Annie knew they had built a good life together.

But one day, everything changed. It was just another shift at the power plant for Pedro, like so many before. Annie had kissed him goodbye that morning, expecting to see him back home for dinner. But the call came instead. There had been an accident - something had gone horribly wrong while Pedro was working on a generator. The details were vague and confusing, but what Annie knew for sure was that Pedro wasn't coming home.

Joleen had only been fifteen years old at the time, far too young to lose her father, and the grief had hit her hard. The funeral had been a blur, with friends and family offering condolences, their words never quite reaching both mother and daughter. Pedro was gone, and nothing anyone could say would change that. Annie had tried to be strong - she had no choice but to be. She still had to work because her job at the bank demanded it. She had worked there for most of her life, climbing the ranks to her current position as a supervisor. The hours were long, but it was steady work, and it kept food on the table. And yet, no matter how hard she tried, she couldn't seem to reach Joleen.

Her daughter had grown quieter and more withdrawn in the years after Pedro's death, and there had been nothing Annie could do to bridge the gap that seemed to widen between them. Joleen had always been close to Christine Soriano, her best friend since childhood. The two girls had been inseparable, always laughing, always together, and Christine had acted as an excellent distraction for Joleen after Pedro's death.

She would walk Joleen home from the bus stop after school. They would hang out at Joleen's house and do their homework together while Annie was at work.

Christine's dad would then pick her up in the evenings to take her home. This wasn't every day, of course. But Christine typically spent most of her time with Joleen. That was until 1969... Joleen's high school senior year. Seemingly overnight, things went from good to bad to very bad for Joleen, and there was nothing Annie could do to stop it.

Christine's family relocated to the village of Agat in January of that school year. That meant that she and Joleen would be on opposite ends of the island and going to different schools. Christine's family had been renting a house on the outskirts of the village of Dededo, not far from Joleen's house. But when her dad landed a job down at Naval Base Guam, they could finally afford to buy a house. Rather than making the forty-minute commute between Dededo and his new job at Naval Base Guam, also known as Big Navy, Christine's dad decided to buy a house in Agat, which was much closer to the base.

After the move, Christine and Joleen would speak on the phone almost on a daily basis. But they were in different schools and could no longer do their homework together. As time passed, the two had less and less to talk about. So, Joleen began to shut herself away, as though the loss of her father and her best friend had been too much for her young heart to bear. Annie had hoped it was just a phase, something Joleen would grow out of with time. But things only got worse when she met Ben.

Vicente "Ben" Cruz was everything a good parent

would warn their daughters to avoid. He was reckless, always riding his motorcycle too fast, and to top it off, a high school drop-out. He was also older than Joleen by a few years, and Annie didn't trust him from the moment she laid eyes on him. There was something about the way he carried himself - the swagger and the carelessness in his smile - that set her on edge. And yet, Joleen had been drawn to him. He wasn't all that attractive. And as far as Annie knew, he didn't have a job. *So, where was he getting his money from?* Annie could only imagine the worst, and she desperately hoped that he would not pull Joleen into anything illegal that he might be involved in.

Joleen would hang out with Ben after school instead of heading home from the bus stop like she was supposed to. And when she did get home, Ben would be in the house with her. Annie knew this because her neighbor across the street, Janet Pangelinan, would tell her everything. Annie and Janet often met to chat a little before the Saturday evening mass that they both attended each week. Janet would know when Joleen and Ben came and left the house because Ben's motorcycle was very loud. She reported that sometimes, Ben would walk Joleen into the house and then leave a few minutes later. But most of the time, he would stay for an hour or two.

But Annie couldn't do much about that, being stuck working at the bank until closing time. One evening, Annie told Joleen that she didn't want Ben, or any other guy, in the house when she was not there. If they didn't stop that, she would call the police and report Ben for trespassing.

"You're always listening to gossip, and you don't know him like I do!" Joleen had yelled, slamming the bedroom door behind her.

Annie had stood outside the door, her heart heavy with a mixture of anger and despair. She wanted to protect her daughter, but Joleen's rebellious streak made it nearly impossible to get to her. After their argument, Joleen began getting home later in the afternoon from school. This led to Annie no longer knowing her daughter's whereabouts after school.

The only thing Annie knew about Ben was that he was way older than Joleen, but she didn't know much more about him than that. Her daughter usually tried to avoid talking about Ben or about what they did when they were together. So most of Annie's information on Ben actually came from Janet. Janet always seemed to have the best gossip. It was she who had mentioned that Ben had dropped out of school. When Annie brought it up with Joleen, she would argue that he didn't need school because he made his own money. Annie didn't know what that meant, but it absolutely was not reassuring in any way.

All Annie could really do was pray for her daughter. Trying to talk to Joleen at that time was almost guaranteed to result in an argument. The fact that Joleen was not skipping school and her grades were still okay gave Annie even less to complain about. Joleen graduated from high school that year, and just barely a few months later, without any warning or discussion, Joleen packed her things and moved out of the house to live with Ben.

Annie's house was at the northern end of Dededo. Ben's apartment was in the village of Chalan Pågo. That was about a 25-minute drive from Annie's house, which suited Joleen just fine. Annie never saw Ben's apartment, and Joleen never told her where it was. But she would visit Annie occasionally, though her visits were primarily to ask for money.

It wasn't long after Joleen left the house to live with Ben that Annie began to notice small changes in her daughter during the brief visits they had. Joleen's body language was different - she seemed more withdrawn, her eyes avoiding her mother's gaze more often than before. But there were other, more physical signs too. Joleen's clothes seemed to fit differently, her face was a little fuller, she seemed to be nauseous almost all the time, and Annie couldn't help but notice how tired she looked.

At first, Annie tried to push the thought away. It was too much to consider, too frightening. But the more she saw Joleen, the more convinced she became. Annie's mind raced with worry. *Could Joleen be pregnant?* And if she was, what did that mean for her future? For their relationship?

Annie tried to broach the subject gently, but Joleen

quickly shut her down. "I'm fine, Mom. Stop worrying," she would say, her tone dismissive and defensive.

But Annie couldn't stop worrying. Every time she saw Joleen, her suspicions grew stronger. She wanted to confront her daughter directly, but she was afraid of pushing her further away. The tension between them was already thick, and Annie feared that bringing up the possibility of a pregnancy would be the final blow to their fragile relationship. As the year neared its end, Annie was sure that Joleen was pregnant. She brought it up once again and suggested that Joleen see a doctor, but her daughter refused, saying that she didn't want to be waiting for hours at the Public Health clinic.

It was no surprise that Annie had started spending a lot of time at Santa Barbara Church. She had lived in Dededo her whole life, and Santa Barbara had always been her parish. Her job at Guam Savings and Loan was just a ten-minute walk from the church, making it easy for her to attend mass more frequently. What had started with her usual Saturday evening masses, soon turned into her attending weeknight masses after work. Annie went, of course, to pray for her daughter, Joleen. But the truth was, she also went to avoid the loneliness of sitting at home alone with her thoughts.

This had been her routine, until just a few days later.

The evening news reported that a young man had been killed in a motorcycle accident earlier that week. He had been speeding through the village of Sinajaña on wet roads late at night. Annie's heart sank when she heard it. *What would Ben have been doing in Sinajaña so late at night?* She couldn't understand it, but deep down, a terrible feeling crept over her. She just knew it was Ben in the accident.

And then, before she could stop herself, a shocking thought flashed through her mind, *I hope it's him.* The moment the thought formed, Annie gasped in horror at herself. "God, please forgive me!" she cried out loud, shaken by the awful thought she had just had. How could she even think such a thing? Annie had always taken pride in her faith, in her kindness, and in her Catholic values. She had always tried to be compassionate and nonjudgmental. But now, she felt ashamed. "Lord, forgive me. I didn't mean it," she whispered again, her voice trembling.

But she knew why the thought had surfaced. Deep down, all she wanted was for Joleen to come home.

Annie tried to reach Joleen after hearing about the accident. She tried calling her over and over, but there was no answer. Each time the phone rang, Annie's worry grew stronger. *Where was she? Was she okay? Had something happened to her too?* Annie's thoughts raced with fear, but she had no way to reach her daughter. She didn't even know where Joleen and Ben's apartment was. All she could do was wait, her heart heavy with worry as the hours passed.

That night, Annie lay in bed, staring at the ceiling. The soft hum of the fan and the sound of the trees outside did nothing to calm her mind. She couldn't stop thinking about Joleen and the accident. But there was nothing she could do except wait, pray, and hope that Joleen would come back to her before it was too late.

Chapter 2

The Spirits That Linger

Joleen sat on the edge of Ben's bed, staring blankly at the wall opposite her. The morning sun poured through the window, illuminating dust motes dancing in the air, but it brought her no comfort. Two days had passed since she received the devastating news about Ben's death in a motorcycle accident, and the shock still felt raw, like an open wound. She felt disconnected from reality, as though she were trapped in a fog that wouldn't lift.

Her mind raced with different emotions - grief, anger, confusion. The memories of their time together played in her head, reminding her of both the love they shared and the difficulties that had marked their relationship. The disagreements, the moments of betrayal, the laughter - it was suddenly all jumbled together, and she couldn't make sense of it all.

She looked around the small apartment in Chalan Pågo, feeling lost among Ben's belongings that were scattered around the apartment. His clothes all over the place, with his favorite leather jacket hanging over the back of a chair, the smell of gasoline lingering on it, and his motorcycle helmet sat on the table, reminding her of the reckless life he had led. To her, each item told a story, whether of laughter or pain. Even the walls seemed to be lined with memories of them together - the pictures of their adventures and the small notes he had hung for her on the walls.

Joleen couldn't help but still feel attached to him, and with each breath she drew, it was as if the apartment had a tight hold on her.

"Why can't I just leave?" she whispered to herself, the words hanging in the air.

She knew she should go back to her mother, Annie, who had been calling her nonstop, worrying about her well-being. But the thought of leaving this place felt impossible because she felt bound by the memories of their time together.

She got up and went to the window, pushing it open to let in the warm island air. The sounds of everyday life could be heard all around, including kids laughing, neighbors chatting, and the distant hum of the passing cars below. Life continued as usual outside, but Joleen felt like she was stuck in a time loop of never-ending grief. She shut her eyes in the hopes that the sunlight would drive away the cold that was beginning to seep into her bones, but it didn't do much to relieve the pressure on her chest.

*****

Days passed in a blur, each one blending into the next. Joleen fell into a routine of waking up, staring at the ceiling, and feeling overwhelmed by the memories of Ben. She woke up every morning with the same thought, *Ben was gone.* She would then sit in silence, staring at the wall and feeling the emptiness in her chest growing larger day by day. However, the nights were the worst. She would lie in bed and stare at the shadows dancing on the walls as the darkness crept into the corners of the room.

At times while she lay in bed, she often felt as if something was lurking just beyond her vision. At first, she dismissed it as her mind playing tricks on her, the result of too much grief and not enough sleep. However, the sensation was persistent, growing stronger each night. She would hear the faintest rustle - a whisper of movement in the darkness - as if the shadows on her wall were alive and watching her.

One evening, as she lay in bed, a strange noise broke the silence; it seemed to be coming from the living room.

Joleen sat up, her heart racing and breath quickening. The cool vinyl floor sent a chill up her spine as she swung her legs over the edge of the bed. *Was someone in the apartment?* She told herself it was nothing more than her imagination playing tricks on her, but the doubt tormented her.

Gathering enough courage to go and check what the noise was, she crept toward the door, her heart pounding like a drum in her chest. With a shaky hand, she turned the doorknob and peeked into the hallway. The shadows seemed to swallow the light, stretching out like long fingers reaching toward her.

"Hello?" she called out, her voice trembling, but there was only silence.

Moving forward, she stepped into the living room, and her gaze fell upon the coffee table. A picture frame had fallen over, and its glass was shattered on the floor. "How did that happen?" she wondered out aloud, her heart racing. Careful not to hurt herself, she bent down to pick up the pieces, but as she reached for the frame, a cold draft brushed by her, raising the hairs on her arms and legs. Suddenly, the air around her felt electric and thick with tension.

"I'm just tired," she murmured, trying to dismiss the feeling of dread. "It's just my mind." But as she straightened up, the air seemed heavier, settling around her, making it hard to breathe. She looked around the apartment, searching for an explanation, but all she found was an eerie silence.

Her days slipped into a repetitive cycle of fear and exhaustion. Every night, she would lie in bed, haunted by dreams that felt too real. In one, she saw Ben standing at the edge of a dark abyss, his face hidden by shadows. He reached out to her, but his hand was cold, almost skeletal. "You have to help me," he pleaded, his voice echoing in the darkness.

"Help you?" she gasped, but as she stretched her hand forward, the dream shattered, and she woke up gasping for air, her pulse racing. Each time she fell asleep, the nightmares returned with more intensity. One vivid dream showed Ben standing at the foot of her bed, his eyes dark and accusing. "Why didn't you save me?" he screamed, a mixture of rage and sorrow twisting his features.

With each passing night, the dreams drained her spirit further. She felt like a hollow shell whenever she woke up, and her energy was constantly drained as if something were feeding off her despair. The line between what was real and what was just a dream blurred, and soon, she couldn't tell what was happening anymore. *Was Ben really gone? Or was he trapped here, reaching out to her from the shadows?*

One afternoon, while trying to distract herself, Joleen searched through some old boxes in the corner of the living room. She stumbled upon a collection of items that belonged to Ben, including old photos, concert tickets, and notes he had written. As she flipped through the memories, a sense of nostalgia washed over her, mingled with pain. She smiled at a picture of them at the beach, arms wrapped around each other, showing them as carefree and happy.

But as she moved deeper into the box, something strange caught her eye. Ben's motorcycle keys were nowhere to be found. She could have sworn she had left them on the table that morning, but they were gone. "Where are you?" she muttered, searching through the box, pushing aside papers and trinkets. A deep sense of unease settled in her stomach.

She decided to head to the kitchen for a glass of water, hoping to shake off the feeling. As she poured the water, a cold breeze swept through the room, making her shiver. She glanced around, noting that the windows were closed, yet the chill lingered, seeping into her bones. It felt as if the walls were breathing and alive with some unseen energy.

"Maybe I just need some fresh air," she thought, shaking her head. She stepped outside, letting the warm island afternoon sun surround her, but the feeling of dread lingered. So she walked along the street, trying to clear her head.

When she got back to the apartment that evening, the sun had already set and the shadows were growing darker around her. As she entered the apartment, she felt the usual chill and heaviness of the darkness pressing down on her. She forced a smile and told herself, *I can do this*, but the atmosphere felt oppressively heavy that night.

As she settled into bed, the nightmares returned, clear and terrifying. She dreamed of Ben again, his face twisted in anguish. "You don't understand!" he shouted, reaching out as though to pull her into the darkness. She woke with a start, the room cold, and her breath visible in the air. "Why is it so cold?" she gasped, wrapping her arms around herself for warmth.

Suddenly, she heard it - a soft whisper, just barely audible, drifting through the silence in the room.

"Joleen..."

It was faint but unmistakable, and it was a voice that sent shivers down her spine. She sat up, straining to listen as her heart raced.

"Ben?" she called out, her voice trembling, but there was only silence in response.

She was unable to sleep that night because she had an unsettling feeling of being watched. As the hours passed slowly, she sat in the dark, staring at the shadows. The feeling grew more intense the longer she remained awake. The shadows in the room's corners appeared to move, growing longer and twisting.

She finally gathered enough courage to go investigate, getting out of bed and tiptoeing into the hallway. The sound of the floor creaking beneath her feet could be heard in the silence. As she reached the living room, she noticed the curtains fluttering even though the windows were closed, their fabric shifted as if someone had just brushed past them. A shiver went up her spine and her pulse quickened.

In the dim light, she could see Ben's jacket hanging on a chair. As she approached it, she noticed something odd, the jacket was draped in a way that made it look as though someone had just taken it off.

"This is ridiculous," she scolded herself, shaking her head. "It's just the wind."

But deep down, she felt the unease settling in her gut. With a deep breath, she turned to head back to bed, but as she reached her room, she caught a glimpse of movement in her peripheral vision. A shadow had swiftly flitted past the open doorway.

Joleen froze, her heart thumping in her chest. She squinted into the dark hallway, her breath quickening as she struggled to see what had just passed by. A thousand thoughts raced through her mind. *Was it just her imagination? Perhaps the traces of a nightmare lasting in her waking hours? Or was there truly something there, something that was watching her from the shadows?*

"Hello?" she called out, her voice barely above a whisper.

The word hung in the air, swallowed by the deafening silence. She took a hesitant step forward, the floorboards once again creaking under her weight. The faint light from the streetlamp outside spilled through the window, creating shadows across the walls.

As she entered the hallway again, the chill intensified. It was as if a cold hand had brushed against her skin, sending a wave of goosebumps rippling down her arms.

She glanced over her shoulder, half-expecting to see Ben's familiar figure standing behind her in their bedroom, but only darkness greeted her.

Taking a deep breath, she continued back to the living room, her eyes scanning the space. The curtains fluttered again, and she noticed the faint outline of her own reflection in the window. It seemed distorted, almost ghostly. Shaking her head, she tried to dismiss the fear that nagged her. She was alone in the apartment - she had to be.

But as she turned back toward the hallway, she felt something brush across her ankle. Heart racing, Joleen jumped back. She looked down to find Ben's motorcycle keys lying on the floor; however, she was certain that they had not been there earlier. "How did you get here?" she breathed, picking them up and holding them tightly in her palm. The metal felt cold against her skin, sending another shiver coursing through her.

Suddenly, the apartment was filled with a loud crash that boomed off the walls. The noise seemed to have come from the kitchen, and for a moment, Joleen felt paralyzed and rooted to the spot in fear. A thousand scenarios played out in her mind, each one worse than the last. Could someone be in the apartment with her? *Was Ben's spirit truly here, or was it something more sinister?*

With her heart hammering, she took a cautious step toward the kitchen. The moment she stepped into the threshold, she froze again. The kitchen chairs were all neatly pushed in, but one chair had been pulled slightly away from the table. It seemed out of place, which was very strange to her. The water droplets from the tap dripped into the sink, creating a steady beat in the silence.

She glanced back at the living room, where the shadows twisted and flickered, and swallowed her panic. "It's just the wind," she whispered to herself, trying to regain her composure. She walked over to the chair, her breath hitching as she reached for it. Just as her fingers brushed against the backrest, a blast of cold air swept through the kitchen, making the curtains billow as if they were alive.

Panic swelling in her chest, Joleen staggered back. "Stop it!" she screamed, her voice filled with desperation.

She could feel a heavy and oppressive energy seeping into her bones, and she wanted nothing more than to get out of the suffocating apartment. Just then, the landline on the kitchen countertop rang, the sound piercing the silence and startling her. She jumped and quickly snatched it up, her hands trembling.

"Hello?"

"Joleen? Finally!" Christine's voice, thick with relief, and a bit of tension was on the other side of the call. "I've been trying to call you for days, and you never picked up. Are you okay?"

Joleen swallowed hard, struggling to find the right words. "I'm... I'm alright, Christine. Just... need some time here."

"Your mom's worried sick," Christine finally said, her tone gentle but firm. "She thinks something bad has happened to you. She's been trying to reach you, but you never answer."

"Thanks, Christine," she whispered finally. "I'll call her soon."

With those final words to her friend, she ended the call. Joleen let out a shuddering breath, feeling the heaviness of her friend's words. Although she secretly wanted to just up and leave Ben's apartment and the stuffy atmosphere there, she couldn't get herself to do so because she felt too attached to the memories they had created together.

"What if I forget him?" she whispered to herself, clenching the keys in her hand.

The shadows around her seemed to vibrate in response, and for a moment, she swore she could hear Ben's voice murmuring her name in a faint whisper that floated through the air.

"Joleen..."

"No!" she yelled, whirling around as fear took hold.

Her heart pounding, she tumbled back into the hallway from the kitchen. She was losing herself in the grief and the memories that plagued her, failing to retain her grip on reality. She desperately needed to find a way out.

As she walked back toward her bedroom, she caught sight of the photo that had fallen from the coffee table a few days earlier, now resting on a shelf in a new frame. Something twisted in her stomach as she remembered that day clearly - a day that had been full of love and laughter - before everything had spiraled into chaos.

With a heavy heart, she picked up the frame. The image of them smiling and carefree felt like a harsh reminder of what she had lost. She wanted to scream and rage against the unfairness of it all, but instead she cradled the photo in her hands with tears running down her cheeks.

Her voice broke as she choked out, "I miss you, Ben. Why did you leave me?"

The apartment seemed to groan in response, the air becoming heavy and thick, and the shadows growing deeper around her.

*****

Back in Dededo, Annie sat at the edge of her couch, clutching her phone tightly in her hands. She had called Joleen countless times, but each attempt went unanswered. The silence on the other end filled her with dread and a deep worry that something was terribly wrong. She had tried to tell herself that Joleen just needed space and time to grieve after the accident, but Annie's instincts wouldn't let her rest.

In her heart, she felt something deeper stirring. A mother's intuition, perhaps, or maybe it was simply fear for her only daughter, now seven months pregnant and so young. Annie had always tried to protect Joleen, but how could she protect her from something she didn't even understand?

That morning, she lit a few candles in her living room while whispering prayers for Joleen's safety, guidance, and strength. As the flames flickered, she closed her eyes and clutched her hands together tightly, murmuring a short prayer.

"Please, God, watch over my child. Show her the way back to me."

The soft sound of her own voice in the quiet house was comforting, but the worry remained, weighing heavily on her heart.

Later, as the sun began to set, Annie made her way to the Santa Barbara Church, as she did most Saturdays. The small steel-framed building stood at the corner of her neighborhood, with two towering flame trees offering shade over the entrance. A cool breeze blew steadily through the streets - a welcome relief from the island heat - but even the calming weather couldn't ease the anxiety Annie carried with her.

As she approached the church, her friend Janet was waiting under one of the flame trees. Annie barely had to say a word; Janet could see the worry on her face, and the lines of tension across her forehead had deepened in the past few days.

"Have you heard from Joleen?" Janet asked gently, her voice low as she glanced around to ensure no one else was listening.

Annie shook her head, her grip tightening around the strap of her purse. "Not yet. I've tried calling so many times, but she won't answer. I don't understand... why won't she call me back?"

Janet reached out, placing a comforting hand on Annie's forearm. "It was Joleen's Ben in that accident, wasn't it?"

Annie looked up at her friend, her eyes filled with unshed tears. "It has to be. The name, the motorcycle... everything matches. I'm so worried about Joleen, Janet. She's so young, and she's pregnant. How is she going to handle this on her own? She doesn't have any money, and now, she's completely alone." Her voice cracked, and the tears she had been holding back spilled over. "Why won't she call me? Why won't she let me help her?"

Janet squeezed Annie's arm more firmly, her own expression softening with sympathy. "Maybe she's in shock. Or maybe it's her pride. You know how young people can be. But she'll come around, Annie. She doesn't have a choice anymore."

Annie nodded, though her heart ached with uncertainty. She reached for her handkerchief, dabbing at her eyes as Janet continued, "Let's talk to Father Tony before mass. We can ask him to dedicate prayers for Ben and Joleen. Maybe a little extra prayer will help bring her back to you."

Annie agreed, feeling a sliver of comfort in the suggestion. As they waited together at the church entrance, watching the sun dip lower on the horizon,

Annie silently prayed for her daughter's safety. She prayed for Joleen to come home, where she belonged.

*****

As the days went by, Joleen, haunted by her nightmares, began to remember stories from her childhood about the *taotaomo'na*. She had grown up hearing warnings from elders about the importance of respecting these spirits, stories of those who had crossed them and faced dire consequences.

"What if they're angry with me?" she thought, the idea sending a shiver down her spine. The strange occurrences in the apartment reminded her of those tales. What if Ben wasn't just lingering because of his love for her? What if there was something more... something ancient tied to the land that was now reaching out to her?

Her thoughts spiraled further as she found herself pacing the apartment, feeling a shadow lurking just behind her. She glanced over her shoulder, convinced she had seen a figure darting into the corner of her vision.

"You're just tired," she muttered to herself, the words familiar in her ears since they seemed to be the only explanation she could provide herself with for comfort.

In the days that followed, her fear deepened, and her physical health began to deteriorate drastically, leaving her drained and weak. The nightmares became more disturbing, with Ben's face morphing into something monstrous, his eyes dark and filled with rage. Each time she woke, she felt like a part of her spirit had been chipped away, leaving her hollow.

Desperation gripped her. *I can't stay here anymore,* she thought, her heart pounding in her chest. She needed to leave, but the thought of returning home filled her with dread. *What would she say to her mother? How could she explain the nightmares, the shadows, the feeling of being watched?*

She couldn't let this darkness consume her. She decided to visit her friend Christine for a few days, and perhaps she could tell her about everything that had been troubling her. With her mind made up, she began to pack a small bag - a few clothes, her toiletries, and a picture of her and Ben. The apartment felt darker, with an unsettling energy that made her skin crawl.

Just as she reached for the front door, a voice whispered, low and menacing, *"Ti siña hao humånao."*

It sounded like Ben, but it was twisted, dark, and spoke in their ancient CHamoru tongue. The hairs on the back of her neck stood on end.

"No!" she cried, her voice trembling with fear. "I'm not staying here. Not tonight!"

Joleen took one last look at the apartment, feeling the burden of everything she was leaving behind. With tears in her eyes, she stepped into the world outside, ready to face whatever was ahead.

Chapter 3

Joleen Comes Home

Joleen sat across from Christine on her friend's cozy living room couch, the familiar sounds of Christine's family moving around the house filling the air. She glanced at Christine's mother, who was bustling in the kitchen with an ease that felt comforting, even nostalgic. Sitting here, in the warmth of her best friend's home, Joleen felt a strange mix of relief and anxiety. She hadn't realized how much the past days had worn her down, leaving her more exhausted than she wanted to admit. For the first time in a while, she didn't feel as burdened by the constant weight that had heavily settled on her shoulders.

Christine poured a cup of tea for Joleen and herself, then took a seat, her gaze soft but searching as she handed the cup to Joleen. "Jo," she started gently, "I know you've been dealing with a lot... more than most people could understand." Her voice was soft, and her words carried a warmth and familiarity that had always reassured Joleen.

Joleen's eyes drifted down to her cup, swirling the tea absently, finding it hard to meet Christine's gaze. She felt as though if she looked directly at her friend, all the emotions she had been burying would come rushing to the surface.

"Jo," Christine continued, her hand reaching over to rest on Joleen's arm, "have you thought about talking to your mom? Even just letting her know you're okay?"

Joleen nodded and let out a long, tired sigh. "I've thought about it... I really have. But... there's so much she wouldn't understand," she said, her voice barely above a whisper. "And what could I even say to her that would make any sense?"

Christine's gentle smile was understanding but persistent. "Sometimes, you don't have to explain everything. Maybe it's enough just to let her be there, to let her help you, even if you can't say everything that's going on. You know how moms are; sometimes, just being around each other is enough."

Joleen felt the slightest crack in her own defenses, Christine's words gave Joleen a small window of time to think that perhaps... perhaps her mother's presence would be helpful. But along with the thought came a flicker of fear since she couldn't shake the memory of what she'd seen and felt in Ben's apartment, and the dread that somehow, those spirits might have followed her.

"I don't know... I feel like I'd just be bringing all of this with me if I went home. What if..." Her voice trailed off, not knowing how to put her worry into words.

"Joleen, your mom loves you, and I know she's worried," Christine said in a low assertive tone. "Let her see you. Allow her to be there for you in whatever way she can. It doesn't have to be about explaining everything. Maybe being home will help you find a way through this."

Joleen looked up, meeting Christine's eyes for the first time. She could see the care and the determination there, and it struck her how lucky she was to have Christine by her side, someone who wouldn't let her face everything alone. Joleen managed a faint smile, the first in days. "You're right. Maybe... maybe I need to be there. Maybe she needs me there too."

Christine's face softened, a warm smile lighting up her features. "Exactly. And just take it one step at a time, okay? You've been through enough. Give yourself time to feel safe again, to find your footing."

Joleen nodded, the knot in her chest loosening just a little. For the first time, she allowed herself to imagine what it might feel like to step into her mother's home again, to be in the familiar, grounding presence of her mother after everything that had happened.

The following day, her conversation with Christine still fresh in her mind, she decided to borrow the Sorianos' telephone to call her mom and tell her she was ready to come home.

*****

Annie was still hanging out some laundry to dry on the clothesline in her carport when she heard the phone ring. She rushed inside the house to answer. "Hello," she said slightly out of breath. She pressed the handset firmly to her ear with both hands, as if she was worried she might miss something if she allowed even the smallest gap.

"Hi, Mom."

"Hi, Jo! How are you?"

"I'm okay."

"I heard about what happened to Ben. I'm so sorry! I have been trying to get hold of you, to no avail... Do you need anything? Is there anything I can do?" Annie was close to stuttering as she felt a flood of words and inquiries wanting to come out, but she was also clinging to caution as she didn't want to chase Joleen off by prying too much.

"Mom, I, uh... I..." Joleen's voice was low and weak. "Can I move back in with you?"

"Of course, my girl. Please come home. I'll help take care of you. Please just come home," Annie answered immediately and thought to herself, *Thank you, God!*

"Thanks, Mom."

Joleen didn't sound too excited about the warm welcome. Perhaps embarrassed would be more accurate.

Joleen continued, "Christine is going to be helping me pack up the apartment over the next couple of weeks."

"Oh! You're still in touch with Christine? That's so good to hear." Annie's grip on the phone relaxed a bit.

"Yeah. She visits once in a while." Joleen didn't feel like telling her mom that she was currently at Christine's house, not wanting her mom to probe her with any further questions.

Annie offered, "I could come by to help grab some things."

But Joleen was quick to reply, "No. That's okay. We can take care of it."

"Okay. Please let me know if there's anything I can do, though." But that wasn't all Annie wanted to know about. She continued, "Do you need anything for the baby? Have you seen a doctor lately?"

"I don't have money for a doctor, Mom. And I'm not going to sit for hours in a crowded lobby at the Public Health clinic."

"I didn't mean anything like that, Jo," said Annie in a bit of a panic. "I'm sure you are under a lot of stress, and I'm just worried about you and the baby. I'm not judging you in any way. I just want to help you, and this is one way I think I can help."

"That's okay," Joleen quickly replied. "We'll be packing in the next couple of days, so I will start bringing some things over soon enough."

"That's good! I'll clear some space."

"Bye, Mom," Joleen said quickly.

"Bye, Jo. I'm so gla - " and the phone line cut off, signaling the end of their call before Annie could finish her sentence.

A myriad of questions and emotions were still swirling around as Annie hung up the phone. *That jerk wasn't paying for doctor's visits? The news said he was drunk when he had his accident! How did he have money to go out drinking but he couldn't take care of his own child?*

Annie hated herself for thinking it, but a part of her considered that Ben's death was a good thing - that it might have been God's way of bringing Joleen back to her. Maybe with more time and faith, God would also help turn Joleen back into the loving daughter she used to be.

Annie wanted to try to take control over Joleen's life. She imagined that Joleen would accept her mothering and would follow her guidance now that she had seen how bad life could get. But Annie knew firsthand what it was like to lose someone you loved. So she asked God for the strength to give Joleen her love and support... and to also help her bite her tongue.

*****

Joleen arrived at her mother's house just as rain began pattering against the car's windshield. She felt a mix of relief and tension as she approached the house - relief in knowing she was still welcome at her childhood home, but tension from the heaviness of old memories and uncertainty about the future. She stared at the small home, taking in the neatly painted shutters, the faint glow of the porch light cutting through the gray afternoon, and the flower bed in the front yard where her mother still tended to her plants.

She didn't stare at the house for long. After grabbing some of her luggage, she quickly got out of her car and headed toward the front door. Clearly her mother was home, seeing as her car was parked in the garage. *Wasn't she supposed to be at work or something?* Joleen wondered. As she got closer, the front door opened, revealing Annie's familiar face, with a warm smile that quickly softened into a gentle, curious gaze as she watched Joleen approach.

Joleen returned a curt nod and continued inside, keeping her tone light but brief.

"Just bringing in my things," she said, her gaze fixed on the narrow hallway ahead, avoiding the searching look in her mother's eyes.

Annie seemed to hesitate, her mouth opening as if to say something, but she stopped herself, offering only a quiet, "Let me know if you need anything." Her words were a simple offering, but Joleen continued past her without meeting her gaze.

Joleen stepped into her old room and let out a breath she hadn't realized she was holding. Everything was just as she remembered it; the bed was neatly made with her old comforter, the walls a familiar shade of blue, and even the small stack of books she had left behind on the dresser were now dusted and waiting for her. She set her bag down and ran a hand along the edge of the dresser, her fingers trailing over the faint grooves where she'd once scratched doodles as a restless child. Being back felt strange, as if she had stepped into a picture of her life before everything changed.

Annie's footsteps shuffled softly down the hall to the kitchen. Joleen sat on the edge of her bed, half-listening to the faint rustle and gentle clinking from the kitchen where Annie had started making tea. It was an old habit, one she'd picked up whenever there was something heavy in the air. For a moment, Joleen considered going out to join her, but the thought of sitting across from her mother, trying to find something to say as a way of breaking the strained silence felt overwhelming.

In the days that followed, Joleen kept to herself and avoided her mother as much as possible. As she brought more of her things back home, she would slip in and out of her room when her mother wasn't around, moving through the house in silence, and quickening her steps whenever she heard her mother nearby. She felt burdened by her mother's concerns and her gentle invitations - "I made some soup if you're hungry," or "There's fresh bread in the kitchen" - were usually left unanswered or met with a murmured "I'm fine."

Annie's worry never turned into words; she would watch Joleen with that quiet, observant stare, her expression flickering with concern whenever she passed her daughter's closed door. At one point, she gently knocked and called through the door, "Joleen? If you don't mind, I was thinking we could have supper together." Joleen stayed silent, waiting for her mother's footsteps to move from her door before letting out a slow breath. Lately, she only felt safe in her room, alone, free from her mother's worried stare and without having to explain herself. However, each time she heard her mother moving around the house, a pang of guilt twisted in her stomach.

On a quiet morning, Joleen woke to the sound of soft clinking from the kitchen. She knew her mother was up early, preparing breakfast as she always did. The smell of coffee drifted down the hall, mixing with the faint smell of toast, drawing Joleen out of bed. She hesitated by the door, wondering if she should join her mother. But the thought of sitting across from her, trying to make conversation, felt overwhelming. She waited until she heard Annie moving into the living room before slipping down the hall, grabbing a piece of toast and a cup of tea in silence.

Annie appeared in the doorway as Joleen turned, her face lit with a gentle but hopeful smile. "Joleen," she started softly, "I was hoping we could have breakfast together. It's been a while since we really talked."

Joleen froze, her grip tightening on her cup. She glanced down, her voice barely above a murmur. "I think I'm just going to eat in my room. I... I'm not feeling very social."

Annie's smile faltered, but she nodded, stepping back. "Of course, honey. Just let me know if you need anything." Her voice was soft, understanding, but a flicker of disappointment showed in her eyes as she moved back toward the kitchen. Joleen watched her for a moment, a pang of guilt settling in her chest before she turned and returned to her room.

*****

As the days passed, Joleen became more troubled and could hardly sleep. Each night, she experienced a slight uneasiness that crept into her dreams and woke her up at strange hours. As the house settled around her with soft creaks and sounds that felt both familiar and unfamiliar, she would lay there in the quiet, staring at the faint shadows on her ceiling. She couldn't pinpoint the reason, but as of late, she had a nagging feeling that something wasn't quite right.

One night, just as she was drifting into a light sleep, she thought she heard a faint tapping from the far corner of her room. It was barely noticeable, so soft that she thought it might just be the house settling. She closed her eyes again, forcing herself to relax. But then it came again, this time a bit louder - a soft, rhythmic tapping that seemed to echo through the quiet.

Joleen sat up, her heart pounding as she scanned the room, searching for the source of the sound. She felt foolish, telling herself it was nothing, just a random noise in an old house. Still, the restlessness remained, making it hard to sleep as her thoughts drifted back to that strange feeling she'd had at Ben's place, the shadows that seemed to follow her in the edges of her mind.

In the morning, she stayed in her room longer than usual, trying to shake the creeping anxiety. However, Annie's quiet presence and the faint concern in her eyes served as a reminder to her that there was only so much distance she could keep before her mother's worry turned into questions she wasn't ready to answer.

*****

Annie had begun noticing small, unsettling things around the house. At first, she brushed them off as quirks - an odd draft here and there, sometimes a momentary flickering of the lights. But it was getting harder to ignore the incidents as each day went by. It was after a long, tense night that Annie decided to take matters into her own hands.

Around midnight, Annie had gone to get a glass of water in the kitchen and found the living room TV flickering on, though neither she nor Joleen had been in there all evening. The air was thick and still, like something was holding its breath right beside her. When she went to turn off the television, she felt a prickling chill run down her spine. She glanced over her shoulder, half-expecting to see a figure lurking in the shadows, but there was no one, only silence and a sense of dread that seemed to hold her in place for a moment before she could pull herself back to bed.

By morning, Annie resolved that this was beyond anything she could handle alone. She needed help, someone who could provide comfort but also the spiritual support she felt was now necessary. As she reached for her coat, Annie felt her hands tremble slightly.

"Maybe he can help us," she murmured, her thoughts drifting to Father Rogelio, the parish priest who had long been a good influence in the local community.

His wisdom and calm manner had reassured Annie through her most trying times. *Perhaps he could do the same now.* She hesitated before speaking to Joleen, uncertain how her daughter might react. But Annie couldn't wait any longer. She found Joleen in the kitchen, her eyes weary, looking older than her years.

"There is something wrong in this house, Joleen, and I want to go to the church to see Father Rogelio about it," Annie said softly, watching for any sign of acceptance or resistance in Joleen's face. "I think he might be able to help with whatever it is."

Joleen barely looked up from her cup of coffee. Her face was impassive, and her expression remained neutral. Annie knew that to Joleen, the idea of spiritual guidance felt outdated and ineffective. But Annie had always been a woman of faith and had relied on its quiet strength to carry her through life's storms.

"You don't have to come if you don't want to," Annie said gently. "But I need to speak to him. I have to believe there's a way to bring peace back into this house. To help you and the baby feel safe."

A hint of doubt crossed Joleen's face, but she shook her head. "I don't believe it'll work, Mom. But... if you need to do it, I won't stop you."

Annie reached out to touch Joleen's hand, but her daughter recoiled slightly, as if unsure how to accept comfort. A flash of hurt crossed Annie's face, but she hid it quickly, aware that Joleen was in her own internal battle. With or without her daughter's faith, Annie felt she had to try. If anything could cast light on the shadows that seemed to cling to Joleen, it would be Father Rogelio and his guidance.

Chapter 4

Threads of Fear

Annie sat up in bed, her gaze fixed on the clock hanging on the wall, the time read 2:47 a.m. She sighed softly and shifted under the covers, trying to find a comfortable position, but sleep wouldn't come. The conversation with Joleen earlier still lingered in her mind and pressed heavily on her chest.

I don't believe it'll work, Mom. The words rang in her ears. *But if you need to do it, I won't stop you.*

Joleen's tone had been flat, distant. She had refused the idea of meeting Father Rogelio, just like she had rejected every other thing Annie had tried to offer since her return. The old, familiar pang of helplessness twisted inside her, making her chest tighten. Joleen didn't believe in the same things Annie did anymore: faith, God, the power of prayer. She used to, but now... now, it was as though everything that used to matter no longer did.

Annie's fingers clenched around the edge of the blanket, her thoughts drifting to the noises she'd been hearing for the past few nights. They had begun as some sort of rattling, like the soft click of a baby's rattle, just faint enough to sound like it might be her imagination. But it wasn't her imagination. She was sure of it.

Every time she woke in the night, needing to use the restroom or just restless from the heat, she'd hear it again - a small, hollow sound coming from somewhere outside, as if something was moving around the edges of the house, something not quite human.

She turned her head toward the window, the thin sliver of moonlight creeping through the blinds, casting long shadows across the floor. The house was still, too still. The familiar hum of the refrigerator, the soft whirring from the pedestal fan, and the distant sounds of the crickets - everything that usually made the house feel alive - were absent.

Just the quiet.

Her breath hitched. There it was again.

A soft rattle.

Her heart skipped, and she stiffened, eyes darting toward the ceiling. The noise wasn't loud, but it was unmistakable. It was as if something or someone was pacing outside. The rattle followed a rhythmic pattern, a sharp click-click-click that made her stomach churn.

She was almost afraid to move as if some unseen presence would notice her every movement. Was it the wind? Could it have been the trees?

But no.

She knew what it sounded like.

It was a baby's rattle.

She swallowed hard and slid out of bed, the cool, smooth surface of the vinyl floor beneath her bare feet feeling oddly cold. The familiar smell of old wood from the furniture and faint dust filled her nose, but the house didn't feel comforting tonight. The air was thick, and heavy in a way that felt wrong, as if something was pressing down on her chest. Her hands trembled slightly, but she forced herself to walk to the window, one slow step at a time.

She hesitated at the blinds for a moment, unsure whether she wanted to see what was out there.

The rattle stopped.

She exhaled sharply and shook her head. *It's nothing*, she told herself. *Just nerves. It's late, and you're tired.*

But her hands still shook as she pulled the blinds open just a bit. The outside world greeted her with shadows and the soft, swaying branches of the trees. Nothing unusual. She leaned closer, her breath fogging up the glass as her eyes scanned the yard.

Nothing.

The rattling began again, and this time, the sound was coming from the direction of the living room. She froze, straining her ears. The house was quiet again, but she had heard it, and she wasn't imagining it.

She moved slowly, carefully, each step deliberate, as though something might jump right in front of her. When she reached the living room, she paused and turned toward the counter where Joleen's car keys usually rested. She always checked the counter to confirm that her daughter had returned home safely. But tonight, as her gaze lingered on the empty counter, a cold shiver slid down her spine. The keys were gone.

Did Joleen go out again? Annie wondered, but that thought barely had time to take hold before another sound sliced through the quiet.

The rattle.

It was coming from outside, faint but distinct. And it was moving... moving around the house, following the perimeter like a shadow. The soft clicking of the rattle circled the exterior, as though something was walking just beyond the edge of the shadows, teasing her with its presence.

She pressed her palm to the cool kitchen counter, trying to steady herself. Her breath was shallow, and her pulse quickened. She had to stop this. *It's just the wind,* she told herself. *It's nothing. Maybe it's the trees rustling or an animal.*

But the chill that had settled in her bones refused to be dismissed.

Annie's mind flickered to her childhood, to the stories her mother used to tell her about the *taotaomo'na* - the spirits of the land, ancient protectors of the islands. Spirits drawn to the vulnerable, to those who were in a delicate state, like pregnant women or newborns. Her mother had warned her of their curiosity, their interest in children, and their tendency to watch and follow when the time was right.

Her stomach clenched.

But no. She wasn't going to let fear win.

Still, the rattle came again. Moving, soft, like the sound of a baby's rattle gently shifting across the yard. Then it stopped. But only for a moment.

Annie's eyes flicked to the dining room sliding door. Beyond the door, through the sheer curtains, she could make out the vague silhouette of the carport; empty, except for her old, faded blue sedan parked in the corner. The lamp above the door was her only source of light outside.

Could someone be out there? Could it be a person? She took a slow, cautious step toward the door, almost as if she could feel the presence on the other side.

No footsteps. No rustling. Nothing.

But then, click! A sharp, unmistakable sound.

She winced, her hand gripping the door frame for support. Something moved just outside the glass. A shadow. Then it vanished.

Annie quickly stepped back from the door. She tried to shake it off, but she couldn't ignore the growing sense of dread. This wasn't just a noise or a passing sound that could be explained away. This was something more.

Her mother's warnings came flooding back. The *taotaomo'na*, the restless spirits, their fascination with children. Annie couldn't deny it any longer; something was out there.

The feeling of being watched intensified.

She hurried back down the hallway, back to the safety of her room. Her feet were light, but her mind was heavy, filled with doubt.

She glanced back over her shoulder at the dark house. The shadows seemed deeper now, darker. The space between the walls felt somehow larger.

Was something really out there? Or was it just the house playing tricks on her mind?

Her mother's voice echoed in her head, *Do not ignore the signs, Annie. The taotaomo'na will not leave until they have what they want.*

As she got back in bed, the sound of the rattle lingered in the back of her mind.

*****

The next afternoon, Annie's eyes were heavy, red from the sleepless night, but she had made her decision. She couldn't keep pretending that everything was fine. The rattling sounds, the creeping feeling of something watching her, and the strange presence that seemed to grow stronger with each passing day were all more than she could handle alone.

She stood by the kitchen counter, her hands

trembling slightly as she picked up the small, silver crucifix pendant she had received at her Confirmation. The pendant had always been a symbol of her faith, something she clung to in moments of doubt, and right now, it felt like the only thing that could offer any hope. She wasn't sure if it would work, but she had to try.

For Joleen, she thought. *For the baby.*

Her thoughts were interrupted by the sound of Joleen moving around in her bedroom down the hall. Annie took a slow, deep breath. Joleen had said she wouldn't stop her from going to church, but she knew how her daughter felt about these things. It made Annie's chest tighten just thinking about it.

But there was no time for doubt. If she didn't act now, the fear would consume her and Joleen, though she tried not to show it.

*****

Annie arrived at Santa Barbara Parish late in the afternoon and parked in front of the Parish office, the sun still hanging high in the sky. The office was actually a small concrete house that was converted into office space. Annie was happy that there were no other cars there. She didn't want anyone else to know about the issues she was having.

"Hi, Marie," Annie said as she stepped into the Parish office.

Marie San Nicolas was usually the only person

working in the office. "*Hafa adai*, Annie." Marie greeted Annie with a more formal CHamoru greeting since they were in the office. "How have you been?" Marie asked.

"Well, my daughter's back home. So, that's good."

"That's good to hear." Marie had noticed that Annie had been attending mass on her own for a while now.

"Yeah. I'm happy to have her back. But she's pregnant and moody, and she won't come to church with me. I'm worried about her and her baby." Annie reached into her purse to pull out the pendant. "So, I was hoping I could get this pendant blessed for her." Annie placed the pendant on Marie's desk.

"Oh, that's pretty, and it's a good idea," Marie said. "But Father Tony and Father Rogelio are both out. Father Tony will be at his mom's all evening, and Father Rogelio is at the hospital. He won't be back until just before the seven o'clock mass tonight. If you'd like, you can leave the pendant. I'll leave a note so one of them can bless it tonight... then you can pick it up tomorrow."

"I appreciate it, Marie. But I think I'll just come back later. Thanks, though." Annie picked up the pendant and headed back to the door. "Have a good evening, Marie."

"You too, Annie. It was good to see you."

Father Rogelio will be saying mass tonight, Annie thought to herself. *He is always very approachable.* She decided she would attend mass and ask Father Rogelio for his help after. He may be willing to bless the pendant right then and there.

Thankfully, after mass had finished, Annie had

Father Rogelio to herself. She waited for him at the bottom of the stairs from the altar.

"Good evening, Annie," said Father Rogelio with his usual welcoming smile.

"Hello, Father. I'm sorry to bother you, but I need your help."

"Oh, you are not bothering me, Annie," he replied in his mild Filipino accent. "How may I be of service?"

"I have a necklace that I would like to have blessed, Father. It's for my daughter."

"Of course. I would be happy to bless it for you. Is this a gift? Are things okay? I haven't seen her in a long while."

"Well, things are okay. We aren't on the best terms, but she recently moved back in with me. I thank God for that! I'm trying to get her to come to mass with me, but that might take some time. Also, I've heard... things at night. Strange noises, like rattling, outside the house. It happens at odd hours, and I feel like I'm being watched." Annie paused just a bit. "I fear for Joleen. She is pregnant. So I'm hoping that she will agree to wear the necklace at least. I am deeply worried about her and the baby."

"I understand, Annie. This is your only child... and your only grandchild. This is good, what you are doing. Let's get this necklace blessed for now," said Father Rogelio as he started back into the church toward the Sacristy to bless the pendant. "The prodigal daughter has returned and that is already something to give thanks for."

Father Rogelio said his prayer over the pendant and sprinkled some holy water on it. "Almighty Father, we humbly ask that, through the intercession of St. Benedict, you pour out your blessings upon this necklace. May it protect the person who wears it. In the name of the Father, and of the Son, and of the Holy Spirit." He finished the blessing and said to Annie as he gently placed the pendant in her hands, "Don't push her, but keep inviting her to join you at mass."

"Thank you, Father," Annie said. "It was easier when she was smaller because I could just make her come with me. I'm still tempted to try," she said with a little giggle. "But I understand what you're saying; she's so... angry. She doesn't believe any of this can help. I don't know what else to do."

Father Rogelio reached out, resting a firm but gentle hand on her shoulder. "Faith is not something we can force, Annie. It must come from within, especially when people are lost. You must be patient. She will find her way in her own time."

Annie nodded slowly, trying to absorb his words. "I just... I'm so scared," she admitted. "I don't want to lose her. Or the baby."

"You won't," Father Rogelio assured her, his voice steady. "But you must trust in God's plan, even if it's hard to see right now. Sometimes, the darkest paths lead to the brightest light."

The two said their goodbyes, and as Annie stood to

leave, she felt a small spark of hope ignite in her chest. The pendant was blessed, and she had spoken her fears aloud to someone who understood. But as she stepped out of the church and into the cool evening air, a sudden chill washed over her, causing the hair on the back of her neck to stand on end.

She paused, glancing around the church grounds. The courtyard was empty, but the sensation was so strong, so sudden, that it felt like something was watching her from the darkness beyond the church walls.

Her grip tightened around the blessed pendant as she quickened her pace, eager to get back to the safety of her car. She tried to shake off the feeling, telling herself it was just her nerves, but the eerie chill stayed with her, lingering like an unwelcome presence as she drove home.

*****

Meanwhile, back at the house, Joleen lay in bed, staring up at the ceiling. The hum of the pedestal fan did little to drown out the silence that pressed against her ears. She wished for sleep, but it had become elusive, slipping away each time she tried to grasp it.

She turned on her side, adjusting the blanket, but couldn't shake off the uneasy feeling that had been creeping up on her since her mother left for church. Annie had been acting more paranoid than usual, constantly urging Joleen to pray, to keep herself protected. At first, Joleen had dismissed it as her mother's usual overprotectiveness, but tonight, the house seemed different.

Joleen let out a frustrated sigh, rubbing her eyes. She wanted to blame it all on her mother's paranoia. But the truth was, there was something else gnawing at her, something she had been trying desperately to ignore.

Closing her eyes, her thoughts drifted back to Ben's apartment, the memories of that night coming back to her in vivid, uncomfortable flashes. Joleen's eyes snapped open. She was back in her bed, the house around her silent. She sat up, clutching the blanket to her chest as she listened.

There it was again, the sound of that baby rattle, so faint she almost thought she was imagining it. The sound seemed to drift from the hallway, accompanied by soft, barely audible whispers. Her skin prickled with goosebumps, and she felt a cold sweat break out along her neck.

No, she told herself firmly. *This is just stress.* But as the sound grew louder, her grip on rationality began to slip. It didn't make sense, how could the same sounds follow her here, to her mother's house?

Her hands trembled as she tightened her grip on the blanket. Joleen's breath came in short, panicked bursts as she listened to the sounds around her. For a moment, she thought she heard her name being whispered, but when she turned her head, there was nothing there.

Joleen tried to calm herself down, reminding herself it was all in her head, but a part of her - the part that had grown up listening to her family's stories - wasn't so sure anymore. Maybe her mother was right. Maybe there were things in this world that couldn't be explained, things that didn't care whether she believed in them or not. However, her pride wouldn't let her outwardly admit to her mother that she had probably been right all along.

She shut her eyes tightly, hoping that it would all go away and this would have all been a dream. She lay back on the bed and covered herself with her blanket, hoping her mother would get home soon.

*****

The front door creaked as Annie stepped into the house. She set her purse on the dining table and exhaled slowly. In her hand, she held the freshly blessed pendant. Its silver surface glinted faintly in the light, a small but potent symbol of her hopes.

"Joleen?" Annie called out, her voice echoing slightly in the quiet house. There was no answer. She sighed, rubbing her tired eyes. After hours spent at the church, speaking with Father Rogelio and attending the evening mass, she had felt a momentary sense of peace. But now, standing alone in the stillness of their home, that feeling quickly faded.

She walked down the short hallway, where the doors

to the three bedrooms lined the narrow space. Joleen's door was shut, a faint line of light visible underneath. Annie hesitated before knocking gently.

"Joleen? I need to talk to you."

The door creaked open, and Joleen stood there, her face shadowed and weary. She looked like she hadn't slept in days, dark circles under her eyes.

"What is it, Ma?" Joleen asked, her voice edged with irritation while trying to conceal her relief at her mom finally being back home.

Annie took a breath, holding out the pendant. "I had Father Rogelio bless this for you. I really think you should wear it."

Joleen stared at the pendant for a moment, her lips pressing into a thin line. "I told you, it won't make a difference," she muttered, crossing her arms. "A necklace isn't going to change anything."

Annie's heart clenched, a mix of frustration and fear bubbling up. "Joleen, please. I know you don't believe in this, but it's not just a piece of jewelry. It's protection. For you... for the baby."

Joleen's eyes flashed with annoyance. "You think a necklace is going to protect me from whatever's happening? It's not..." She stopped herself, shaking her head. "It's not real, Ma. You're just... making things worse by acting like this."

The air between them was thick with tension, each word like a small cut to Annie's heart. She could see the exhaustion in Joleen's eyes, but there was something else there too - fear. Joleen was trying to hide it, trying to stay rational, but Annie knew her daughter well enough to see the cracks forming.

"Fine," Annie said softly, lowering the pendant. "I just... I just want to help."

Joleen didn't respond. She turned back into her room, closing the door firmly behind her. Annie stood there for a moment, staring at the closed door, her hands shaking slightly. She could feel tears prickling at the corners of her eyes but swallowed them down. She had to stay strong. For both of them.

That night, Annie fell into a restless sleep, exhaustion finally claiming her. But just as on previous nights, she woke with a start at exactly 3 a.m. The house was utterly silent, the kind of silence that made her ears ring. However, she needed to use the bathroom.

After coming out of the bathroom, she headed to the kitchen for a glass of water, but then she suddenly jumped back and almost fell over. She pressed her back against the hallway wall as her hand swept up and down frantically looking for the light switch. But she didn't feel any safer as the lights came on. Her skin crawled and her knees slowly buckled as each beat of her heart seemed to pump icy cold fear throughout her body.

There were footprints... wet, baby-sized footprints... clear as day on her flooring. The footprints seemed to come from the front door and through the hallway. They led straight to Joleen's bedroom door. These weren't strange noises outside her house. These were *inside* the house! All of a sudden, prayers and the holy relics seemed useless.

Annie fumbled through Joleen's bedroom door, still trembling. "Jo, wake up!" Annie began nudging Joleen's leg. "Joleen! Wake up!"

"What?" Joleen started off annoyed until she noticed how frantic her mother sounded.

"There are baby footprints in the hallway. I followed them, and they led right to your room, Jo!"

Joleen sat up in bed and peered out toward her bedroom door. "Where? I don't see anything."

"Out in the hallway."

Joleen stepped out of bed and looked out through the open bedroom door. She was able to make out what looked like wet spots on the floor just before they completely evaporated. Even if she didn't believe that they were footprints like Annie said, Joleen did acknowledge that it was a little strange to see the wet spots at all.

"Jo! I'm really scared for you and the baby. You really need to go to Church with me."

"Mom," Joleen replied. "I get that you're scared. But I'm fine."

"Hold on," Annie said as her brow furrowed even more than it already was. Her legs were a little more stable now as she carefully walked over to her room. She grabbed the pendant from her dresser and brought it into Joleen's room. "At least wear this, please," said Annie as she handed Joleen the pendant. "It will make me feel better to know you have it on."

Joleen looked at the pendant again, her shoulders sagging. She seemed too tired to argue. "Fine. I'll wear it," she muttered, holding out her hand.

Annie's eyes filled with relief as she carefully placed the chain around Joleen's neck. "Thank you," she whispered, her fingers lingering for a moment on the cool metal. She could feel the faint warmth of her daughter's skin underneath, a small comfort in the growing darkness.

Joleen looked down at the pendant, touching it lightly with her fingers. "Not that anything is going to happen, but how is this supposed to help with anything anyway? You have blessed things all over this house and you're still worried."

As much as she wanted to argue, Annie couldn't. Joleen was right.

"Please, just keep it with you." Annie pleaded. She didn't want to admit it, but she no longer felt protected by the items that were once so sacred and powerful to her. She couldn't go back to sleep. How could she? The thought of something walking freely through her house kept swirling around in her head.

At that moment, Annie thought to pray for Joleen, though she wasn't sure how her daughter would take it.

"Let me pray with you, Joleen. Just this once."

Joleen hesitated but nodded reluctantly. Annie took her daughter's hands in hers, bowing her head. "Dear Lord," she began, her voice trembling with emotion, "please protect my daughter and her child. Keep them safe from whatever darkness has entered our lives."

Joleen stayed silent, her eyes closed, her hands gripping Annie's tightly. For the first time, she didn't pull away, didn't scoff, or roll her eyes. There was something fragile in her expression, something almost like belief.

As Annie finished her prayer, she kissed Joleen's forehead. "We'll get through this," she said softly, more to herself than to Joleen.

But even as she spoke the words, a cold shiver ran down her spine. The air in the room felt heavy again, like a storm cloud waiting to burst. And somewhere around the house, faint but unmistakable, came the sound of a baby's giggle, echoing from the shadows.

Chapter 5

Spirits Take Hold

Annie jolted awake, her heart pounding in her chest. The room was pitch dark, and for a moment, she didn't know where she was. Her mind was still tangled in the remnants of a dream, *or was it a nightmare?* She wasn't sure anymore. Lately, waking up in the middle of the night had become all too familiar.

She reached out blindly for the nightstand lamp, her fingers shaking as they found the switch. The light clicked on, flooding the room with a weak glow that only made the shadows seem darker. Annie glanced at the clock. 3:02 a.m. - the same time as always. That hour had started to feel cursed.

Annie sat up slowly, swinging her legs over the side of the bed. The cool vinyl floor sent a shiver up her spine as her bare feet made contact. She rubbed her temples, trying to clear her head. Despite her exhaustion, sleep had become a restless struggle, filled with strange noises that lingered just beyond her hearing.

She pressed her hands together and whispered a quick prayer. "Lord, please protect us... please." But the words felt thin, as if the house itself was swallowing her voice.

The events of the past days replayed in her mind like a broken record - the wet, baby-sized footprints, the sound of giggles that seemed to drift from nowhere, and the cold drafts. Annie had tried everything: prayers, holy water, blessed items placed in every corner of the house. But none of it seemed to stop whatever was creeping in. She had hoped the new pendant she'd given Joleen would help, but now she wasn't so sure.

Annie stood up, wincing as her knees cracked. She pulled on her robe and stepped into the hallway. The house was silent, the kind of silence that made her ears ring. The air felt heavy, almost damp, as though it was pressing against her skin. She glanced at Joleen's closed bedroom door, a faint strip of light peeking from underneath. At least Joleen was home; that gave Annie a small sense of comfort.

Upon reaching the kitchen, she headed toward the sink and filled a glass with water, her hands still trembling. The cold water was a small comfort as it soothed her dry throat.

But then, she heard it. A soft, almost playful giggle. Annie froze, the glass slipping from her fingers and shattering on the floor. The sound was faint but unmistakable, it was the same baby's laugh she had heard before.

Her breath caught in her throat as she whipped around, eyes wide, scanning the shadows. "Joleen?" she called out, but there was no response. Her heart was racing now, each beat louder than the last. It felt like something was squeezing her chest, making it hard to breathe.

Annie pressed her back against the counter, her eyes darting toward the hallway. The light under Joleen's door was still on, but the house was so quiet, it felt like time had stopped. For a moment, she thought about waking Joleen, but she didn't want to scare her daughter any more than she already was. She could see that Joleen was trying to stay strong for the sake of the baby, and Annie wasn't about to jeopardize her daughter's efforts.

She didn't dare move for a moment, her back still pressed against the counter. Then, mustering every bit of courage she had left, Annie whispered another prayer. "Our Father, who art in Heaven..."

The words were barely out of her mouth when a sudden gust of cold air blew through the room, making the lights flicker. It was like a breath, a whisper of something unseen brushing past her cheek. And just like that, the air settled again. The coldness was gone, leaving only the quiet hum of the refrigerator and the distant tick of the clock in the living room. Annie stood there, her breaths coming in shallow gasps. She knew it wasn't over. Whatever it was, it was toying with them, waiting for the right moment.

Finally, she forced herself to move, stepping carefully around the shards of glass she hadn't yet cleaned. She didn't dare turn off the lights as she made her way back to her bedroom. As she passed by Joleen's door, she paused for a moment, listening. But all she heard was the faint sound of Joleen's breathing, steady and calm.

Annie closed her bedroom door behind her, turning the lock as if that could keep the darkness out. She climbed back into bed, pulling the covers up to her chin. But sleep was out of the question. She lay there, eyes wide open, waiting for the next sound, the next sign that the house wasn't as safe as it seemed.

Her mind kept drifting to the *taotaomo'na* and their legendary tales. She didn't want to believe that these occurrences were their doings. *Taotaomo'na inside a house that was blessed? Inside a house with holy symbols blessed by the church. How is that even possible?* Annie now realized that her faith would not be enough to get them through this. Why were the *taotaomo'na* being so bold? Why were they so interested in her, Joleen, and the baby? Annie couldn't understand it. But she knew someone who might.

The next morning, Annie's eyes felt heavy as she

forced herself out of bed. She hadn't slept at all after last night's unsettling encounter. The faint light of dawn was filtering through the thin curtains, casting a soft, gray glow over the room. She could hear the quiet hum of the refrigerator and the distant sound of a car passing by outside, but the house itself felt eerily quiet.

Taking a deep breath, Annie pushed herself to her feet. The cold floor made her shiver, and her joints were stiff from a night of tense, restless waiting. She needed coffee, something strong to clear the fog from her mind and chase away the lingering dread that clung to her.

As she stepped into the kitchen, the scent of freshly brewed coffee greeted her, a welcome surprise. Joleen was already up, standing by the counter with a steaming mug in her hand. Her dark hair was pulled into a messy bun, and the soft glow from the window cast shadows under her eyes, making her look even more exhausted than usual.

"Morning, Ma," Joleen said, her voice thick with sleep. She was trying to sound normal, but Annie could hear the strain behind it.

Annie gave her daughter a small, tired smile. "Morning, sweetheart." Her eyes went straight to the silver pendant resting on Joleen's chest. The fact that Joleen was actually wearing it brought her a tiny bit of relief, though it did little to erase the anxiety gnawing at her.

Joleen noticed her mother staring and sighed. "I'm wearing it, okay? Like I said I would." She touched the pendant with her fingers, the silver chain glinting in the weak morning light.

"I appreciate it," Annie said softly, pouring herself a cup of coffee. The rich scent filled the air, comforting and familiar. "I know you don't believe in these things, but it makes me feel better."

Joleen just shrugged, taking a sip from her mug. She looked out the window, her gaze distant. Annie watched her closely, noticing how Joleen's shoulders were tense, her movements stiff. She was trying to act like everything was fine, but Annie could see the cracks. Her daughter's usually bright eyes were dull, shadows etched deeply beneath them.

"Did you sleep okay?" Annie asked, trying to keep her tone light.

"Yeah, I slept," Joleen replied, but her voice was flat. She then turned away from her mother and headed toward her room.

As Joleen walked away, Annie couldn't shake the feeling that something bad was coming. She stood there for a moment longer, the warmth from her coffee cup seeping into her cold hands. The morning light was getting brighter, but it did little to dispel the shadows lurking in the corners of her mind.

"Please, God, keep her safe," she whispered a silent prayer for her daughter.

*****

The late morning sun hung high in the sky as Annie drove along the winding roads, her hands gripping the steering wheel tightly. The sun's warmth spilled into the car, but it did nothing to ease the chill that had settled deep into her bones. Each mile felt longer than the last, the scenery outside blurring together as Annie's mind raced.

She was on her way to her aunt's house, Rosa Perez, known in the community as *Tan* Chai, the *suruhåna*. Although *Tan* Chai was her aunt, Annie hadn't visited her for quite some time. She didn't know *Tan* Chai's phone number, but she did remember how to get to her house. Annie now needed her help. So, she got in her car and hoped *Tan* Chai would be willing to see her although she would be arriving unannounced.

Tan Chai's house was surrounded by the jungle in the Macheche area of Dededo, and though the route was familiar, for some reason the drive felt different on this particular morning. Annie kept her eyes on the road, trying to focus, but her thoughts kept drifting back to Joleen. The memory of her daughter's tired eyes and the way she had brushed off Annie's concerns had left a knot in her stomach.

When Annie finally pulled up to *Tan* Chai's small house, she let out a shaky breath. The house was surrounded by a lot of herbs for her natural remedies - ones she grew at her house and many others available in the surrounding jungle area. Annie pulled into *Tan* Chai's driveway and was surprised to see her standing outside the front door as though she had been waiting for her. Annie stepped out of the car, the gravel crunching under her feet.

"Long time no see, *Tan* Chai," Annie said as she closed her car door. "Remember me? I'm Francisco and Maria's daughter, Annie." She looked around as she walked up the driveway. There were beautiful, healthy plants all over the place.

Annie walked up to *Tan* Chai to greet her with the traditional CHamoru *man nginge'*. "Ñora," Annie uttered respectfully to her aunt in greeting.

"*Dioste ayudi*," replied *Tan* Chai as a blessing given in response to receiving *man nginge'* from her niece.

"How did you know I was coming?" Annie asked *Tan* Chai.

Tan Chai smiled. "I didn't. But I had a feeling that someone was coming and that it was important," she explained as she held the screen door open to let Annie in.

"Really?"

Tan Chai chuckled as she admitted, "I'm just kidding. I just finished trimming some plants here in the front and was walking in when I heard a car slowing down. My driveway is the only one here, so I figured someone was visiting." *Tan* Chai noticed that Annie didn't really laugh, so she knew this wasn't just a casual visit. "Come in, *nene*. Come in."

It had been a long time since anyone referred to Annie as *nene*, a term of endearment similar to "sweetie." Strangely, it made her feel safe, as though she was now in *Tan* Chai's care.

As Annie stepped in through the door, she remembered being there sometime in her teens. She didn't remember, though, what the visit was about. *Tan* Chai then directed Annie to a couch in her living room. "Sit... sit and tell me why you have come."

Tan Chai sat on a matching chair near the end of the couch where Annie sat. Her house had translucent, flowing white curtains covering the tall windows, letting the sunlight in while keeping some of the heat out. There was little traffic through *Tan* Chai's street, so it was very quiet and cool as the ladies spoke.

"It's my daughter, *Tan* Chai. She is pregnant, and I'm getting scared. She's okay, though. She was living with her boyfriend until he died in an accident recently. Now she's back home living with me. What scares me is that strange things have been happening at my house ever since she moved back in. I think it's *taotaomo'na*."

"Do the two of you go to church?"

"I do," says Annie. "But she won't."

"Mmm," *Tan* Chai hummed with her lips pursed as she nodded. "No church. Pregnant. And she's suffering from a recent death. This makes her spirit weak and vulnerable to the *taotaomo'na*."

"I have been hearing baby rattle sounds outside the house. Then, a few nights back, I saw wet baby footprints inside the house." Annie leaned in toward *Tan* Chai as she continued. "*Tan* Chai, I have blessed crosses, blessed palm leaves, and even my shelf with a statue of the Virgin Mary. How are the *taotaomo'na* coming into my house?"

Tan Chai's head tilted back and wrinkled her forehead in disbelief. Even she had never heard of something like that happening. "Get your house blessed again, *nene*. Call your priest to go there as soon as possible," *Tan* Chai said. That was all she could think of.

"Okay. I'll go to the church right after here," Annie responded. "But is there anything you can do to help?"

"I'm sorry, *nene*. I can pray for you. I can pray with you. But I'm not very good with *taotaomo'na*," admitted *Tan* Chai. "I'll ask around. Maybe I can find a *suruhåna* or *suruhånu* who knows what we can do."

"Please, *Tan* Chai. I'm really scared."

"Okay," *Tan* Chai said. She stood up and walked over to a shelf where she grabbed a pencil and a notepad. "Give me your phone number. I will call you as soon as I find something out. You need to also watch your daughter. Watch to see if she starts behaving differently. Try to limit her exposure to *taotaomo'na*. Staying indoors at night is best." *Tan* Chai affectionately reached over and touched Annie's forearm gently. "Try to bring her here when you can. Maybe I can help you convince her to go to church."

"I will try."

"But for now, try to get someone to bless your house right away. I will start making some calls."

They both stood up and headed to the front door.

Annie turned and hugged *Tan* Chai. "Thank you, *Tan* Chai!"

"Of course, *nene*! I'll be praying for you and your family."

Annie went straight to the Santa Barbara Parish office after seeing *Tan* Chai. She was able to schedule a blessing for the next day... Friday. Father Tony would be available, and he understood the urgency. Having grown up in Guam, he was very familiar with the *taotaomo'na*. He, too, was concerned when Annie explained what had been happening. He would go on Friday evening after Annie got home from work.

Tan Chai made some calls as she promised. She found a couple of people who might be able to help; Frank 'Kiko' Aguon, a fairly young *suruhånu* with experience helping with *taotaomo'na*. Kiko was in his early forties and lived in the village of Chalan Pågo. He would be able to stop by Annie's house. Another was *Tan* Paro Martinez, a *suruhåna* from the village of Umatac. *Tan* Chai was just waiting for her contacts to get her the phone numbers for Kiko and *Tan* Paro. She decided she would talk to them before getting back to Annie.

Annie got home from the Parish office and was eager to talk to Joleen. But Joleen wasn't there. Instead, Annie found a note on the counter from Joleen saying that she was going to be at Christine's house because Christine was throwing her a baby shower. But Annie didn't know where Christine lived, and she didn't know Christine's phone number. Christine's family had only moved to

Agat last year, so their phone number was not listed in the phone book yet. Annie remembered what *Tan* Chai said about trying to have Joleen stay home at night. But what could she do now? Her only comfort at this point was that Joleen was wearing the pendant she gave her.

*****

Agat was a small, quiet village nestled along the southern coastline of Guam. Christine's house sat close to the Ga'an River, at the end of a short cul-de-sac. It wasn't anything grand, but its location gave it a calm, peaceful feel, tucked away from the busier parts of the island. Because the house tended to get too warm for gatherings inside, Joleen's baby shower was held in the carport. A large twenty-foot canopy had been set up to the side of the house, with folding chairs and tables arranged neatly underneath it. The shade from a sprawling banyan tree kept the guests cool, and the breeze from the river added to the comfort.

There were about a dozen guests, mostly close friends and a few family members. It wasn't a big enough group to hire a DJ, but Christine had some cassette tapes and her dad's dual cassette player to keep the atmosphere lively. They played old favorites that brought back memories of high school days, when Joleen and Christine were inseparable.

The food was simple but satisfying: platters of red rice, barbecue chicken, lumpia, and desserts like latiya and mango cake. Laughter filled the air as Joleen caught up with old friends she hadn't seen in years. It felt more like a small reunion than a baby shower, and for a little while, Joleen seemed to relax. Even though the strange events at home weighed on her, she tried to focus on the positive and enjoy the moment.

As the evening wore on, the party began to wind down. It was a weeknight, and Christine wanted to be mindful of the neighbors, so the music was turned off just before ten. The guests worked together to clean up, folding chairs, packing leftovers, and gathering trash. Christine offered to drop off the baby shower gifts at Joleen's house the next morning to save her the trouble of loading them into the car, and Joleen accepted gratefully.

Once the last of the guests had left, Joleen thanked Christine and got into her car to start the drive home. It was her second time visiting Christine in Agat since she moved there, but the house was close to the main road, so this made finding her way back straightforward even though she still wasn't very familiar with the area. The night was clear, with only a few wispy clouds in the sky. The moonlight reflected off the ocean, creating a soft shimmer along the coastline as Joleen drove. She kept her window cracked to let the cool night air in, hoping it would help her stay alert.

As she left the coastline behind, the road grew darker. The stretch of highway she was driving on passed through a part of the island that had once been the village of Sumay, before the Navy took over the land. Now, it was nothing but thick jungle on either side of the road. The trees loomed high, their branches weaving together to block out the moonlight. Without streetlights, the road was almost pitch black.

Joleen turned up the volume on the radio, hoping the music would keep her company. But something was wrong. The sound started to distort, growing faint and hollow. It was as if the music was coming from far away, echoing through a tunnel. Frowning, Joleen twisted the volume knob back and forth, but it didn't seem to help. Her stomach tightened with unease.

A sudden sense of heaviness came over her. The edges of her vision blurred, narrowing into a dark tunnel. Joleen's hands tightened instinctively on the steering wheel, but she couldn't feel it under her fingers. It was as though her body was floating, detached from the car. Panic surged through her chest. She blinked hard, trying to clear her vision, but her eyelids felt heavy, almost glued shut.

Somewhere in the distance, she heard chanting. The voice was low and rhythmic, speaking in a language that sounded like CHamoru, but the words were too muffled to understand, and it sent chills down her spine. Joleen struggled to focus, willing herself to wake up, to snap out of whatever was happening.

Then, a blast of light filled her vision. A car horn blared, jolting her back to reality. Joleen gasped, her heart racing as she realized she was now driving through the village of Asan. She had no memory of passing through the Sumay area or the village of Piti. A stretch of 10 minutes or more was just... gone. Her hands were gripping the steering wheel so tightly that her knuckles ached, but she couldn't recall when she'd regained control.

Joleen's breaths came quick and shallow. She felt disoriented, and her head was pounding as if she'd been holding her breath for too long. All she wanted was to get home. The road ahead was better lit now, lined with homes and businesses as she neared the more populated villages. The familiar glow of streetlights helped ease some of her anxiety.

By the time she pulled into her driveway, her head was throbbing. Joleen dragged herself out of the car, her legs heavy with exhaustion. She didn't even bother to change clothes. As soon as she stepped into her bedroom, she sank onto the bed, her mind spinning with questions she didn't have the energy to answer.

What had just happened? Was it just fatigue or something else entirely? Joleen wasn't sure, but one thing was certain, she needed to sleep. Maybe in the morning, things would feel normal again.

So she just closed her eyes and let the darkness take over.

*****

The next morning was a workday for Annie. She saw

Joleen's keys on the kitchen counter. Peeking into Joleen's room, she found her fast asleep and thought there's nothing to worry about, so Annie headed out to work.

When she got home from work that afternoon, she was surprised that Joleen's car was still there. She opened her bedroom door and found Joleen still in bed. However, her forehead was all wrinkled and covered in sweat. Annie walked in to check on her and found her burning up, unresponsive to her efforts to wake her.

"Jo. Jo, wake up." Annie nudged Joleen on the shoulder. "Jo? Joleen? It's time to get up. Are you feeling sick?"

Joleen was breathing, but that didn't reassure Annie. She ran to grab a thermometer and slipped it under Joleen's tongue. When she pulled it out, it read 104 degrees Fahrenheit! Annie ran to the phone and called the Dededo Police precinct. She always kept the police phone number taped to the wall because she lived alone and would sometimes see strangers taking their time walking past her house.

"Guam Police Department. This is Officer Quitano. How can I help you?"

Annie frantically responded, "Officer! I need help! I think my daughter is unconscious and she has a very high fever! I just got home from work, and I think she's been like this all day!"

"Okay, Ma'am. What is your name?"

"I'm Annie Leon Guerrero."

"And how old is your daughter?"

"Umm… nineteen! She's nineteen and she's eight months pregnant!"

"And you said you are home? Are you both inside the house?"

"Yes, Officer. Please send an ambulance! We're at 2586 Wusstig Road. It's a blue house. Please hurry."

"Alright, Ma'am, I have your address. Please stay with your daughter, we're sending an ambulance out to you right away."

About fifteen minutes later, an ambulance arrived. The lights were flashing, so that quickly drew Janet's attention from across the street. She peeked out through her curtains to see what was going on. When she saw the ambulance, she ran across to Annie's house and arrived just as Joleen was being lifted into the ambulance with Annie climbing in as well.

"Annie! Annie, what happened?" Janet tried to get Annie's attention. "Annie!"

Annie finally noticed Janet. "I don't know, Janet." That was all the attention she managed to give to Janet before the paramedics closed the ambulance doors.

Janet started to walk back to her house when Father Tony and Christine drove up just a couple of minutes apart. They both saw the ambulance leave Annie's house. Janet didn't have much to tell them other than that Joleen seemed unconscious and Annie was with her. Christine said she would head to the hospital to be with Annie and find out more about what was going on.

Father Tony said he would check in on them later.

Joleen was taken to the Emergency Room at Guam Memorial Hospital. She had not responded to anything the paramedics tried during the drive there. As they brought her into the ER, they directed Annie to the waiting area. That's where Annie was when Christine ran in.

"Mrs. Leon Guerrero! How's Joleen?"

Annie had a rosary in her hands as she prayed. "I don't know. She was unconscious and had a really high fever." She looked over to Christine as she sat down next to her. She asked her, "How did you know we were here?"

"Your neighbor across the street told me. She saw me drive up looking for you guys, so she came over and told me an ambulance took Joleen. Oh, and Father Tony was there. He said he would come by the hospital after mass to check on you and Joleen."

"Did Joleen seem sick at all last night at your house?" Annie asked.

"No. She was fine. We wrapped up around ten o'clock. I told her to just leave her baby shower gifts behind so she wouldn't have to worry about unloading when she got home. I had come to drop them off when Mrs. Pangelinan noticed me and told me what had just happened."

"Do you know if anyone got food poisoning or something from the food?"

"Nobody has said anything. We were outside, so we

made sure the food was in warmers and covered," Christine explained. "We all ate the same things and none of us were sick before or after the party."

Wait! Did Christine just say they were outside? "Christine, where is your house? Is it near the jungle?" Annie was starting to suspect the *taotaomo'na*.

"Yeah. We are at the end of the street and the Ga'an River is behind our house."

Annie turned more to face Christine directly. "Were you guys laughing or talking loudly? Playing loud music?"

"Yeah." Christine was wondering where this line of questioning was going. "But we turned everything off and everyone went home by ten o'clock so that we wouldn't be bothering the neighbors."

The look of panic on Annie's face seemed to intensify with every answer Christine gave.

Just then, a doctor walked in from the Emergency Room and went straight to Annie. "Are you Mrs. Leon Guerrero?"

Annie slowly stood up. "Yes. I'm Joleen's mother. Is she okay?"

The doctor reached out and gently placed his hand behind Annie's arm. "I'm Doctor Brooks. Let's sit over here," he said as he guided her to a corner farther from the entrance. The waiting room was empty, but he wanted them farther from the door just in case someone else walked in. "Your daughter is currently in a coma. She is not responding to any stimuli, and we have been unable to wake her." Annie was already trembling, but now the tears came streaming down from her eyes. Dr. Brooks continued, "However, she is stable enough that we want to move her into a room. We didn't find any internal bleeding or head injuries. We also didn't find any kind of infection or toxins in her initial blood work."

Annie was shaking her head in confusion. "So, what could have caused this? What's happening with my daughter?"

"It's unclear at this point," replied Dr. Brooks.

"So, you don't know? How can that be? How can she end up in a coma when nothing happened?"

"I'm sorry, Mrs. Leon Guerrero. We haven't found a direct cause, yet. We are going to send some blood work off-island for more tests, though. Now, the medics said that you found her in bed unconscious. Did all of this happen suddenly, or were there any signs that she might have been sick, and she just got worse over time?"

"It just came out of nowhere, doctor. She was fine." Annie turned and gestured at Christine to come over. "This is her best friend. She was with Joleen last night, and even she didn't notice anything wrong." Annie paused and looked directly at Dr. Brooks. "What about the baby?"

Dr. Brooks replied, "The baby is fine. It seems that whatever is going on is only affecting Joleen. But we want to keep a close eye on both of them. Since this came on so suddenly, we want to be ready just in case any other unexpected changes occur."

"Please find out what's going on, doctor! This is my only child... and my only grandchild!" Annie pleaded.

Dr. Brooks nodded. "We are doing all we can, Mrs. Leon Guerrero. So, what we're going to do is move Joleen over to a room where we will keep an eye on her. Doctor Ramirez will be here in the morning, and we will be working together to help Joleen and watch the baby. For now, a nurse will be coming out shortly with some forms for you to fill out."

"Thank you doctor," replied Annie as she wiped away her tears with her handkerchief. "You said you were sending blood work off-island for more tests. Do you know how long it might be before you get the results?"

"It usually takes about a week for the off-island lab to receive the blood work," replied Dr. Brooks. "The tests take a couple of days. Then, they fax the results to us. So, we would be looking at getting results in about a week and a half to two weeks."

"Alright. Thank you, Doctor Brooks."

As Dr. Brooks walked back into the Emergency Room, Annie turned to Christine and asked, "Can you be here around eight in the morning to stay with Jo?"

"Sure, Mrs. Leon Guerrero. I'll be here."

"Thanks, Christine. I just need to take care of some things, and I don't want to leave Jo alone."

*****

Father Tony stopped by the hospital that night. He

sat and prayed with Annie for a while, learning about her concerns regarding Joleen and the *taotaomo'na*, and then he left after about an hour, asking Annie to call the Parish office if she needed anything. Christine left shortly afterward.

It was a long night for Annie. Her mind kept racing. *How could Jo end up in a coma? What happened? What if it was the taotaomo'na?* Annie remembered what Christine said and couldn't help but make connections to local superstitions.

Don't make loud noises at night where taotaomo'na tend to be, which includes jungle areas and areas near rivers or streams. This is exactly what Joleen was doing at the party - making loud noises at night near the jungle with a river. Maybe they did end the party early enough so as not to offend the neighbors. But had they already offended the *taotaomo'na*?

If you are pregnant, don't go to places at night that are not familiar to you. Again, this is exactly what Joleen did - she was pregnant and had never been to Christine's house in Agat before, or so Annie thought. It was a place she was not familiar with, and she had gone there at night.

Annie kept thinking that maybe Joleen had pushed things too far. The *taotaomo'na* were already very interested in Joleen and her baby. *Did she provoke them? Was she too exposed to them?*

Annie prayed the rosary while she watched the clock. As soon as Christine arrived the next morning, Annie drove to *Tan* Chai's house for help. *Tan* Chai was outside watering her plants when Annie drove up.

"*Tan* Chai!" Annie cried as she rushed out of her car.

"What happened, *nene*?" *Tan* Chai replied.

"It's my daughter, *Tan* Chai! She's in a coma at the hospital. She was fine on Wednesday, and then she was unconscious yesterday. The doctors don't know what's wrong!"

Tan Chai dropped the water hose and hugged Annie as tears started to stream down her face. "How can I help?"

"You told me she shouldn't go out at night. But I didn't get to tell her." Annie pulled back from their embrace to face *Tan* Chai. "When I got home the day you told me, she had already left the house. She went to a party in Agat, at her friend's house, and she has never been there before. They had their party outside... it was nighttime... and the house is near the jungle along the Ga'an River." Annie started trembling again and crying. "I didn't know where the house was, and I didn't know how to get a hold of her to warn her! I think the *taotaomo'na* got to her, *Tan* Chai!"

Tan Chai hugged Annie again. "Let me get my bag and you can take me to her."

"Thank you, *Tan* Chai!"

Tan Chai noticed that Annie was still trembling, so she grabbed Annie's car keys and said, "Maybe I should drive."

It only took about fifteen minutes to get to the

hospital. *Tan* Chai walked in with Annie toward Joleen's room. However, she slowed down as they got closer to the room.

Annie noticed and asked, "*Tan* Chai? What's wrong?"

"I'm sorry, *nene*. I think you were right. I can feel the *taotaomo'na*. And the smell is very strong."

"What smell?" Annie asked.

"You probably can't smell it. If the *taotaomo'na* are nice and are happy with you, they can give off a sweet smell, almost like that of the fadang tree." *Tan* Chai took a couple of deep breaths as though she was feeling nauseous. "But if they are mean or angry, then they give off very bad smells. In this case, I'm smelling something like sulfur." *Tan* Chai nodded in the direction of a room in the ward and said, "Is that your daughter's room? That's where the smell is coming from."

Annie was stunned. "Yes. That's her room."

They walked into Joleen's room and tears started trickling down *Tan* Chai's face. Just her expression made Annie's heart sink.

"I've never felt anything like this before. I can feel a very mean and powerful *taotaomo'na*." *Tan* Chai looked scared and started to stammer a little as she spoke. "I don't know how to help with this." However, in that moment, *Tan* Chai's expression changed to confusion. "Annie, I'm feeling another very strong force, though this one doesn't feel mean. I was so nauseous outside the room, but close to the bed, it's not so bad." *Tan* Chai looked directly at Annie and asked, "Did the doctor say anything about the baby?"

Annie paused and took a breath. "He said the baby seemed fine. But what about Joleen, *Tan* Chai?"

"I don't know what we can do for your daughter. I'm so sorry. But the baby is also at risk. It feels almost like the *taotaomo'na* is frustrated and angry, but I think the baby is resisting, though I don't know how this is possible."

Tan Chai then began sifting through her purse and pulled out a small statue of the Blessed Virgin Mary. She placed it on the table next to Joleen's bed. "I think this is why the *taotaomo'na* were so interested in your daughter and her baby. We have to keep praying. If this is the baby resisting, we need to pray to help the baby."

Annie was holding Joleen's hand and crying as she sat next to her. Then she reached over and placed a hand on Joleen's belly. She knew it wasn't rational, but she was hoping she could feel some kind of connection to the baby. To her surprise, it was almost like the baby knew what she wanted and pushed up into Annie's hand. It wasn't a kick or the feel of the baby moving around. To Annie, it felt like an intentional gentle push to return the affection. She didn't tell *Tan* Chai, though.

Tan Chai went through her purse again and pulled out a piece of paper with some phone numbers on it. "*Nene.* I'll be right back. I'm going to make some calls to try to find out more about what we are dealing with." She stepped out of the room and headed for a pay phone that she saw out in the lobby.

About 30 minutes later, she walked back in. "Okay. I just called a couple of *suruhånos* who have more experience with *taotaomo'na* than I do. Kiko Aguon is a younger *suruhånu* from Chalan Pågo. He said he can be here this afternoon. *Tan* Paro Martinez is a *suruhåna* from Umatac. But she's older and can't come. I spoke to her and told her what was going on and what I was feeling. She thinks your grandchild has the gift of the *makåna*," said *Tan* Chai. "That would explain why the *taotaomo'na* have been so interested."

"*Makåna*? What's that?" asked Annie.

"The *makåna* were the *suruhånu* of ancient times. They were healers like us, but they also had a strong connection to the spiritual world. Legend says that they could see and even communicate with the spirits. I think the reason the *taotaomo'na* are interested in this baby is because of that connection. The evil *taotaomo'na* may want to use the baby as a vessel. Then the baby would become a *kakahna*; which is a dark version of a *makåna*."

"WHAT?! Are you telling me that kind of thing is real?" Annie scowled. "How is that even possible?"

"Nobody really understands these kinds of things anymore. It's all legend. *Tan* Paro thinks there may have been people who knew more about this before World War II. But so many people were killed by the Japanese. We lost their knowledge and their talents."

"Are you sure *Tan* Paro knows what she's talking about?" Annie scoffed. "I don't believe that! This is just a baby! How can a baby have anything to do with evil spirits and spiritual connections?" Annie turned away and looked at Joleen instead.

"I'm sorry, *nene*. I'm not trying to upset you. I just know that we are dealing with forces stronger than us." *Tan* Chai pulled out her rosary and raised it to Annie. "I believe in God and in prayer. I also know that the *taotaomo'na* can be fearsome and terrible."

"So, what can we do? Is Kiko Aguon able to help? Is that why he's coming?" Annie asked.

"He's coming because I need help. I don't have as much experience with *taotaomo'na*. I would feel safer with his help, and he will pray with us."

Annie turned her head slightly toward *Tan* Chai but still would not make eye contact. "Father Tony was here, though. He didn't smell anything." She turned back toward Joleen. "He also didn't say anything about *taotaomo'na*, yet he knew what's going on."

"Not everyone can sense the *taotaomo'na*. Sometimes, you only feel them because they want you to know they are there. I think the *taotaomo'na* here wants to scare me away," *Tan* Chai said as she dropped her head. "That's why I asked Kiko to come. I *am* scared."

Chapter 6

Father Rogelio's Burden

The sacristy was quiet, save for the faint creak of the wooden floorboards beneath Father Rogelio's feet. He stood at the small table by the window, carefully laying out the garments he would wear for the evening mass. The soft, muted glow of the setting sun filtered through the stained-glass window, casting colorful patterns onto the walls and floor. It was a sight that usually brought him peace. This evening, however, his mind was clouded.

He unfolded his stole with accustomed ease, its deep purple color a sign of preparation and penance. However, his mind was elsewhere. His chest felt heavy and uneasy, and it had been getting worse all afternoon. Though he was unable to pinpoint the exact cause, the feeling followed him around like a shadow.

The sudden sound of hurried footsteps in the hallway broke his focus. He turned just as the door to the sacristy opened, and Father Tony stepped inside. Rogelio immediately noticed the look on Tony's face; troubled, almost urgent. Father Tony was not the kind of man to panic easily, which only made Rogelio straighten up more, bracing himself for whatever news had brought Tony here in such a state.

"Father Tony," Rogelio greeted, his voice calm but tinged with curiosity. "Is something wrong?"

Tony exhaled sharply and nodded, stepping further into the room. "It's Joleen," he said, his voice low but steady. "You remember Annie's daughter?"

Rogelio nodded slowly. He had met Joleen a couple of times when she had gone to mass during her younger years. As she had aged, she had stopped going to mass with her mother, and he had also recently learned about her boyfriend's death and her pregnancy. Annie had mentioned the pregnancy proudly, her joy evident in every word.

"What happened?" Rogelio asked.

"She's in the hospital," Tony continued, his tone lowering as though the walls themselves might overhear. "She fell into a coma yesterday, and the doctors don't know why. Annie is devastated."

The words landed heavily on Rogelio's ears. He felt a

pang of sorrow for Annie, imagining the fear and helplessness she must be feeling. But there was something in Tony's tone, a weight that suggested there was more to the story.

"Annie thinks... it's not natural," Tony continued, hesitating for a moment before adding, "She thinks it's the *taotaomo'na*."

The room seemed to grow quieter, as if the very mention of the word demanded reverence. Rogelio remained still, his expression unreadable. He knew enough about the *taotaomo'na* to understand why Annie might feel this way. Since arriving in Guam years ago, he had learned much from Father Tony about the CHamoru people's belief in these ancestral spirits. They were protectors of the land but also forces to be feared if disrespected. Many in the community spoke of them with a mix of awe and caution.

Rogelio clasped his hands in front of him, his thumbs idly pressing together as he processed the information. "What makes her think that?" he asked quietly.

Tony stepped closer, lowering his voice. "Joleen had been at a party the night before she fell into the coma. They were near the jungle, by the river. Annie thinks someone must have done something to offend the spirits. She's convinced this is their punishment."

Rogelio frowned, his mind racing. He thought back to the blessing he had performed at Annie's house. He had taken every step carefully, praying over the rooms, sprinkling holy water, even blessing the pendant at

Annie's request. *Could it be possible that those acts had failed to protect Joleen?* The idea left a bitter taste in his mouth.

"I told her we would pray for Joleen," Tony added. "But Rogelio, you know how strong these beliefs are. For Annie, this isn't just a medical problem. It's spiritual."

Rogelio nodded slowly. He couldn't ignore the cultural significance of the *taotaomo'na*, even if his own Catholic faith didn't align completely with such beliefs. "Thank you for telling me." He said finally. "I'll pray for her as well. And for Annie."

Tony placed a reassuring hand on Rogelio's shoulder. "I know you will. But don't carry this alone, okay? We're both here to guide this community, and that means supporting each other too."

Rogelio managed a small smile, though it didn't quite reach his eyes. Tony gave him a brief nod before turning to leave, his footsteps fading into the distance.

As the door closed, Rogelio let out a slow breath, his shoulders sagging slightly. He turned back to the table, but the task of preparing for mass now felt trivial compared to the storm of thoughts swirling in his mind. He sat down on the nearby bench, folding his hands in his lap. For a moment, he simply stared at the floor, his mind replaying Tony's words.

He had blessed their home. He had prayed for Joleen, for her unborn child, and had also blessed the pendant Annie had gifted her. And yet, something had gone wrong. Joleen was lying in a hospital bed, caught between life and death, and he couldn't help but wonder if he had failed her somehow.

Rogelio stood abruptly, moving toward the small altar in the corner of the sacristy. He knelt before it, clasping his hands tightly as he began to pray. The words came automatically, years of practice guiding his tongue, but his heart felt heavier with each passing moment.

"Lord," he whispered, "I ask for your guidance. Help me to understand what is happening and grant me the strength to support this family. If I have failed them in any way, forgive me. Show me what I must do."

The silence that followed his prayer was both comforting and unsettling. Rogelio remained kneeling for several minutes, his thoughts drifting back to his early days in Guam. He remembered sitting with Father Tony in the rectory, listening to the parish priest explain the stories of the *taotaomo'na*. At first, Rogelio had dismissed the tales as superstition. But over time, he had come to see them as more than just folklore. They were a reflection of the CHamoru people's deep connection to the land, a way of understanding the world that wasn't so different from his own faith.

Yet as he finished preparing for mass, he couldn't shake the feeling that he had missed something. Perhaps he had been too quick to rely on his Catholic rituals, too focused on his own beliefs to fully grasp what was needed. The thought tied his stomach into knots, a sharp pang of unease lingering in his chest.

*****

The hours passed slowly. After the evening mass, Rogelio retreated to his small office, where a worn journal sat waiting on his desk. Writing had always been his way of sorting through complex emotions, and that night was no different. He opened the journal and began to write, his pen moving steadily across the page.

He wrote about Joleen, about Annie's fears, and the possibility of the *taotaomo'na* being involved. He admitted to himself the guilt he felt, the nagging thought that he might have failed to protect them. But as he continued to write, he found himself returning to the idea of faith; faith not just in God, but in his own ability to serve this community.

The *taotaomo'na* were not part of his Catholic training, but they were deeply significant to the people he had been called to guide. He didn't have to fully understand them to respect their importance. And perhaps, he thought, that respect was the key.

Closing the journal, Rogelio sat back in his chair, his fingers briefly tracing the edges of the leather cover. His doubts hadn't vanished, but he felt a renewed sense of purpose. Joleen needed him, and so did Annie. He couldn't let his uncertainty hold him back.

He decided there and then that he would visit the hospital the following day, and he prayed for Annie and her daughter again, hoping to ease some of the burden on his shoulders.

"Lord," he prayed softly, "grant me wisdom and strength. Let me be a source of comfort and guidance for this family. And if there is a lesson to be learned, help me see it clearly."

As he rose to his feet, a sense of quiet resolve settled over him. The road ahead was uncertain, but Rogelio knew he would face it with faith and humility. When the morning came, he would set off for the hospital, ready to offer whatever support he could.

Chapter 7
The Child

The hospital corridor was quiet except for the occasional hum of a passing cart. Father Rogelio walked steadily, his hands clasped behind his back, the weight of his rosary heavy in his pocket. He had been here countless times before, visiting the sick and offering last rites. But today felt different. Today, he was here for Annie, a woman he'd watched endure so much already.

He entered the room softly, not wanting to startle anyone. Annie sat in a stiff chair near the bed, her hands tightly clutching her rosary. Her lips moved in silent prayer, but her red-rimmed eyes betrayed her exhaustion. *Tan* Chai stood nearby, her arms crossed, offering a protective presence despite her small frame.

"Good morning, Annie. *Tan* Chai," Father Rogelio greeted them gently.

Annie looked up, her face lighting briefly with relief. "Father," she whispered. "Thank you for coming."

He placed a comforting hand on her shoulder. "Of course. How is Joleen?"

Annie's eyes filled with tears as she glanced toward the bed. Joleen lay motionless, her face pale, her breathing shallow. The machines around her beeped steadily, reminding Annie of her daughter's fragility.

"She's not getting better," Annie said, her voice trembling. "The doctors... they don't know if she'll make it."

Father Rogelio nodded solemnly. He reached into his pocket and pulled out his rosary. "Let us pray together," he said, his voice steady.

As the three of them bowed their heads, Father Rogelio's voice filled the room, reciting a prayer for Annie, Joleen, and the unborn baby. The words carried a calm authority, and for a moment, the air in the room seemed to lighten. But it was fleeting. The oppressive heaviness returned as soon as the prayers ended. After offering a few more words of encouragement, Father Rogelio left the hospital.

*****

Kiko Aguon lived a simple but purposeful life as a woodcarver and craftsman. His home in Chalan Pågo was more than a house; it was a legacy. The workshop he worked in had belonged to his father, who was also a skilled carver. As a boy, Kiko learned the craft by watching his father work, carving furniture from ifil wood - furniture so sturdy and beautiful that it became highly sought after on the island.

But Kiko's skills went beyond furniture. Under the guidance of his uncle Joe, a respected *suruhånu*, Kiko learned the old ways: the prayers, the chants, and the art of creating talismans for spiritual protection. Joe passed on all he knew before his death, leaving Kiko not only with the tools of the trade but the weight of responsibility to carry on their family's spiritual legacy. By his mid-thirties, Kiko had earned a reputation for crafting charms and talismans to ward off *taotaomo'na*. These ancient spirits were feared by many, and Kiko's creations were often the first line of defense.

When Kiko received *Tan* Chai's call from the hospital, he wasted no time. Gathering a small bag with his tools and supplies, he made his way there, his mind focused. He arrived later in the day, and as he approached the hospital room, a sense of unease gripped him. The air felt thick, almost electric, and the presence of something otherworldly was undeniable. He had felt such presences before, but this one was particularly strong.

Inside the room, Joleen remained unconscious, her body still but her face marked with the stress of her condition. Annie sat close to her daughter, worry etched deeply into her features. *Tan* Chai stood near the small table, her Virgin Mary statuette perched on top.

"Kiko, thank you for coming," said *Tan* Chai, motioning him forward. "Annie, this is Kiko. Kiko, this is Annie and her daughter, Joleen."

Annie scrutinized Kiko, her eyes scanning his face, then dropping to the worn bag slung over his shoulder. Her expression was guarded and skeptical.

"I'm sorry we're meeting under these circumstances," Kiko said, his voice calm but serious. "*Tan* Chai explained what's happening. Let's begin."

Without waiting for a response, Kiko opened up the bag that he brought with him. He pulled out a kind of talisman and placed it on the table where *Tan* Chai's Virgin Mary statuette stood. The talisman contained blessed palm leaves woven into the shape of a cross. It had some other plants woven in as well. Kiko also pulled out a small bottle that contained some kind of oil. "*Tan* Chai, can you help me massage this onto her arms and legs?"

Tan Chai nodded and got up from her chair.

"What is that?" Annie asked, her voice sharp with worry. "What are you doing?"

Kiko was so focused on getting started that he had forgotten that Annie might have questions. "My apologies, Annie. The cross and this *palai* are meant to help ward off *taotaomo'na*."

"That oil is *palai*?" Annie asked.

"Yes, it is," Kiko explained, holding up the bottle. "It's made with specific plants and coconut oil. When we massage it into the skin, it acts as a protective barrier since the smell from the other ingredients is supposed to be unpleasant to *taotaomo'na*. Also, the oil keeps the mixture from evaporating from the skin after we massage it in."

"And this will help my daughter?" Annie's doubt was plain, but her desperation kept her from outright dismissal.

"It is part of the process," Kiko replied evenly. "The *taotaomo'na*'s hold on her is strong. I will ask the *taotaomo'na* to release your daughter, however, I have to warn you once again that this *taotaomo'na* is very strong. It seems to really want this baby." Kiko turned to look at *Tan* Chai and Annie and continued, "We will keep praying. Hopefully, we can chase off this spirit."

Kiko and *Tan* Chai began the ritual, massaging the *palai* into Joleen's arms and legs in slow, deliberate movements. As they worked, they prayed, reciting the rosary in unison throughout the night. Almost every hour, Kiko would break from the rosary to ask the spirit to leave Joleen. Annie understood the solemn plea spoken in CHamoru and followed Kiko as he repeated, "*Espiritu, påtgon Yu'us este. Sotta put fabot.*"

The first time Kiko spoke the words, Joleen's body trembled, and a low, guttural growl escaped her lips. Her head lifted slightly off the bed, as though an unseen hand had grabbed her by the neck. Annie gasped, clutching

Joleen's hand tightly, her knuckles white with fear.

"What is happening to my daughter?" Annie whispered, her voice trembling.

"We must keep praying," Kiko said, his tone steady despite the unease he felt.

The eerie occurrences continued through the night. Each time Kiko uttered the prayer, Joleen's body would shudder, and the guttural noises would return. At one point, a nurse entered the room and froze in horror at the sight. Her scream was brief, but it shattered the already tense atmosphere before she fled the room. Another nurse replaced her but kept her distance, her fear evident in her cautious movements.

Why is this happening to my girl? What did she do, God? Why are you letting this happen to her? Annie was firmly pressing her face into her hands with her fingers almost digging into her flesh. *Why, God? Why?*

Each time Joleen's body shuddered and made that beastly sound, Annie would pull Joleen's hand to her cheek with one hand, and she would rub her shoulder with the other hand, nodding side-to-side with tears falling from her closed eyes. "I'm here, Jo. I'm right here." *Please, God. Let me take her place. Let it be me, not her.*

With everything going on over the past couple of days, Annie didn't realize just how tired she was. Her exhaustion eventually overtook her, and she drifted into a restless sleep. Her dreams were vivid and unsettling. In one of her dreams, she found herself sitting on a lawn chair, watching a young boy playing in a backyard. He was playing near the edge of the jungle but then stopped suddenly. He just stood looking straight at her. As she looked more closely, she could see that he was actually frozen with fright.

The whole sky darkened, and her focus seemed to zoom in on the boy. Maybe it was the motherly instinct in her, but she felt that something horrible was about to happen. So, she started running toward the boy. However, she couldn't reach him. A haunting silence filled the air as she ran, and time seemed to stand still. She could feel herself running, but she couldn't seem to reach the boy.

Just then, a pair of massive, ghostly white hands with bloody claws emerged, reaching for the boy from the bushes. A deep, menacing voice growled through the air proclaiming, *"Iyo-ku hao på'go."* Instantly, Annie recognized this as a *taotaomo'na* claiming, "You're mine now" as it approached the boy. The horrible hands then grabbed the boy and pulled him into the jungle.

Before she could even react to the dream, Annie was awoken by *Tan* Chai's nudging and the rush of nurses entering the room. A couple of nurses crowded Joleen's bed while others rushed in and out to call for additional help.

"Jo?" Annie shouted as a nurse was escorting her out of the room. "Joleen!"

Tan Chai grabbed Annie by the hand to help move her out of the way. "Come, *nene*. Give them room."

"What's happening? Jo? What's happening to my baby?"

"I'm sorry, Mrs. Leon Guerrero. We need room so we can try to help your daughter," replied one of the nurses.

Dr. Ramirez was just down the hall and rushed into the room as Annie, *Tan* Chai, and Kiko were escorted to the nearby waiting area. A few minutes later, a couple more nurses rushed into the room with a cart that had what looked like an incubator attached. Tears kept streaming down Annie's face as she watched all the commotion. *Tan* Chai held Annie's hand while she and Kiko continued to pray the rosary.

An hour later, Dr. Ramirez emerged, his face heavy with the burden of what he had to say. "Mrs. Leon Guerrero," he began, his voice soft but firm, "I'm very sorry to say this, however, because Joleen was in a coma, the pregnancy became too much of a strain on her body; we had to perform an emergency C-section to try to save the baby as well as to reduce the stress on Joleen's body. Because the baby was very close to term, we were able to save him."

Dr. Ramirez paused for a second. But it felt like so much longer to Annie. She struggled to listen. Her heart was sinking so deep that she felt she might pass out.

Dr. Ramirez continued, "But we weren't able to save Joleen. Once her heart stopped, we were unable to revive her. I'm so sorry."

Annie's legs gave out and she collapsed from the edge of the seat onto the floor. She didn't say anything at first, almost as if her body didn't have enough energy to even form words. But then an intense frown formed on her face and the tears flowed stronger than ever. "Myyyy baaaby!" She started shaking *Tan* Chai's hands as *Tan* Chai held hers to try to console her and keep her from falling over.

Tan Chai knelt down beside Annie to hold her, wrapping her arm across Annie's back. "My Jo! My Jo! She's just a girl! She's my baby girl!" Annie's head rolled onto *Tan* Chai's shoulder as she continued crying.

Dr. Ramirez also got down on one knee to hold Annie by the arm in support. "We will be monitoring the baby for at least a day to make sure there are no lingering health concerns," said Dr. Ramirez. "I will still be around. If you have any questions, please let a nurse know so they can page me."

Annie didn't respond, but *Tan* Chai nodded to the doctor.

"Let's get you off the floor for now," said Dr. Ramirez. He and *Tan* Chai then guided Annie back up onto the chair.

Kiko flagged the doctor to the side and asked if they could have the nurses keep the talisman with the baby.

"We can't keep anything inside the incubator with the baby," said Dr. Ramirez.

Kiko pleaded, "Can it be hung on the cart to stay with the baby? It doesn't have to be inside the incubator. It's just important to us, especially considering that we've just lost his mother."

Dr. Ramirez could not allow it. Because the baby was a newborn and because the cart he was in would be placed in the nursery with other newborns, they needed to try to keep things as sterile as possible.

The best thing that Kiko and *Tan* Chai could do, was to stay as close to the baby as they could get and continue praying.

A nurse helped Annie onto a wheelchair and pushed her alongside *Tan* Chai and Kiko to the nursery waiting area. Once there, they all helped Annie onto a cushioned bench where she quickly fell asleep. Kiko and *Tan* Chai continued to pray for the baby as Annie slept.

A couple of hours later, Annie awoke and asked about the baby. "My grandson. It's a boy, right?" she asked as she sat up and got oriented. "Is my grandson okay?" she asked *Tan* Chai.

"Yes, *nene*. The doctor said he's strong and healthy," *Tan* Chai replied. She slid closer to Annie on the bench to rub her back. "They are just keeping him for observation."

"He's very strong, Annie." Kiko stood facing the nursery. "I can feel him from here." He turned to face Annie and added in a solemn tone, "We're very sorry that we couldn't do more to help your daughter."

Annie didn't know how she still had tears left, but a few still managed to make their way down her cheeks. She wasn't so overwhelmed with grief though.

Tan Chai noticed. "That's the boy," she said.

"Huh?" Annie asked, confused.

"You noticed that you feel a little calmer than you expected. That's the boy. He senses that you are hurting, and he is trying to help you," explained *Tan* Chai. "This is a very special boy."

Tan Chai told Annie, "The nurses may come by again soon. They want to know what to name the baby."

Annie had calmed down a little more. "Name?" she said as she wiped her nose. "I don't know. It wasn't supposed to be my choice. I never really thought about it."

Just then, Annie remembered a discussion with Father Rogelio when she brought the pendant to him to be blessed. "You know, Father Rogelio suggested a name a while back," she told *Tan* Chai. "He was talking about how Joleen was my prodigal daughter who had returned."

Tan Chai chuckled a bit. "That sounds like Father Rogelio."

"He said that when he was a boy in the Philippines, his youngest brother was not expected to live through birth. But he survived and they all saw it as a miracle. His parents named the boy Matias, which means gift of God. If Joleen's baby was a boy, Father Rogelio suggested that she consider naming him Matias or Mateo."

Kiko chimed in. "Gift of God actually sounds good. I like it."

Annie decided, "I do like the name Mateo. Mateo it is."

"He should be baptized as soon as possible," Kiko said. "I don't feel the *taotaomo'na* anymore. But I feel the boy. He has a strong spiritual presence. The *taotaomo'na* will still want him."

Tan Chai added, "So, get him baptized. I also think we should take him to see *Tan* Paro. We won't go until after he is baptized, though."

"Yeah. That's good," Kiko agreed. "He is still too vulnerable. You should limit his exposure."

Tan Chai then turned to Annie, "One more thing, *nene*, your house is too close to the jungle. That's partly why the *taotaomo'na* had been bothering you so much when Joleen moved back in," she added. Kiko nodded in agreement.

"What?" Annie said, stunned. "What am I supposed to do, then? I can't sell my house! My husband, my daughter, all the memories are there in that house!"

"Maybe you can rent it out," suggested *Tan* Chai. "Then you can use the rental money to help you rent a smaller place closer to the church. Some place with more houses around you and less jungle."

Annie's head dropped and she just stared at the waxed vinyl hospital floor as she rocked slightly back and forth in her seat. She did not like the idea of leaving the home that she had shared with her husband and her daughter. But it was slowly sinking in that she didn't really have a choice if she wanted to keep baby Mateo safe.

Mateo was released from the hospital a couple of days

later. Annie didn't really have any other close relatives. Her older brother had passed away years before from a stroke. Her parents had also passed on many years prior, and she didn't see much of her in-laws after her husband's funeral. Therefore, it was *Tan* Chai and Janet who helped Annie with Joleen's arrangements. They handled the traditional nine nights of rosaries as well as Joleen's wake and funeral. They also helped with arranging Mateo's baptism shortly afterward.

Tan Chai felt a responsibility to protect Mateo. She understood that he was rare and precious. She also understood that evil spirits would always want him because of his connection to their world. As soon as Annie was up to it, *Tan* Chai coordinated for them to visit *Tan* Paro in Umatac.

*****

It was mid-March when *Tan* Chai and Annie brought Mateo to visit *Tan* Paro. Umatac, nestled in the southern-most part of Guam, was a long drive by local standards. The journey, however, was breathtaking. The winding roads meandered through picturesque beaches and lush, green mountains, their beauty offering fleeting moments of calm for Annie's anxious heart.

When they arrived late that morning, the scent of the ocean lingered in the breeze as they approached *Tan* Paro's humble home.

"Hello?" called *Tan* Chai, her knuckles lightly

rapping the screen door.

The door creaked open, revealing a boy in his early teens. His face was shy but polite. "Hello. Are you, *Tan* Chai?"

"Yes, that's me."

The boy turned to call over his shoulder. "Nana, they're here!" He then turned back, holding the door wide open. With a quick dip of his head, he greeted her in the traditional *man nginge'*. "Ñora."

"*Dios te ayudi,*" replied *Tan* Chai warmly as she stepped inside.

The boy turned to Annie and offered the same respectful greeting.

Annie, still adjusting to these customs, hesitated before replying, "*Dios te ayudi.*"

The living room smelled faintly of herbs, and a gentle breeze from a standing fan carried their earthy scent. Seated near the window in her wheelchair, *Tan* Paro radiated an aura of calm wisdom. Her gaze immediately fixed on Mateo, her eyes softening as if they were tracing unseen threads that bound the child to the spirit world.

Annie held Mateo close as they approached, feeling uneasy under the intensity of *Tan* Paro's attention.

"Hello," the older woman said, her voice soft yet resonant. Her eyes never left Mateo as she spoke. "He's beautiful. Such warmth."

"He's special, isn't he?" said *Tan* Chai as they all took their seats.

Annie, however, was puzzled. "What do you mean?

You haven't even touched him."

Tan Paro turned her focus to Annie, her smile warm yet knowing. "It is not a physical warmth, child. It's a deeper one; a light you feel with the soul."

Annie stiffened. She had learned to trust the intuition of those like *Tan* Chai and Kiko, but this still felt alien to her.

Seeing Annie's doubt, *Tan* Paro's expression softened further. "Let me explain. All of us come from the spirit world. Before we are born, our souls wander between that world and this one, tethering to our bodies only shortly before birth. This connection makes babies vulnerable, especially to spirits seeking to slip into our world."

Tan Chai chimed in, "That's why there are so many taboos and traditions about protecting pregnant women and newborns."

"Exactly," agreed *Tan* Paro. "As a child grows, the connection to the spirit world weakens, and baptism helps to sever it completely for most. But this one..." She paused, her eyes returning to Mateo. "This one is different. His connection is powerful, and it will remain strong."

Annie's heart tightened. "Is that why the *taotaomo'na* were after him?"

"Yes," said *Tan* Paro solemnly. "They see what he is - a rare gift, a *makåna*. In our ancestors' time, *makåna* were powerful healers, using their connection to the spirit world for good. But such gifts come with risk. That connection, like a window, allows the spirit world to reach back. When a *makåna* fails to protect themselves, they can become a vessel for darkness, turning into what our people call a *kakahna*."

Annie felt a cold dread settle over her, but she forced herself to ask, "Will getting him baptized protect him? Closing that window?"

"For most children, yes," replied *Tan* Paro. "But Mateo's gift is from God Himself. Even God does not wish to cover it." Her smile returned as she gazed at the baby, who was now fast asleep in Annie's arms. "His connection to the spirit world is part of who he is. What we can do is guide him, teach him, and protect him until he learns to protect himself."

"What do we do next?" Annie asked, her voice trembling but resolute.

"Stay close to the church," said *Tan* Paro. She turned to *Tan* Chai. "When he's old enough, we'll teach him everything we know about healing, the *taotaomo'na*, and the spiritual forces of this world." Her smile widened. "But in the end, I think he'll teach us even more."

For a moment, the room fell silent, filled only with the quiet hum of the fan and the rhythmic breathing of baby Mateo. Then, *Tan* Paro closed her eyes, her face serene. "Thank you for letting me meet him. He truly is extraordinary."

*****

Annie took *Tan* Paro's advice to heart. Over the following weeks, she and Mateo moved into a cozy duplex in Dededo, just a short walk from the Santa Barbara Church. Though leaving her home on Wusstig Road was painful, she knew it was necessary to keep Mateo safe.

The house found a new tenant - Janet's cousin - through what felt like divine providence. Janet handled the paperwork eagerly, happy to keep family close by.

With Mateo's safety secured, Annie faced one final challenge: finding someone to care for him while she worked. But this, too, resolved itself almost effortlessly. *Tan* Chai stepped in without hesitation, agreeing to watch Mateo at her house.

As Annie settled into her new life, she often heard Father Rogelio's voice in her mind, full of that warm, knowing humor, *"And so we see yet again... God works in mysterious ways."*

Chapter 8

Shadows in the Village

The village of Dededo, often humming with its normal life, was unusually quiet. People went about their routines, but something felt wrong. The air seemed heavy, as though everyone was waiting for something to happen. Even in the busyness of daily life, there was a tension that no one could explain. At Santa Barbara Church, where villagers gathered for mass and community events, people talked in hushed voices. They exchanged uneasy glances and shared stories that left others nodding in agreement.

"I don't know what it is," one woman said to her neighbor outside the church, her voice barely above a whisper. "It's like there's something in the air. My husband says he heard footsteps outside our window last night, but when he looked, no one was there."

Another parishioner nodded gravely. "Our dog's been acting strange too, barking all night at nothing. It's like... it knows something we don't."

Parents waiting outside Santa Barbara School to pick up their children exchanged similar stories. Some shared accounts of animals behaving oddly, while others spoke of shadows moving just beyond the edge of their vision. The unease was subtle but unmistakable, spreading like a ripple through the community. The parents watched their children closely, their faces lined with worry.

"Don't stay out after dark," one father warned his son as he took his hand. "It's not safe these days."

Even people who didn't usually believe in superstitions couldn't ignore the strange things happening. Everyone felt it, the sense that something was wrong.

*****

Annie tried to focus on her newborn grandson, Mateo, and keep her mind off the rumors. Since his birth, she had stayed home as much as possible, telling herself it was to keep him safe. But in truth, she was scared.

The outside world didn't feel the same anymore.

Every time she stepped out, she felt as though unseen eyes were following her. The village streets were still, but it wasn't the kind of stillness that brought peace. It felt unnatural, like the calm before a storm.

Inside her house, things were no better. Mateo was her joy, but some of his behaviors unsettled her. He had a habit of staring into empty spaces in the house, his dark eyes wide with curiosity. Sometimes, his eyes would lock onto a corner of the ceiling or an empty chair and smile or even giggle at nothing, reaching his tiny hands into the air as though someone, or something, was there.

At first, Annie dismissed it as typical baby behavior. "Babies are just like that," she told herself. "They don't know what they're looking at." But the longer it went on, the harder it was to ignore.

One afternoon, Annie was feeding Mateo when she noticed his gaze shift to the corner of the room. He stopped drinking from his bottle and began smiling at something she couldn't see. His hands reached out, his little fingers grasping the air.

"What are you looking at, Mateo?" she asked softly, trying to keep her voice steady. She turned her head to look at the corner, but it was empty. The sunlight streaming through the window lit up every inch of the space, leaving no room for shadows.

Still, Mateo's eyes stayed fixed on that spot, his smile growing wider. Annie felt a shiver run down her spine. She quickly picked him up and carried him to another room. That same evening, as Annie was folding laundry in the living room, a sudden commotion outside caught her attention.

The sharp, frantic barking of a dog echoed through the neighborhood. At first, she ignored it, thinking it was just a stray. But the barking didn't stop. It grew louder, more insistent, and distinctly angry. Curiosity got the better of her, and she peeked out through the curtains. Across the road, a dog was pacing back and forth, its body rigid and its teeth bared. Its eyes were locked on Annie's house.

Her stomach tightened as she scanned the street for anything unusual. There was nothing; no movement, no people, not even the rustling of leaves in the still night air. Yet the dog continued to bark, its growls low and guttural.

Annie stepped away from the window, pulling the curtains closed with trembling hands. "Just a crazy dog," she muttered under her breath, but the unease lingered. Even after the barking finally stopped, the memory of the dog's relentless attention stuck with her. She double-checked the locks on her doors and windows before going to bed that night.

*****

The days passed, but the strange occurrences only increased. Annie heard from a neighbor about some chickens found dead in their coop. The story made its rounds at church, each retelling more detailed and unsettling than the last.

"They weren't even torn up," the neighbor said. "It's not like a dog or a cat got to them. Just dead. And their bodies felt cold... so cold it didn't seem natural."

Another neighbor mentioned hearing footsteps on their roof late at night. "I thought it was just a flock of birds," he said. "But when I went outside to check, there was nothing there."

Annie felt a chill creep up her spine as she listened. She didn't want to believe it had anything to do with her or Mateo, but the stories were piling up. She tried to focus on caring for Mateo, but even he seemed affected by whatever was happening. One morning, as she was changing his diaper, she noticed faint bruises on his arms.

The marks were small, like tiny handprints, and they weren't there the night before. Annie stared at them, her heart pounding. She gently ran her fingers over the bruises, but Mateo didn't cry or show any sign of pain. In fact, he smiled up at her and cooed as if nothing was wrong.

"Maybe I held you too tight," she whispered, trying to convince herself. But deep down, she knew the bruises weren't from her.

Annie also became more and more aware of the strange things happening around her. Mateo's habit of staring into empty spaces continued, and he seemed to be doing it more often. The laughing and little giggles continued, and Annie tried to distract herself, but it wasn't easy. She kept remembering the stories she had heard from others in the village - the whispers about shadows and footsteps and cold spots.

One night, she was woken by Mateo's cries. She sat up in bed, groggy and disoriented, when she heard it: a soft knock, coming from somewhere inside the house. The sound was faint at first, but it grew louder, echoing through the walls. It didn't seem to be coming from the door or any one place. It was as though the house itself was knocking.

Annie froze, clutching the blanket tightly around her. The knock came again, sharper this time. Her heart raced as she reached for the rosary hanging from her bedside lamp. She began to pray aloud, gripping the rosary tightly.

The knocking stopped. Mateo's cries quieted, and the house fell silent once more. Annie didn't sleep for the rest of the night. She sat by Mateo's crib, the rosary still in her hands, and waited for the first light of morning.

The next day, Annie made a decision. She couldn't ignore the signs anymore. Something was happening, and she needed help. She hadn't been attending church as regularly as before, but that was about to change.

"We're going to mass today," she told Mateo as she dressed him in his Sunday best, even though it was a weekday. She packed his diaper bag and headed out, her steps more purposeful than they had been in weeks.

At the Santa Barbara Church, Annie felt a small

measure of peace. The familiar smell of incense, the soft glow of the candles, and the comforting murmur of prayers eased some of her tension. She knelt before the altar, Mateo cradled in her arms, and whispered a fervent prayer for protection.

"Lord, I don't know what's happening," she prayed, her voice low but steady. "But please, keep Mateo safe. Keep us safe and watch over our home."

As she left the church, Annie felt a renewed sense of resolution. Whatever shadows lingered in the village, she wouldn't let them take Mateo. She was determined to keep her grandson safe, no matter what it took.

Chapter 9
Mateo

Santa Barbara School was a Catholic private school for children from kindergarten through eighth grade. Located on the same property as Santa Barbara Church, the school served as both an educational institution and a central part of the community. Annie had saved carefully to afford Mateo's tuition, believing that a Catholic education would help guide him as he grew.

Every morning, Annie made sure Mateo was dressed neatly in his uniform before walking him to the school bus stop. After school, he would take the bus to *Tan* Chai's house, where he waited until Annie came to pick him up after work. As Mateo grew older, his days at school and afternoons at *Tan* Chai's became part of a steady rhythm. By the time he was eight years old, Mateo started helping her care for her plants.

Tan Chai's garden was more than a simple hobby; it was the heart of her traditional medicine practice. Annie was pleased to see Mateo learning from *Tan* Chai, especially since the tasks were becoming harder for her as she aged. On weekends, Annie and Mateo would spend additional time at the house. Annie helped with cleaning and cooking, while Mateo assisted in the garden, watering plants, pulling weeds, and carrying cuttings for drying. Though it started as a small responsibility, his connection to the garden would soon grow into something extraordinary.

When Mateo was ten years old, he began to take on more advanced tasks in the garden. He watched closely as *Tan* Chai showed him how to care for the plants and identify the parts used for medicine. "Not all leaves are ready to be picked," she would explain, holding up an example. "The plants tell you when the time is right."

Mateo didn't entirely understand her words at first, but he paid attention, determined to do well. By the time he turned eleven years old, he had learned how to harvest the plants himself. One evening, Annie arrived at the house to see Mateo carrying a basket filled with fresh cuttings. "Is it okay for him to be harvesting?" she asked, looking at the basket. "Isn't he too young for that?"

Tan Chai giggled a little as Mateo handed her some fresh cuttings from one of the plants. She said, "Nene," and paused to receive the cuttings, then she looked back at Annie and continued, "Age doesn't matter. It's his hands. *Maolek... maolek kannai-ña!* His hands are so good!" she exclaimed.

Annie had never heard the expression before. "What do you mean his hands are good? Do you mean to tell me that he has a green thumb?"

"That's part of it," *Tan* Chai nodded. "But it's more than that." She started laying some cuttings between sheets of newspaper to begin drying them out. "With a green thumb, you can grow plants and keep them healthy. But being able to harvest the ingredients and keep their essence intact is also important."

"So he has to make sure not to damage the plant?" Annie was confused. "But isn't he already damaging the plant by harvesting it?"

Tan Chai pursed her lips to one side as she struggled to find a way to explain. "Mateo can feel when the plants are ready to be harvested. But it's even more than that." *Tan* Chai leaned closer to Annie. "When he harvests, it's almost like he can make the plants proud that they will be put to good use." *Tan* Chai then turned back toward the cuttings and continued. "It sounds crazy, but the plants take much longer to wilt when he cuts them. It's like he preserves their energy even though they have been cut."

Annie's confusion turned to amazement. She had

never heard anything like this before. "Okay, I get it. But how can he do that?"

"I know how he can do it. But I don't know why," *Tan* Chai admitted. "Everything in the physical world and in the spiritual world is made up of energy. Somehow, Mateo is able to work with those energies. That's how he can do what he does with the plants. He works with both the physical and spiritual energies of the plants. That makes the plants more potent when they are used in the medicines." Then *Tan* Chai started shaking her head as if in defeat and said, "But as far as why he can do it, that's a question only God can answer."

*****

One Friday afternoon, Annie went to *Tan* Chai's house to get Mateo, as was their ritual. As Annie and *Tan* Chai were talking, Mateo had been inside the house packing up his homework so he could go home with Annie. However, as he came out of the house to head to Annie's car, *Tan* Chai called him over. She was excited to share more with Annie about what she was discovering in Mateo.

"Boy, come tell your grandma how you helped me today in the jungle back here," *Tan* Chai said.

Annie was shocked. "In the jungle? You let him in the jungle?" Annie didn't say more than that in front of Mateo because she didn't want to bring up all that had happened leading up to his birth. But she knew *Tan* Chai would understand her very justified concern.

"Wait until you hear this," *Tan* Chai said as she signaled with one hand to Annie to calm down.

Mateo paused and looked down as he scratched his head. "I forgot how to say it, *Tan* Chai."

"*Håle' tinanom katso*," *Tan* Chai replied.

"Oh yeah." Mateo then turned to Annie. "*Tan* Chai needed more ingredients to make more medicine... uh, *åmot tininu*. So, some of the leaves were easy to find because their plants are big and easy to spot. However, she also needed *håle' tinanom katso*."

"What is that?" Annie asked.

Mateo shrugged, "Some kind of root. But the plant is harder to see in all the jungle areas here. Tan Chai asked me to go with her to look for some so she could show me what it looked like and how to harvest it. She planted them in a couple of areas in the jungle and she wanted to see if I could find them without her giving me directions."

Annie was listening but would still give an occasional glare at *Tan* Chai. "Okay," she said as she nodded to Mateo that she understood what they were doing.

Mateo continued, "So I looked at the jungle and said, 'Okay. If I was some *håle' tinanom katso*, where would I be hiding?' Then all of the sudden, *Tan* Chai and I both got chills like there was taotaomo'na here. It was very weird."

"What?!" Annie shouted.

"No. Not bad taotaomo'na," Mateo said. "I felt really

comfortable, like when you or *Tan* Chai are with me. And there was a strong, flowery smell, like the scent of perfume."

Tan Chai chimed in, "It was *kalachucha*, the plumeria flower. I smelled it, too."

Annie nodded. "Mmm. So it was friendly taotaomo'na?"

Tan Chai nodded, "Yes, *nene*. Very friendly."

"Yeah," Mateo continued. "I wasn't even scared when I heard a voice saying, *'Sigi mågge'* and I saw some leaves shaking a little in one spot in the jungle."

Annie had lost her daughter to taotaomo'na and now her grandson was talking about voices in the jungle calling him to them. She was very furious with her aunt for taking Mateo into the jungle. "*Tan* Chai! What do you think you are you doing?"

Tan Chai tried to reassure her. "Don't worry, *nene*. Remember there are good *taotaomo'na* and there are bad ones. There are some very kind ones around my house. I think they're here because they like that I help people."

"Grandma?" Mateo said as he turned to Annie with a slightly perplexed look on his face. "Now, I hear someone saying, *'Tåya' guaha. Man familia hit'*. I think I'm supposed to say it to you."

Annie's jaw dropped. The *taotaomo'na* were saying they were family? But before Annie could say anything, *Tan* Chai slammed her hands together in one loud clap and then pointed at Annie.

"That's it! The *taotaomo'na* say they are related to us. Now it makes sense why they are so friendly." She started waving her index finger at Annie to make a point as she said, "I can bet you they have been watching over him whenever he is here. That's why there have been no bad *taotaomo'na* around all these years, even though my house is surrounded by jungle."

Annie thought to herself, Mateo has extra protection here? She shook her head as if to get reoriented. "Thank you, God", she said out loud. She quickly followed with a thank you to the *taotaomo'na* who had been protecting Mateo by saying, "*Guella yan guello, dångkulu na si Yu'us ma'åse'!*"

Tan Chai walked over to Annie and hugged her. She let out a little giggle, then looked at Annie. "Guess whose voice I'm hearing in my head right now?"

"Hahaha!" laughed Annie. "Father Rogelio saying God works in mysterious ways?"

Tan Chai smiled, and with a lift of her eyebrows and a nod of her head, she said, "That's right. But wait! My boy didn't get to finish his story yet."

"Oh yeah. Sorry," Annie said. "Continue, Mateo. The voice called you, and the leaves were shaking."

While Annie and *Tan* Chai were talking, Mateo had been distracted by a beetle that had landed on his shoulder. He had it crawling on a finger as he replied to Annie, "That was all."

Annie raised an eyebrow at Mateo.

"Just kidding," he said with a big smile.

"Uh-huh?" Annie replied as she smiled back. "So, what happened?"

Mateo turned back toward the jungle behind *Tan* Chai's house. "The leaves were moving just in that one spot near that avocado tree," he said as he pointed. "But before we went, I asked for permission first, like we're supposed to. Then we walked to the spot, and that's where we found it. The *håle' tinanom katso*."

Annie asked, "So you know how to ask permission, too?"

"Yeah. *Tan* Chai made me memorize it, and I'm always supposed to ask before doing anything in the jungle. To ask permission for picking plants, we say *guella yan guello, kao sina yu' manule' tinanoum-mu ya yanggen matto hao gi tano'-hu fanule' ha' sin mamaisen.*"

Tan Chai was so proud. "I didn't give him any hints. He knew where he was going. I actually planted some in a couple of other places a while back, but this one was ready for harvesting. He didn't just find the right plant. He found the one that was ready to harvest." She walked up to Mateo, wrapped her hands on his cheeks, and kissed him on his forehead. "My boy has a gift, and he's only eleven years old."

Annie was amazed, worried, but amazed. Her head was filled with a number of thoughts. Why is this happening to him? What does it mean? Are these signs of something good... or something bad? Either way, it was definitely reassuring to know that there were good spirits watching over Mateo.

*****

Mateo spent much of his childhood in and around the Santa Barbara Church. Annie attended mass almost every day, and Mateo was always by her side. As he matured, he had grown so familiar with the church's prayers and all of the procedures that it felt natural for him to become an altar server. Wearing the cassock for the first time, standing beside the priest at the altar, filled him with pride and a sense of purpose.

At first, Mateo was assigned to assist during weeknight masses, which were smaller and quieter. As he gained experience, he was gradually included in weekend masses, which were usually packed with parishioners. Over time, as his familiarity with the ceremonies and various tasks increased, he started serving at special ceremonies like baptisms and weddings. He loved the responsibility and took pride in helping with the sacred services.

Mateo quickly grew close to the other altar servers, many of whom were pairs of brothers around the same age. There were the Duenas brothers, the Ninete brothers, the San Nicolas brothers, and the Cruz brothers, and working alongside them felt like being part of a larger family.

One thing that always made Mateo laugh was Father Rogelio's playful sense of humor. The priest who oversaw the altar servers had a habit of adjusting their schedule. Since the schedule was kept on a clipboard hanging in the Sacristy, it usually showed who would be serving which masses each week. Father Rogelio would then look through the whole schedule, and wherever he found Chris San Nicolas on the schedule, Father Rogelio would write a 't' at the end of his first name to change it from "Chris" to "Christ." Mateo thought it was hilarious every time he spotted the little edits.

Also, Father Rogelio knew Mateo's story well. He had been there to comfort Annie during the tragedy of Joleen's death and the miraculous birth of her son. Perhaps because of this, the priest seemed to hold a special place in his heart for Mateo. Often, when he saw Mateo, he would trace a small sign of the cross on his forehead as a blessing.

One day, as Father Rogelio was blessing him, Mateo pulled a piece of candy from his pocket. "Would you like some, Father?" he asked earnestly.

Father Rogelio smirked. "Hmm. You are like the serpent," he teased, giggling a little.

Mateo tilted his head, confused. "What do you mean?"

"I'm on a diet," the priest explained, patting his round belly with a chuckle. "You're tempting me, like the serpent with the forbidden fruit!"

Mateo burst into laughter, finally understanding that the priest was joking. Over time, he had grown close to Father Rogelio and had come to see him as a funny uncle and as someone who could always make him smile.

One day, Father Tony, Santa Barbara Church's other priest, was admitted to the hospital, leaving Father Rogelio as the only priest at the parish to handle all the responsibilities. One of those duties was visiting the hospital to administer last rites. With so much to manage, he asked Annie if Mateo could accompany him to help carry supplies. Annie trusted Father Rogelio completely and agreed, though she was surprised by the request.

At the hospital, Mateo proved to be a natural helper. He stayed organized, managing the supplies the priest needed and assisting with small tasks while Father Rogelio focused on comforting the patients and their families. By the time they got to the third patient, Father Rogelio had noticed something about how the patients and family members responded to Mateo being in the room. Some of them recognized Mateo from church, but they didn't know him personally. However, the patients that happened to be conscious seemed to be calmer and more at peace when Mateo was around, their families included. So, Father Rogelio asked Mateo to join him as they said prayers over the patients and then again to say prayers over the family members who were present.

After finishing prayers in the rooms, the priest turned to Mateo in the hallway. "Are you comfortable helping me with these visits?" he asked gently. "You understand what we are doing here, yes?"

Mateo nodded without hesitation. "Yes, I understand

Father, and I'm fine. A lot of people here are sad and scared, and we're here to help them."

"Yes, Mateo," Father Rogelio said, patting him on the shoulder. "You're right. And you're doing well. I'm proud of you."

Mateo smiled. "So, who's next?"

"Actually, my son, we're done for the day. Let's get you home," the priest said.

As they turned to leave, Mateo suddenly felt a sharp, icy chill run down his spine. The sensation was so strong that his body physically shivered. Startled, he glanced behind him, his gaze falling on the far end of the hallway as Father Rogelio passed in front of him.

There, standing near the end of the hallway, was a large, sinister-looking, black dog. It was unlike any animal Mateo had ever seen before. Its fur was coarse and wild, and its eyes burned with an intense, hostile glare. The dog stood still, its head low, ears pinned back, staring directly at him.

Mateo's heart pounded. Why isn't anyone else seeing this? he thought. He turned to glance at Father Rogelio, hoping the priest might notice the creature. But Father Rogelio was already walking ahead, unaware of Mateo's growing fear.

When Mateo turned back to look at the dog, it was gone, and the hallway was empty. Despite its disappearance, the uneasy feeling lingered. Mateo stayed close to the priest as they exited the building and walked to the car. Even as they left the parking lot, he couldn't shake the sensation that he was being watched. The sooner we get out of here, the better, he thought.

He didn't mention the dog to Father Rogelio or Annie that evening. But as he lay in bed that night, the image of the dog and its piercing stare haunted his thoughts. Mateo didn't know what it meant, but deep down, he felt it was more than just a stray animal. Something had changed, and he couldn't help but wonder if the encounter was a warning, or a sign of things to come.

Chapter 10

Tan Chai's Revelation

The morning air was still cool, but the faint warmth of the sun had begun to seep through the leaves of the papaya tree outside. *Tan* Chai stood on the porch of her modest home, a wooden structure that had weathered decades of typhoons and the sun. The house, though simple, was a reflection of her life: neat and orderly.

A small grotto in the front yard caught the first rays of sunlight. The Virgin Mary statue, nestled within a careful arrangement of rocks and seashells, stood as a silent testament to her unwavering faith. Flowers that were freshly picked lay at the statue's base, along with a rosary draped carefully around The Virgin Mary's hands.

Inside the house, the living room walls were a gallery of memories. A prominent photograph of a young man in an army dress uniform hung next to her wedding picture. The young man had *Tan* Chai's sharp cheekbones and warm eyes. It was her son, Daniel, who had enlisted in the army during the Vietnam War.

Daniel's loss was an ache that never truly left her. She had been proud of his decision to serve, a choice many CHamoru men made out of pride and a deep sense of duty. But pride had turned to devastation when the news arrived that Daniel was not coming home. The grief had threatened to consume her, but *Tan* Chai had found solace in her faith and her work as a *suruhåna*.

Next to Daniel's photograph was a small picture of Mother Teresa, her weathered face radiating compassion. Another framed piece displayed a simple Vatican flag, a keepsake from Pope John Paul II's visit to Guam in 1981. These images were her anchors, reminders of the strength she drew from her faith and her purpose.

She then moved to the kitchen for a glass of water. As she sat down at the wooden table in her kitchen, her eyes fell on a crotchet plaque that one of her patients had made for her. It had words inscribed on it saying, "May your hands bring comfort and your heart offer peace. May you heal and be healed, bringing light where there is dark." These words pulled a memory from her childhood. It was one she tried not to dwell on, but it lingered in the quiet moments, unbidden and sharp, reminding her of when things had gone dark in her life during those years.

She had been ten years old, a curious girl with a knack for wandering. Her grandmother had sent her to the edge of the jungle to collect *gålak fedda'* leaves for a remedy of external wounds. The jungle was familiar territory as she had often played near its edges, chasing birds or gathering wildflowers.

That day, however, something was different. The air felt heavier, and the usual rustling of leaves and chirping of birds was absent. It was as if the jungle was holding its breath.

She remembered trying to gather the leaves from their tree branches when the world around her seemed to blur. The vibrant greens of the jungle dulled, and a strange humming noise filled her ears. Her hands froze, the leaves slipping from her grasp.

When she woke, hours had passed. She was lying in a tangled web of pandanus roots, her body stiff and her mind foggy. Villagers searching for her found her in that spot, her eyes wide and unseeing.

It took days for her to recover fully, and even then, she couldn't explain what had happened. Her grandmother performed a cleansing ritual immediately to ensure she was free of any lingering spiritual attachments. The elder, assisted by her mother, began by giving her a bed bath with holy water mixed with herbs.

This was followed with *palai* containing coconut oil, ashes of burnt blessed palm leaves, *alangilang* flower, and other herbs. As her grandma was doing this, she continued to mutter prayers and burned dried herbs, waving the smoke around her body as she sat motionless, still grappling with the strange experience. However, her family wasn't deterred by her lack of motion as they continued to pray the rosary as led by her grandmother.

From that day on, she avoided the jungle. It wasn't just fear, it was respect. She had felt the power of the *taotaomo'na*, the ancient spirits of the land, and she understood the consequences of crossing boundaries they guarded.

The villagers whispered about her experience. Some said she had been taken by the *taotaomo'na*, while others believed it was a warning. Whatever it was, it left an indelible mark on her. The jungle no longer felt like a familiar friend. Instead, it was an entity, alive and watchful, one she kept at arm's length.

As the years passed, *Tan* Chai channeled her energy into learning the traditional ways of healing. Her grandmother was a renowned *suruhåna*, and *Tan* Chai was eager to absorb her knowledge. She learned how to prepare teas from *tumon* and sage, how to grind *hågon pi'ao* and *patma* leaves for medicinal paste, and how to read the body's ailments through subtle signs.

Yet, despite her expertise, she remained wary of venturing too far into the spiritual realm. While her grandmother had often communicated with the *taotaomo'na*, seeking their guidance and blessings, *Tan* Chai hesitated. The memory of her childhood experience made her cautious. She focused instead on healing the physical, mending wounds, easing fevers, and soothing aches.

Her garden became her sanctuary. Rows of medicinal plants - *kaktos, tupon ayuyu, halom tano* - thrived under her care. She spent hours tending to them, their growth offering a quiet affirmation of her purpose.

After her grandmother passed on, *Tan* Chai became a trusted healer in the community. People came to her with different illnesses, and she greeted and treated each patient with a calm presence and a deep understanding of their pain.

Then came Mateo in her life. He was different, *Tan* Chai could sense that immediately. His aura seemed to ripple, a mix of light and shadow, as if the physical and spiritual worlds competed for his attention. She was also able to recognize the same pull in Mateo that she had felt as a child: the call of the *taotaomo'na*. But Mateo's curiosity was unrelenting, and his openness was disarming. He reminded her of herself before fear had taken root.

One afternoon, they sat in her garden, the scent of crushed herbs thick in the air. Mateo held a small mortar and pestle, grinding the roots under her guidance.

"Do you feel it?" she asked, watching him closely.

"Feel what?" Mateo looked up; his brow furrowed in

concentration.

"The energy," she replied. "When you grind the roots, you release their spirit. Everything has energy - plants, stones, water. You must respect that energy and work with it, not against it."

Mateo nodded, his hands slowing as he focused on the task.

"You have a gift, Mateo," *Tan* Chai continued. "But it is not just a gift. It is also a responsibility. The *taotaomo'na* are never selfless in their gifts. Accept what they offer with respect, for they always demand something in return."

He looked up, his young face serious. "Do they scare you?"

Tan Chai hesitated, her gaze drifting to the edge of the garden where the jungle loomed. "Sometimes." She admitted. "They scare me because I know their power. I have felt it. But fear is not a weakness, Mateo. It is a teacher. It reminds us to be cautious."

*****

As Mateo's visits became more frequent, *Tan* Chai began to share pieces of her past with him. One day, as they sat under the shade of one of the trees in her yard, she told him about her son, Daniel.

"He was brave," she said, her voice steady but tinged with sorrow. "He wanted to serve, to make us proud. And he did. But the war... it took him."

Mateo listened intently, his young heart heavy with her pain. "Do you miss him?"

"Every day," *Tan* Chai replied. "But I don't let that pain consume me. Instead, I use it to help others. That is how I honor him."

Her voice softened as she continued. "But there is something else I need to tell you. Something I've never told anyone."

Mateo leaned forward, sensing the weight of her words.

"When I was a girl, I was taken by the *taotaomo'na*," she said. Her hands trembled slightly as she clasped them together. "I don't remember everything, but I remember enough to know their power is not something to take lightly."

She described the trance, the tangled roots, the days it took to recover. Mateo listened, his eyes wide with both fear and fascination.

"Why are you telling me this now?" he asked.

"Because you are special, Mateo. The *taotaomo'na* are watching you, just as they once watched me. But you have something I didn't; a strength I can see but cannot explain. You have the potential to do what I could not. To face them."

Mateo's voice was barely a whisper. "What if I'm not strong enough?"

Tan Chai placed a hand on his shoulder, her grip firm but reassuring. "You are. But strength isn't just about courage. It's about knowing when to be cautious, when to seek help, and when to stand firm. We are all here and are willing to help you, Mateo, but you must promise me one thing."

"What?"

"Never forget to respect the *taotaomo'na*. The moment you lose that respect; they will remind you why you should fear them."

*****

Tan Chai's bond with Mateo deepened as she taught him not just about plants and remedies, but about the delicate balance between the physical and spiritual worlds. She showed him how to ground himself, to focus his energy, and to listen to the subtle cues of his surroundings.

Despite her own fears, she found herself inspired by Mateo's determination. He was a reminder of what she had once been: a child, unburdened by the weight of past traumas, willing to face the unknown with an open heart.

As the days passed, *Tan* Chai began to see her role more clearly. She was not just a healer or a mentor; she was a protector. Her purpose was to guide Mateo, to prepare him for what lay ahead, even if it meant confronting her own fears in the process.

In Mateo, she saw hope, not just for herself, but for the connection between their world and the world of the *taotaomo'na*. And for the first time in years, *Tan* Chai felt a flicker of courage in her own heart.

Chapter 11
The Gift

"Mateo, how is the *åmot tininu* coming along?" *Tan* Chai called out from the living room, her voice calm yet warm. Mateo stood in the kitchen, carefully stirring a pot, his focus unwavering.

"It's almost ready, *Tan* Chai. Just letting it cool," he replied, wiping his hands on a towel.

In the living room, *Tan* Chai was massaging an oil mix onto Mrs. Benavente's knees. The older woman winced slightly at first but soon sighed as the relief began to set in.

"This *palai* should help with your knee pain," said

Tan Chai, her hands moving with practiced ease. "I'll just massage it in for a little bit while we wait for your *åmot*."

"What's in it?" Mrs. Benavente asked, curious.

"What's in the *palai*? Well, it's a secret family recipe," *Tan* Chai replied with a small smile. "It's just a few herbs and roots all mixed into coconut oil."

Mateo soon entered, carrying a small cup of *åmot*. "Here it is. It's all cooled down a bit and ready to drink," he announced, setting it on the table next to them.

Mrs. Benavente looked at Mateo with admiration. "It's nice to see someone so young learning how to do all of this."

Tan Chai smiled proudly. "It really is," she agreed as she handed the *åmot* to Mrs. Benavente. "And between us, I think his *åmot* might work better than mine now. But I'm afraid that we can't do much about the taste," she added, chuckling along with Mrs. Benavente.

Mateo's journey as a healer had begun at the age of thirteen, when *Tan* Chai had begun teaching him her recipes for *åmot* and *palai*. Most of the *palai* recipes were fairly simple, involving adding ingredients to coconut oil. The *åmot* recipes, however, sometimes required a little more finesse. But Mateo's natural talent for growing and harvesting the ingredients seemed to carry over into preparing them and turning them into traditional medicines.

In time, *Tan* Chai started training him to perform massages and apply *palai*. He was still very young, so he couldn't perform any of the massages requiring stronger pressure. However, he was able to learn some of the lighter massages. Patients who had seen Mateo learning to make the medicines welcomed the chance for him to assist with massages because they saw and trusted his natural healing talents.

One afternoon, Mateo was helping in the garden when a car pulled into the driveway. A strange, uneasy feeling gripped him. His hands trembled, and sweat formed on his brow.

"*Tan* Chai? I don't feel good. Can I stay in the back?" he asked, his voice shaking and desperate to be away from whatever it was that was heading toward the door.

"Of course, my boy," she replied, though she, too, felt an unusual heaviness in the air as the visitor walked up to her front door.

There was a very bad *taotaomo'na* feeling that came with the visitor. The newcomer's name was Mike Blaz, and he had heard about *Tan* Chai and had come to her for help with what looked like a *taotaomo'na* illness. He had called about thirty minutes before heading over, so *Tan* Chai was expecting him. However, he hadn't mentioned what he needed help with. He had come off as cocky and rude over the phone, nevertheless, *Tan* Chai was always willing to help anyone if she could.

Regardless of how she was feeling, *Tan* Chai opened the door to welcome them. As the man approached, *Tan* Chai could see that he had a large welt on the left side of his neck that seemed to keep his head tilted because of the swelling. He walked in with crutches because it seemed as though he also couldn't use his left leg. As he walked in, his girlfriend held the door open for him. Before walking outside toward the back, Mateo caught a glimpse of the couple.

"*Hafa adai*, Mr. Blaz. How can I help you?" asked *Tan* Chai, her voice steady but cautious. She could already tell what his problem was, but she didn't want to just turn him away right at the door.

Just as he was on the phone, he spoke with a brash but strained voice. "The doctor doesn't know how to help. He doesn't know why my neck and leg are all swollen. He says maybe it's gout or an allergic reaction, but I think it's *taotaomo'na*."

"I see," replied *Tan* Chai. "I believe you're right. But I'm sorry, Mr. Blaz. I can't help with *taotaomo'na* illnesses or injuries. I don't know the medicines to use or how to make them," she informed Mike. "All I can do is suggest that you retrace your steps and return to the place where you might have upset the *taotaomo'na* so that you can ask for forgiveness."

This seemed to make him more upset. "What the hell? Aren't you a *suruhåna*? Aren't you supposed to help with *taotaomo'na* illness?" he snapped.

"I wish I could, but a lot of the knowledge and skills regarding *taotaomo'na* remedies were lost over time. We learn only what we are taught, and we all have different specialties," *Tan* Chai explained patiently. "There is a *suruhånu* in Chalan Pågo who can help you.

His..."

"This is a waste of time. Let's go. We need to find a real *suruhåna*," Blaz muttered, cutting her off. He turned and hobbled back to the car, muttering angrily to his girlfriend as they drove away.

After they left, *Tan* Chai couldn't help but think, *he probably got what he deserved.* She then went outside to check on Mateo.

"Mateo, they're gone," she called out. However, she didn't see him, and he did not respond.

"Mateo?" She turned the corner to the back of the house and found him curled up on the ground, leaning up against the wall with his arms around his knees. "Are you okay, my boy?"

"I'm sorry, *Tan* Chai. I was so scared. I felt that *taotaomo'na*, but it was so angry," he whispered, his voice trembling.

"You felt it correctly. It was angry, but not evil. Sometimes they're just mad because they've been disrespected," she explained, hugging him tightly.

"But it was like I could feel how it was hurting. I was feeling its anger. It made me feel so nauseous and dizzy." Mateo looked at *Tan* Chai and said, "I felt like it was trying to make me angry, too."

Tan Chai just continued to hug Mateo for a while before urging him to get up. "You have a strong gift, Mateo. It lets you feel these things deeply. Now come on, let's go inside so you can rest."

*****

As Mateo grew older, his responsibilities as an altar server expanded. He began assisting with more masses and ceremonies at the church. One day, he was assigned with the Ninete brothers to serve at a funeral where Father Tony would be presiding. This was Mateo's first funeral, so he would be following the lead of the brothers, and he was nervous but eager to learn. Peter, the older brother, was fifteen while David, the youngest, was thirteen. The funeral was actually for one of their uncles.

The ceremony began with a viewing at the church, where Mateo caught his first glimpse of the deceased: an elderly man dressed in a sharp suit, lying peacefully in his casket. Mateo thought the Ninete brothers' uncle looked nice in a suit and tie as he lay peacefully in the casket.

After the mass, a hearse then transported the casket to the cemetery where the deceased would be buried. Everyone in attendance hopped in their cars to follow the hearse in a procession to the cemetery. Prior to the procession, arrangements had been made to have the Police Department stop traffic at intersections in order to allow the procession to pass through uninterrupted, so that went by smoothly.

At the interment ceremony, Father Tony and the altar servers waited by the interment site as the procession of family and friends arrived and gathered around. A canopy had been set up over the site to offer shade for the immediate family during the service. It was late afternoon, but it was still hot under the shade of the canopy. As the interment services began, something seemed out of place to Mateo.

There was a man in a suit and tie standing among the grieving family. The man then placed his hand on his loved ones' shoulders as a gesture of comfort while they cried. Suddenly, he seemed to notice Mateo looking at him, and as their eyes met, he closed his and nodded his head toward Mateo as if to acknowledge him. The man then walked through the crowd and disappeared. Mateo could have sworn that the man was the same person he had seen lying in the casket earlier. He didn't want to upset anyone, so he kept it to himself. *Maybe it was just someone else who looked like the deceased*, he thought. After all, it could have been a possibility since he didn't know the family very well.

However, the same thing happened at subsequent funerals that Mateo assisted with. He would see the deceased in their casket before it was closed at the church. Then he would see the deceased again, saying goodbye to their loved ones before walking into the crowd and disappearing. There was nothing threatening about them, but he knew it wasn't normal.

The last thing he needed was people teasing him saying, "Who 'ya gonna call?" The coincidence of these sightings happening just after the release of *Ghostbusters* only made him more certain no one would believe him.

The spirits he saw looked like normal people. They weren't like the horror movies portrayed, bloody and scary. So, he couldn't really tell if they were spirits or not. It was only at the funerals where he could tell because he would see their bodies in the casket, and he would also see them walking around at their interment ceremony. But they always faded away shortly after.

Mateo wanted to understand more about what was going on, but he didn't know who to ask. Annie and *Tan* Chai both knew about the friendly *taotaomo'na* around *Tan* Chai's house. Maybe they would believe him if he told them he could see ghosts. While on the topic, he thought he could also ask about his parents. He felt he was old enough to know who they were and what had happened to them. *And if people say those who love you are always with you even after they die, then why do I never see my parents?* There were so many things that didn't make sense.

So, one day when Annie came to pick up Mateo from *Tan* Chai's house, Mateo took the opportunity to ask them. They had just finished eating some food that Annie brought over for dinner. His grandma and *Tan* Chai were still sitting at the table when Mateo finished clearing and washing the dishes.

As they sat at the table, he blurted out, "Grandma, *Tan* Chai, do you believe in ghosts?"

The women exchanged glances before nodding. "Yes, Mateo. Why do you ask?" Annie replied.

"Are ghosts and *taotaomo'na* the same thing?" he asked.

Annie nodded again but looked at *Tan* Chai to confirm. *Tan* Chai responded, "Yes. They are the same. But usually when someone says *taotaomo'na*, they are referring to the spirits of our ancient CHamoru ancestors."

"Has anyone ever seen *taotaomo'na*... or ghosts?"

This time, Annie clearly deferred to *Tan* Chai who replied, "I've heard stories. Usually, the stories say that they will only let you see them if they want you to see them. But I don't really know for sure."

Mateo seemed a little disheartened when she said that.

"There was an old *suruhåna* that I knew who survived World War II when the Japanese controlled Guam. Your grandma and I took you to visit her when you were born. She remembered hearing stories about people who could see and talk to the spirits. She didn't know much about it herself because she was still young when she heard the stories. But when we took you to visit her, she said that she could feel something from you that reminded her of those stories. She said that she thought you had the gift of the *makåna*. They were like *suruhånos* who could see and talk to spirits."

Annie smiled. "You're referring to *Tan* Paro, right?"

"Yes, I am."

Tan Chai continued, "I don't know why I didn't think of it before. But the way you are with the plants and medicines... and the way the *taotaomo'na* around here seem to help you, I guess I wouldn't be surprised if you could also see and talk to the *taotaomo'na*. You have already heard them talk to you before."

As *Tan* Chai said that, both she and Annie were now starting to wonder if that was why Mateo started the discussion.

"So, yeah. Uhmm..." Mateo started but paused and fidgeted. "So, I think I do see ghosts." He looked at both *Tan* Chai and Annie to see how they reacted. He was relieved that they didn't seem to doubt him. Instead, they both shifted their chairs to face him more directly.

"How do you know they're ghosts?" Annie asked.

"I've only noticed when I serve at funerals. I would see the person in the casket at the church. But then at the cemetery, I see them again, like they're saying goodbye to their family, and then they disappear."

"Wow!" Annie said, amazed. "That's very touching and..." her voice then took on a more solemn tone, "and even reassuring. Nobody ever sees that kind of thing, but they say you can sometimes feel the spirit of your loved one after they've passed away." She was thinking of her late husband as she said that.

Tan Chai added, "My boy, you really are something special."

"I have a question, though." Mateo asked. "If I can see spirits, and they say that the people you love who have died are always with you, then why have I never seen my parents?"

There it was. Annie knew that one day he would ask about his parents. She figured that no matter when it was that he asked, she would never be ready to answer. She was right. She had no idea where to start.

Tan Chai jumped in saying, "I think it's like I said. Sometimes you only see them if they want you to see them."

Annie pulled out the chair in front of her and gestured for Mateo to have a seat. She held his hand and said, "Your dad... I don't think your mom and your dad were getting along before you were born." Annie knew he was old enough to know, but still wanted to protect him. "So maybe you don't have a strong connection to him. He passed away before he could get to know you."

"Yes. Your parents were very young and made some mistakes." *Tan* Chai tried to help Annie with explaining. "Most people get more time to learn from their mistakes. A lot of times, having children helps them learn and become better people. Your parents didn't get that chance."

"I know my dad died in a motorcycle accident. I guess it makes sense that we didn't have time to connect and that's why I don't see him. But what about my mom?"

Annie took in a deep breath before continuing. "Your mom was actually in the hospital because of a *taotaomo'na* illness."

"What?" Mateo asked.

"She was already eight months pregnant with you when she went to a party at night in a place she had never been to before. They were partying outside near a river along the jungle and with a big banyan tree in the yard." Tears were starting to trickle down Annie's eyes as she spoke. "She didn't know how bad it could be to do all of that when you're pregnant. I was supposed to warn her, but she left before I could."

Tan Chai reached out to hold Annie's hand. "It wasn't your fault, Annie."

Mateo thought for a while. "Is that how we know Kiko?" he asked. "Did he try to help my Mom?"

Tan Chai was quick to respond. "Yes, my boy. We called him to help."

"Then why did she still die?"

Tan Chai continued, "We think it was because the illness hit her too fast and too hard. Kiko also said it was a very strong *taotaomo'na* that had made her sick." Nobody wanted to tell Mateo that Kiko had thought the *taotaomo'na* was actually after Mateo. They didn't want the boy to start thinking it was his fault that his mother died.

The thought of his mother having *taotaomo'na* illness brought tears to Mateo's eyes. He couldn't help but to draw parallels to what he witnessed with Mike Blaz. Mateo remembered how he could feel the anger of the *taotaomo'na* that made the man sick. He could easily imagine what his mother had to go through. Knowing that it got so bad that it killed her filled him with a deep sorrow that weighed heavy on his heart.

*****

A couple of days had passed, but Mateo still couldn't shake the thought of his mother suffering because of a *taotaomo'na*. The idea lingered in his mind, growing heavier each time he thought about it. Even the excitement of being on a field trip, which was a rare treat for the students, couldn't distract him.

Mateo sat by the window on the school bus, staring at the blur of trees and houses as they sped past. Normally, he would've been eager to visit Gef Pa'go, a living replica of an ancient CHamoru village nestled in Inarajan. The field trip promised lessons in weaving, demonstrations of traditional baking, candy making, and other hands-on activities to immerse students in the daily lives of their ancestors. Mateo had looked forward to it for weeks, but now his thoughts were elsewhere.

Even as his classmates chatted excitedly, swapping snacks and planning how they'd spend their time at the village, Mateo remained quiet. His thoughts kept circling back to his mother and the ominous connection Kiko had hinted at - a powerful *taotaomo'na* causing her suffering.

It was going to be a long ride. The teachers on the bus, knowing how restless middle schoolers could get, decided to entertain them with local stories and legends. Each teacher took turns narrating as they passed notable landmarks. Mateo only half-listened at first, his thoughts elsewhere.

The first story began as they approached the Two Lovers' Point, a towering cliff overlooking the sea. The teacher recounted the tragic legend of two lovers - one a CHamoru maiden, the other a Spanish soldier - who leapt to their deaths rather than be separated by the girl's arranged marriage to another man. Some students gasped at the story's dramatic end, while others whispered about the bravery of the lovers.

Later, as they passed the Sirena statue in Hagåtña, another teacher told the story of the girl cursed to become a mermaid. Mateo found it mildly interesting but didn't engage much. He mumbled a quick answer when the teacher asked the class how Sirena had earned her fate - she had defied her mother by swimming instead of helping with chores.

As the bus entered the village of Asan, the story shifted to a more cosmic legend. This one was about the sibling deities Puntan and Fu'una, who used their own bodies to create the earth, sea, and skies. Mateo found it harder to ignore this tale, with its themes of sacrifice and creation. Still, he remained mostly quiet, his thoughts straying back to his own life. However, the next one caught his full attention.

Then, as the bus passed the shores of Agat, the tone of the stories changed. This time, the teachers spoke of the *taotaomo'na* - the spirits of the ancestors who lived in the land, trees, and caves. The legends of the *taotaomo'na* were both fascinating and terrifying, blurring the line between folklore and lived experiences for many of the students.

Mateo leaned forward slightly, his attention fully captured as the teachers described three particularly powerful *taotaomo'na*: Gamson, Gatos, and Anufat.

"Gamson," one teacher said, "is known for his incredible strength. He is said to inhabit the Pago Bay area. If you're ever in those parts, you'll feel his presence; like the weight of the air around you changes."

Another teacher picked up the thread. "Then there's Gatos. They say he commands other spirits who act as his minions. He's not one you'd want to cross, but he's not as feared as the third."

The bus fell into a hushed silence as the teachers described the final spirit: Anufat. "Anufat is monstrous," the teacher said. "They say he has fangs and claws, and there's a hole in his side, big enough to see right through him. People who encounter him speak of overwhelming dread. Some even say he can curse someone with just a glance."

Mateo's skin prickled. He had never heard of these spirits before. Growing up, he had thought all *taotaomo'na* were more or less the same - some friendlier, others more vengeful. But these three seemed in a league of their own. Could one of them have been responsible for what happened to his mother?

The thought unsettled him. Mateo glanced at the other students, who seemed equally captivated by the stories, though for different reasons. Some whispered nervously, while others joked to mask their unease. For

Mateo, the tales hit far closer to home.

Chapter 12

The Taotaomo'na's Warning

The dream began in silence. Mateo was in the middle of a jungle. The air felt heavy, thick with humidity, and his skin was damp with sweat. The towering trees around him were ancient, their branches twisting together to block out the sky. It was dim, but not completely dark. Rays of light fought their way through the gaps in the leaves, casting shifting patterns on the ground.

At first, nothing moved. Everything was still, the kind of stillness that made Mateo feel like he wasn't alone. The air itself seemed alive, as if it were watching him.

Then he saw it - the banyan tree. It was massive, its roots thick and gnarled, sprawling across the forest floor like giant serpents. The tree stood out, more alive than the others, its presence dominating the jungle.

Beneath the banyan tree was a figure. Mateo couldn't see it clearly, but it was there, standing motionless in the shadow of the tree. The figure was tall and shrouded in darkness, its outline blurred as if it were part of the shadows themselves. Mateo's breath caught in his throat. He couldn't explain why, but he felt drawn to it, even as his heart pounded in his chest.

The figure raised its arm, moving slowly, deliberately. Its hand stretched out, beckoning him to come closer. Mateo tried to step back, but his feet wouldn't move. He felt frozen, as though the air around him had turned solid.

Then the whispers began. At first, they were faint, like the rustle of leaves. But they grew louder, sharper. They were everywhere, coming from the trees, the ground, even the air. The words were in CHamoru - familiar but not fully understood. Yet Mateo didn't need to know their meaning to sense their hostility.

"*Suha, sigi humånao,*" the voices hissed. "*Adahi. Sa guaha un ya'u.*"

The whispers grew more frantic, overlapping until Mateo couldn't tell one voice from another. They weren't just warnings; they were accusations, a chorus of angry spirits. His chest tightened, and his hands clenched into fists. He wanted to run, but his legs refused to obey.

Then he saw her. Instinctively, he knew it was her.

His mother stood behind the shadowy figure. Her face was pale, her eyes red as if she'd been crying for hours. She reached out to him, her lips moving as though she were calling his name, but her voice was lost in the chaos of the whispers. Mateo's heart ached seeing her like that, so sad and desperate.

"Mom!" he shouted, finding his voice at last. He tried to move toward her, but the shadowy figure stepped forward, blocking his path. Its presence was overwhelming, pressing down on him like a weight he couldn't lift. The whispers swirled around him, louder and louder, until everything went black.

Mateo woke up with a gasp, his chest heaving as if he had been running. His heart pounded so hard it hurt, and his shirt clung to him, soaked with sweat. The room was dark, but it didn't feel like it should. Something was off. The shadows in the corners seemed deeper, heavier, like they were hiding something.

He rubbed his face, trying to steady his breathing. His hands trembled as he reached for the glass of water on his bedside table. The cold liquid barely helped. He still felt the weight of the dream, like it had followed him out of sleep.

His eyes drifted to the window. It was closed, but the room felt cold, too cold for Guam's humid nights. Mateo pulled his blanket tighter around him, his body shivering. The dream replayed in his mind: the banyan tree, the shadowy figure, his mother. The whispers echoed faintly in his ears, even though he was awake.

*****

Over the next few days, Mateo's dreams didn't stop. Every night, they returned. The jungle. The banyan tree. The whispers. Each dream felt more real than the last. The shadowy figure was always there, waiting under the tree. And his mother; she looked worse each time, her figure fading like a photograph left in the sun.

Mateo's body felt heavier with each passing day. He was exhausted. His appetite was gone, and he struggled to concentrate at school. When his friends talked to him, their voices sounded far away, like they were underwater. He barely responded; his mind stuck in the dreams.

At home, strange things started happening. The garden, which was usually Mateo's favorite place, felt different. It was quieter than usual, the buzzing of insects and chirping of birds barely audible. The air there felt colder, just like his room at night. Mateo found himself avoiding the garden, even though he couldn't explain why.

One afternoon, while sitting on the veranda, Mateo noticed scratches on one of the wooden beams. The marks were deep and jagged, as if an animal had clawed at the wood. At first, he thought they were random. But as he looked closer, he realized they weren't. The scratches seemed to form letters, though they were faint and hard to read.

Annie had been watching Mateo closely. She noticed how quiet he had become, how he jumped at small noises, or stared off into space for long stretches of time. Finally, she called *Tan* Chai, hoping she could help.

When *Tan* Chai arrived, she didn't say much at first. She walked slowly around the house, her sharp eyes taking in everything. When she stepped into the garden, she paused. Her brow furrowed, and she made the sign of the cross.

"There's something here," he said quietly. "A presence."

When *Tan* Chai went back inside the house, Mateo hesitated before telling her about the dreams. As he described the shadowy figure, the banyan tree, and the whispers, she listened carefully, her face growing more serious with every word.

"Mateo," she said, her voice steady but grave, "we've seen how your gift is a blessing... but it is also a curse. It draws attention from the spirit world, and not all spirits are kind."

Mateo felt a chill run down his spine. "What do they want from me?"

"They want to test you," *Tan* Chai replied. "To see how strong you are. The *taotaomo'na,* especially the dark ones, don't let people like you go unnoticed. You've crossed into their world, and now they've noticed you."

That night, Mateo woke to a sound that made his blood run cold. It was a voice, deep and guttural, speaking in CHamoru. The words were sharp and harsh, filled with anger. Mateo couldn't understand all of it, but he caught enough to know it was a warning.

"*Ti siña hao umiscapa,*" the voice growled. "*Hu tungu i fuetsa mu, ya ti atman iyo-ku.*"

Mateo's room felt colder than ever. The shadows in the corners seemed alive, twisting and shifting as the voice echoed around him. He wanted to scream, to call for Annie, but fear held him frozen in place. The voice faded, but its presence lingered, pressing down on him like a weight.

The next morning, he lay in bed thinking about what he had heard during the night. It was still in the wee hours of the morning, and he had to use the restroom; however, he couldn't help but shudder at the thought of getting out of bed. When he finally found the courage to move, Mateo turned on the light. His heart nearly stopped when he looked at his arms. Red scratches ran down them, thin and sharp, as if made by claws. They hadn't been there the previous night when he went to bed.

*****

As the days passed, he continued visiting *Tan* Chai and learning more from her. Mateo hadn't forgotten the mysterious voices or dreams, however, despite his fear, he couldn't ignore the pull of the jungle. It was as if something was calling him, urging him to come closer.

One evening, just before the sun disappeared below the horizon, he followed the narrow path behind *Tan* Chai's house.

The jungle was eerily quiet. The usual hum of insects and rustle of leaves was gone, replaced by a silence that pressed against Mateo's ears. The light was dim, the shadows growing longer with each step he took.

As he walked, he heard whispers again, soft and faint, but unmistakable. They were calling his name. Mateo stopped, his breath catching in his throat. He turned slowly, his eyes scanning the trees.

Then he saw her again.

His mother was standing beneath a tree, her figure bathed in the faint glow of the setting sun. She looked just like she had in his dreams; her face pale and her eyes filled with sadness. She raised her hand, palm out, as if warning him to stay back.

"Mom?" Mateo whispered, taking a hesitant step forward.

She opened her mouth to speak, but no sound came. Her expression shifted to one of urgency, her hand shaking as she pointed to something behind Mateo. He turned quickly, his heart pounding, but there was nothing there. When he looked back, she was gone.

Mateo stood frozen, his mind racing. The whispers had stopped, and the jungle was still once again. But he didn't feel alone. Something was there, watching him.

Chapter 13

Into Hiding

In the weeks that followed, another funeral appeared on the Church schedule and Mateo was the only altar server assigned to assist. He didn't mind too much because Father Rogelio would be presiding. Serving alone was always easier when Father Rogelio was present because he had a calm demeanor and was patient when mistakes happened. But as Mateo stepped into the church that day, his chest tightened. He immediately recognized the man in the casket: Mike Blaz, the man who had come to *Tan* Chai for help after offending the *taotaomo'na*.

Unlike before, Mateo didn't feel the same angry, heavy presence he had noticed when Mr. Blaz was alive and suffering from the *taotaomo'na* illness. Yet, the atmosphere was still unsettling. The ceremony at the church ended as normal, and Mateo rode with Father Rogelio to the cemetery. This time, the interment was at the Pigo Catholic Cemetery. The cemetery was at the base of a hill, bordered by a river on one side and dense jungle along the back. Mateo felt strange as soon as he stepped out of the car. The space felt tight and stifling, almost as if he were being boxed in. It wasn't like the usual peaceful cemeteries he was used to.

The interment services went on as usual. However, during the services, Mateo realized that he didn't see the deceased. He looked around the crowd but didn't see Mr. Blaz's spirit anywhere. Then, out of the corner of his eye, he caught a glimpse of something standing at the edge of the jungle at the back of the cemetery. He didn't turn right away to get a better look because... well, because he got the same spine-chilling feeling that he had once felt at the hospital. But he had to know what it was. So, he slowly turned to look. It was the same ugly, horrible, big black dog that he saw at the hospital before. It just stood there, staring straight at him with its head dropped low and baring its enormous fangs, making its gaze even more menacing.

Unlike at the hospital, the dog didn't disappear right away. It seemed to pace along the edge of the jungle. It was almost as if it was watching Mateo, waiting for a chance to get to him. Mateo was distracted and he fumbled around a bit as he performed his tasks, and this led Father Rogelio to notice that something was up with Mateo. As soon as the service wrapped up, the priest pulled Mateo to the side and hunched over, discreetly asking, "What seems to be bothering you, my son?"

Mateo leaned into Father Rogelio and replied, "There's a really scary dog that keeps staring at me." He didn't look directly at it but gestured with his head to indicate where the dog was.

The priest's expression shifted to concern. "Where? Can you show me?"

Mateo hesitated but eventually nodded in the direction of the jungle. "Over there. Near the trees."

Father Rogelio turned to look but shook his head. "I don't see anything, Mateo. Are you sure?"

"Yes, Father," Mateo said, his voice barely audible. "Can we leave now? Please?"

Father Rogelio didn't press him further. "Of course. Just stay close to me. We will go now."

The priest didn't have to see the dog to believe Mateo. The boy was not the kind who made up things like that, and he could see how shaken the boy was. As they walked to the car, Mateo kept glancing over his shoulder, expecting the dog to lunge at him. Once inside the car, Mateo was quick to lock the door as he sank into the seat to hide. He remained that way as they drove away from the cemetery.

For the first few minutes of the drive, Mateo stayed quiet. His heart raced, and his thoughts were jumbled. He stared at the passing scenery, trying to calm down, and about ten minutes into the drive, Mateo seemed to calm down. He slowly sat back up to look out through the window. Finally, Father Rogelio broke the silence.

"Mateo," he asked gently, "have you seen that dog before?"

The boy stared out the window as he reluctantly answered, "Yes."

"Can you tell me a little about what it looked like?"

"It was big, black, and very mean-looking. It also looked very messy and dirty. But..." Mateo paused for a moment before slowly turning to look at Father Rogelio. "But it felt like a mean *taotaomo'na*."

The priest noticed that Mateo was a little hesitant to mention the word *taotaomo'na*, almost as though he was worried, he would not be believed. But Father Rogelio had no intention of dismissing Mateo's claim. Instead, he nodded thoughtfully and continued with his questions. "I see. Can you tell me where else you have seen this dog?"

"Actually, Father, it was at the hospital... when I went with you." Mateo glanced to see how Father Rogelio would react.

The priest gave a couple of big nods as he thought about what Mateo had been describing. "I do not think this is a real dog that you are seeing. I think you felt the *taotaomo'na* because it was indeed a *taotaomo'na*."

Hearing this, Mateo felt a mix of relief and dread. At least Father Rogelio believed him.

"This would explain why you could see the dog and I

couldn't," continued the priest.

Mateo now seemed more embarrassed than anything. "I'm sorry that I got so scared, Father."

The priest smiled and said, "Do not be sorry. I would be scared as well if I saw a mean dog like that." He tapped Mateo on the shoulder reassuringly.

The priest knew that many cultures had legends about the *ga'lågu* - demon dogs and hell hounds. He had also heard of *taotaomo'na* taking the form of animals, including dogs. Father Rogelio was worried that the dog was actually an evil spirit and that it might be singling out Mateo. But the last thing the priest wanted to do was to make the boy any more scared than he already was.

"Maybe you should not be assigned to serve at funerals anymore. How does that sound?" asked Father Rogelio.

Mateo nodded in agreement and repeated, "I'm sorry, Father."

They were just pulling into Annie's driveway. Father Rogelio put the car in park, then turned to Mateo and said, "There is no need to be sorry, my son. You have done nothing wrong. We have many altar servers to help. But it is important to listen to your heart. If you are truly feeling scared, then you should listen because your heart is telling you to be careful. Do you understand?"

"Yes. I understand," Mateo said.

"Good boy! Now let's go tell your grandmother. That way, she will not be surprised that you are not going to be scheduled to help with funerals anymore."

*****

The next day, Annie dropped Mateo off at *Tan* Chai's house since it was a Saturday. Annie joined *Tan* Chai at her small dining table where she was having some coffee while Mateo sat on the sofa across the way in the living room and turned on the television. Annie shared with *Tan* Chai what Father Rogelio and Mateo had told her about the evening before.

"A big black dog?" asked *Tan* Chai. She didn't look surprised when she asked. It seemed more that she was confirming that she had heard Annie correctly.

"Yes, *Tan* Chai."

Tan Chai asked across to the living room, "And you were the only one who saw the dog, Mateo?"

Mateo replied, "I think so. Father said he didn't see it and nobody else seemed to notice it."

"That does sound like a *taotaomo'na*. And this was at a funeral?" *Tan* Chai asked.

"Uh-huh. It was Mike Blaz's funeral," the boy answered.

She recognized the name right away. "Oh my!" she exclaimed as she adjusted to sit more upright in her chair. "He must have really angered a very bad *taotaomo'na*," she said as she turned to face Annie. She leaned over a bit to whisper to Annie, "The *taotaomo'na* that touched Mike Blaz really scared my boy. I'm glad Father noticed."

With eyebrows raised, Annie nodded in agreement then stood up to leave. "Okay. I'm going to head to work now." She turned to Mateo. "Be good and help *Tan* Chai, Mateo."

"I will, Grandma."

The day passed by very slowly as time seemed to drag on. Since there wasn't much to do after lunch, *Tan* Chai and Mateo decided to take a nap. Mateo lay on the cool linoleum floor near the front door, hoping to catch any breeze that might pass through the screen door.

As he dozed off, he found himself dreaming of the playground at school. He was playing kick ball with some classmates. The sun was high, but a nice breeze kept things cool enough to play. Across the street was an empty lot that had concrete steps and a couple of small slabs in the tall, unkempt grass. They were all that remained of what had been a wooden house many years before. But the lot always seemed dark, giving Mateo chills just by looking in its direction.

At one point during the game, one of Mateo's classmates got in a great kick. However, the ball bounced all the way across the street into the scary lot. Because Mateo was the closest and nobody else wanted to go into the lot to get the ball, he reluctantly started across the street to the lot. Once there, he rushed toward the ball but suddenly felt a spine-chilling sensation travel up to his neck.

He quickly grabbed the ball and turned to run back when he saw two large, ghostly white claw-like hands reaching toward him from the concrete steps. Somehow, he was no longer able to turn his head back to the playground, and he could barely move his legs to run. He was stuck, watching the hands creep toward him. He tried to scream, but his lips wouldn't move. Tears welled up in his eyes as he continued fighting to move or scream.

Just then, he heard a deep voice whispering, "*Iyo-ku hao på'go.*" The voice seemed to be coming from all directions at once.

Then the voice bellowed menacingly as though it were right behind Mateo's head, "*Iyo-ku hao på'go!*"

His chest heaved with uneven breaths, the fear so intense that his heart pounded like a drumbeat in his ears, drowning out everything else. *When would it stop?*

"Mateo." He heard someone calling to him.

"Mateo." The voice came again, but he couldn't turn to see who it was.

"Mateo," he heard one more time. "Wake up, my boy."

Finally, he woke up to *Tan* Chai's voice as she nudged his arm.

"Are you okay?" *Tan* Chai asked. "It looked like you were having a bad dream."

Mateo sat up and looked around to get his bearings, relieved to be back in *Tan* Chai's house. He looked at *Tan* Chai who was on one knee next to him. "Yeah." He took a deep breath. "I'm okay."

"That's good. Come. Get up. I have some ice-cold

lemonade."

He rolled onto one knee to get up and glanced out through the front door. But then he froze suddenly and whispered, "*Tan* Chai!" His eyes were open wide as he stared out through the door.

Tan Chai rushed back to him. "What is it?"

"The dog is here! It's watching me from across the street, *Tan* Chai!"

She couldn't see it. But she got up and headed to the door to try to chase it away.

"Don't open the door! Please don't open the door!" Mateo was trembling as tears rolled from his eyes. It frightened him terribly just to look at it. But he felt even more scared to stop looking because then he wouldn't know where it was if it disappeared.

He lost sight of it anyway as *Tan* Chai rushed back to his side to hold him. He was trying not to cry because he felt he was too old for that. But he couldn't hold the sobs in. Try as he might, the tears still fell down his cheeks.

"Why is it here, *Tan* Chai? Why is it following me?"

The old woman didn't know what to do. Feeling helpless, she rubbed his back and answered, "I don't know, my boy. I don't know."

Tan Chai led him onto the couch where Mateo eventually cried himself to sleep. As he slept, *Tan* Chai called Annie to let her know what had happened. *Tan* Chai also called Kiko Aguon. They had not spoken since Mateo received his First Holy Communion a few years earlier.

Tan Chai had to call a couple of times before Kiko finally answered his phone.

"*Buenas*! This is Kiko."

"Hello, Kiko. This is Chai Perez."

"*Tan* Chai! It's good to hear from you. How are you doing?"

"Well, things were good up until today. It's Mateo."

"What happened?"

"I think there's a *taotaomo'na* following him." *Tan* Chai stammered a little as she continued, "It's really got him scared. I don't know what to do."

"Okay, *Tan* Chai. I'll try to help you figure this out. What signs are you getting that there is a *taotaomo'na* following him?"

"It's not me. Mateo says he has been seeing a big, scary black dog, and he's the only one who can see it." She continued, "He saw it once in the hospital. Then he saw it at a funeral just yesterday. And today, he saw it right across the street from my house."

"Oh boy! Sounds like it is a *taotaomo'na* that takes the shape of a *ga'lågu*, like a demon dog."

"Yes. I've heard they can take the shapes of animals," *Tan* Chai said.

"Has it approached him?"

"No, Kiko. He says it stays at a distance. But it stares straight at him, snarling."

"Okay. So, it's keeping its distance. That means it's either waiting, or it can't get to him." Kiko paused before continuing, "Actually, I think it might be both. I think it's waiting because it can't get to him."

Tan Chai was starting to feel a little relieved. "You know, that makes sense. At the hospital and at the cemetery, Mateo was with Father Rogelio. And today, he was here at my house. I didn't tell you this yet, but we found out that there are good *taotaomo'na* here around my house that I think are the ones protecting him. I have always wondered how we never had incidents like this while Mateo was growing up, even though my house is surrounded by jungle."

Kiko was surprised. "How did you find that out?"

"I have more to share with you about the things this boy can do. But not long ago, I witnessed the *taotaomo'na* here help him find a plant in the jungle for my *åmot tininu*. He even said he heard them call him to where the plant was."

"Whoa! You saw them interacting? They talked to him?"

"Well, I saw a bunch of leaves moving in the exact spot where the plant was. Nothing else was moving. He said he heard them call him to the spot. And later when I was telling his grandma about it, she was getting all worried. That's when Mateo said he heard someone say '*Tåya' guaha. Man familia hit'*, like they knew she was concerned, and they wanted to reassure her."

Kiko was truly amazed. "Honestly, *Tan* Chai, I've never heard of anything like that. And it is definitely interesting that the *taotaomo'na* say they are family. His connection to them is very strong... and very worrying.

And Mateo is still just a kid! If this scares us, I can't imagine how bad it scares him."

"I know!" *Tan* Chai agreed. "At least it looks like my boy is protected. That's what I can tell Annie when she gets here. Thanks, Kiko."

"Sure thing, *Tan* Chai. Oh! I'll come by your place tomorrow. I want to put a couple of charms together that Mateo can keep with him. At least he will have some kind of protection when he is out in public."

Tan Chai was quick to thank him, "*Dångkulu na si Yu'us ma'åse'*, Kiko! That's a very good idea."

They said their goodbyes and hung up. A few minutes later, Annie drove up into *Tan* Chai's driveway. Mateo was still in the living room and woke up as Annie walked in the front door. *Tan* Chai announced that the dog had appeared again. Only this time, it was right across the street. This clearly worried Annie. She walked over to the couch, hoping she might be able to comfort the boy in some way.

"My boy, are you okay?" Annie said to Mateo as she hugged him.

Mateo was still a little embarrassed, but he nodded that he was okay as they hugged.

"I actually just got off the phone with Kiko Aguon," *Tan* Chai said.

Annie looked toward *Tan* Chai. "Yeah? What did he say?"

"He said that it seems Mateo is still being protected. That's why the dog always keeps its distance. The dog might come around, but there should be nothing to worry about as long as it keeps its distance."

This didn't give Mateo any reassurance, though. He didn't want to be anywhere near the jungle anymore. Yet he didn't say anything. He was still embarrassed and worried that his grandma and *Tan* Chai would be disappointed with him. He just wanted to leave.

Annie asked Mateo, "Do you need the restroom before we go?" She wanted to ask *Tan* Chai something while he wasn't there. Luckily for Annie, he nodded that he did need the restroom.

"Okay. Go then, and we will head home after," Annie told him. Once he was gone, she whispered to *Tan* Chai, "So what about when we leave here? What about when we are at my house?"

"Kiko is going to make some charms tonight. He will drop them off tomorrow so that Mateo can keep them with him. Other than that, we will just have to keep an eye on him. Because none of us can see the dog, we'll just have to keep close to him; he will have to tell us if it is getting closer or keeping its distance when he sees it. When that happens, any of us close to him will have pull this out and pray," she said, then pulled out her rosary.

Annie pulled out her own rosary. "Yeah. I keep mine close by, too. But is that all we can do?" she asked.

"Yes. That's the best we can do for him."

"My poor boy. I wish I could trade places with him. Why does he have to go through this?"

"I know, *nene*. He's such a good boy." *Tan* Chai gently

pulled Annie's hands into hers.

They both went silent for a moment. They knew that the rest was up to God, and they both took that moment to say a quick prayer, asking God to help them protect the child.

Mateo and Annie finally said their goodbyes to *Tan* Chai and headed home.

On the drive home with Annie, Mateo was looking out through the car window. As they drove past the Santa Barbara Church, he had a thought. "Grandma?"

"Yes, my boy?"

"Can I stay after school at the Rectory until you get off from work?"

Annie was a little surprised by the question. "You don't want to stay with *Tan* Chai anymore?"

"Never mind," he said defeatedly.

"No, my boy. It's okay. I just want to know." Annie tried to reassure Mateo that she just had his best interest at heart. "Today was very scary, so I understand if you don't want to go back there."

"I'm sorry, Grandma. Do you think *Tan* Chai will be mad at me?" Mateo worried.

"She won't be mad. She's like me. All she wants is for you to be safe and happy. If you are scared at her house, then she will be fine if you don't go there. She can always visit us instead."

Mateo nodded to acknowledge that was what he wanted.

"Okay. So, I will call the Rectory tomorrow while you

are in school to ask. If everything works out, I will call the school to have them pass a message to you letting you know if it's okay or not to go to there after school." She looked at Mateo as she asked, "Does that sound good?"

Mateo nodded again. He was worried that he might be inconveniencing everyone, but Annie's understanding and reassurance made him feel a whole lot better about it.

Things worked out the next day. Annie called the Rectory and spoke to Father Tony. He and Father Rogelio both agreed that it would be best for Mateo, and they would be happy to have him around. He was now old enough to help in the parish office or even to help with cleaning up the church. So, he wouldn't just be sitting around after finishing up his homework.

This just meant that *Tan* Chai would no longer have her magical helper around. But she really did only care that he would be safe. So, there were no complaints from her about Mateo staying after school at the Rectory. But she was definitely going to miss having him around.

Chapter 14

Grandma and Grandpa

Mateo was never one for crowds. His solitary nature had always set him apart at school, with only Jesse Iriarte standing by him since middle school. Jesse, like Mateo, was a bit of a loner. Both Jesse and Mateo were never allowed to attend parties at their classmates' houses. But they never really wanted to, either. Jesse lived with his grandmother, so they also had that in common. Jesse's house was only a ten-minute walk from the school.

Jesse often lingered after school to see Mateo board the bus before beginning his short walk home. So, when Mateo suddenly stopped taking the bus, Jesse noticed.

It was a Friday afternoon when Jesse approached

Mateo, curious about the change.

"Hey, Matt. I noticed you don't take the bus anymore. Are you working at the Rectory now?"

"No," Mateo replied. "I mean, I help out, and I do my homework there while I wait for grandma to get off work."

"Don't you usually go to *Tan* Chai's place?"

"I used to."

"Did she kick you out?" Jesse teased with a grin.

Mateo gave him a little playful shove on the shoulder. "Shut up, man."

The two boys walked over to play on a wooden power pole that was lying on the lawn next to the parish office. They took turns trying to keep their balance as they walked along the pole to see who could go the farthest without falling off.

"Hey, I have a dollar," Jesse said, pulling the crumpled bill from his pocket. "Do you wanna play pinball?"

"Yeah!" Mateo lit up.

The little mom-and-pop store on the corner across from the church and the parish office had an old pinball machine that neither boy could resist. For the first time, they hung out after school, losing track of time as the metallic dings and flashing lights filled the room.

Before they knew it, an hour had passed. They only knew because Marie walked over from the parish office and found them in the store, her presence instantly sobering the carefree mood.

"Mateo!"

Her stern voice cut through the noise, and Mateo froze. "Aren't you supposed to be at the parish office after school?"

"Yeah. But I'm just here across the street," Mateo replied sheepishly.

"And who did you tell so that we would know that you were just here across the street?"

She had a point, and he knew it. Lowering his gaze, he said "I'm sorry, Ms. Marie."

Marie's expression softened, though her tone remained firm. "It's a Friday, and you probably don't have to worry about any homework. So, I don't have any problem with you hanging out with your friend, but as long as your grandma is trusting us to watch over you after school, we need to know where you are and what you're doing. Is that clear?"

"Yes, Ms. Marie."

"I think you've had enough time to hang out. I need you over at the office to help me." She looked at Jesse and said, "You're welcome to help, too, if you'd like, Mr. Iriarte. You just need to ask your grandma first."

Jesse looked at Mateo, then responded, "That's okay, Ms. Marie. Maybe next time." He was pleasantly surprised by the invitation. However, he realized that he was probably going to get in trouble, like Mateo, for not letting his grandma know he was going to hang out with Mateo after school.

From that day on, they got to hang out together every

once in a while at the parish office. They didn't have any other friends, and Marie never heard them talking about any girlfriends.

Mateo did have a crush on someone, though. Her name was Genevieve Ninete. She was the sister of the Ninete brothers who served with Mateo as part of the altar servers at Santa Barbara. Mateo had developed a crush on her for as long as he could remember, but she only ever liked him as a friend. She was always nice to him, though, never being mean to him and never laughing at him whenever he happened to be clumsy in front of everyone.

Mateo specifically remembered one day when they were still at school. He was rushing out of the cafeteria during lunch period because he had seriously needed the restroom, which was down the hall. Upon reaching the door, he pulled the wooden-framed screen door open and got his head through, but his other foot was still just enough behind the door that it stopped it before it opened all the way. However, the force pulled the door handle out of his hand and the door sprung back to close, slamming his head between the door and the door frame.

He could hear all the other kids in the cafeteria laughing at him. The impact gave him a jolt, but it didn't hurt as bad as the embarrassment that came with the incident. He was even more embarrassed because Genevieve happened to be standing in the hallway and witnessed the whole thing. But she didn't laugh. In fact, she was the only person who asked if he was okay.

Genevieve was always interested in the jocks, though. But the guys she dated were not mean or arrogant jocks. They were actually nice guys. So, Mateo really could never complain about them.

In their senior year at John F. Kennedy High School, Genevieve was dating Terry Woods. Terry's family had only moved to Guam the year before, but things between Genevieve and Terry seemed serious. Mateo heard that Terry's family planned to move to San Diego after graduation, and he also heard that Genevieve and one of her girlfriends were also talking about going to college there. They both had relatives living in San Diego and going to school there would mean that Genevieve could stay close to Terry. So, Mateo eventually accepted that he had no chance at winning Genevieve's heart.

However, Mateo's hope for romance got a little boost when he decided to ask one of his other classmates to go with him to their senior prom. Her name was Elizabeth Santos. Mateo used to think she had a boyfriend, but Jesse said she was available. Mateo figured this was his last year, his last chance. So, he asked, and to his surprise, she said yes.

But when prom night finally came, things didn't go as Mateo expected. He and Elizabeth hardly spoke the whole night. Thankfully, Jesse decided to attend even without a date, and he had gotten a seat at the same table as Mateo. During the prom, Elizabeth disappeared a couple of times without a word, and when she came back after the second time, she asked to leave the dance. Mateo drove her straight home and Jesse left with them.

Over the next couple of days, Mateo tried calling her to ask if she'd like to go out again, but she never answered his calls. It wasn't until a week later that Jesse found out Elizabeth only went with Mateo to the prom so that she could make some other guy jealous. Jesse didn't know who the other guy was. All he knew was that he went to a different school.

Mateo was heartbroken, but he didn't have too much time to feel sorry for himself. About two weeks after the prom, Annie collapsed while she was at work. *Tan* Chai was her emergency contact person, so the bank called her right away. They told her that Annie was being taken to the hospital, and since Mateo's school was on the way, *Tan* Chai called ahead to have Mateo ready and waiting when she arrived to pull him out of school early. It didn't take long for her to arrive at the school.

"What happened, *Tan* Chai?" Mateo asked as he got into her car.

Tan Chai was now in her seventies and found it especially challenging to drive and talk while she was also panicked and worried about Annie. She slowly told Mateo what she knew so far. "Your grandma is in the hospital. Her work called me, and I picked you up so you can go with me."

Mateo was really worried, and he could feel *Tan* Chai's anxiety. "Did they say what happened?"

"They're not sure. They just said she collapsed at the

bank."

Mateo turned to look out through his window as he muttered to himself, "Come on, Grandma. Please be okay! Please be okay! Please be okay!"

As they drove up to the hospital, they found that there were no available parking slots near the Emergency Room. So, *Tan* Chai just parked on the side of the road. She and Mateo walked in and asked about Annie at the counter.

"Yes, that's Annie Leon Guerrero," *Tan* Chai repeated to the woman behind the counter. "I was told that the ambulance brought her here. That might have been about thirty minutes ago."

"And what is your relationship to the patient?" the woman asked.

"I'm her aunt and this is her grandson. We are her only family," *Tan* Chai explained.

The woman grabbed the paper she was writing on as she stood up. "Please be seated. I will check with the ER nurses."

Tan Chai and Mateo found a couple of seats together. There were other families in the waiting area, with a couple of people sobbing. The air was thick with worry and fear and the fluorescent lighting, the drab walls, and waxed linoleum floor only made the room feel cold and gloomy. It was almost twenty minutes before a doctor entered the waiting area.

"Leon Guerrero family?" the doctor announced.

Tan Chai quickly waved at the doctor. He signaled for

Tan Chai to follow him into a small office just to the side of the ER entrance. Once in the room, he directed *Tan* Chai and Mateo to take a seat.

"My name is Dr. David Nakamura. I was here when Annie was brought into the Emergency Room. Can I ask how you are related to Annie?"

Tan Chai replied, "I'm her aunt, Rosa Perez, and this is her grandson, Mateo. We are her only family."

The doctor nodded, then looked down at the folded papers in his hand as he took a deep breath. "Mrs. Perez, I'm sorry to say that Annie suffered a major stroke." He paused for a bit before continuing. "She was unresponsive when the medics picked her up, and I'm afraid they were not able to revive her. Her death was officially announced on her arrival. I'm so sorry."

The words seemed to literally knock the wind out of Mateo. He instantly started to feel like a little kid lost in the grocery store for the first time. He didn't know where to turn or what to do. He felt alone and abandoned. Sure, he was an eighteen-year-old young man now. But without warning, he had just lost the only parent he had ever known. He wasn't sobbing uncontrollably, but he absolutely could not stop the tears from welling up in his eyes as he fidgeted relentlessly in the seat next to *Tan* Chai. He started rubbing and scratching at his jeans.

Tan Chai was crying, too. Losing Annie was so sudden. But as stunned as she was, she could only think about how much more it was hurting Mateo. She reached out to hug him, but he dodged her just a little.

Strangely, it wasn't like he dodged her because he didn't want her to touch him. Instead, it was more like she had just blocked his view of something, and he tried to look around her. *Tan* Chai didn't get it but hugged him anyway. The doctor had said some other things, but it was all just a blur. Mateo then shook his head before burying his face in *Tan* Chai's shoulder as he continued crying.

Somehow, they made it to the viewing area just outside the morgue where Father Tony was waiting for them. *Tan* Chai must have mentioned the Santa Barbara Parish office while talking to the doctor and the hospital staff called them. She couldn't really remember what happened but was happy to see Father Tony. The priest led them in prayer over Annie's body. But Mateo seemed distracted as he kept peeking toward the door that led into the viewing area. He had stopped crying and now had more of a confused look on his face.

"*Tan* Chai, I'll be right back. I need to use the restroom," Mateo said as he got up.

Tan Chai nodded and continued praying with Father Tony.

Mateo then walked out of the room and turned around a corner, finding Annie's spirit.

"I knew it! I knew you could see me," Annie said softly.

"What happened, Grandma?" Mateo's voice cracked.

Mateo thought he had seen her earlier when the doctor gave them the news that she had passed on, but he hadn't really gotten a good look at her. It wasn't until he saw her at the doorway to the viewing area that he knew it was her spirit he had seen standing by the door.

"What am I supposed to do now, Grandma?" He started to cry again as he asked.

"I'm sorry, my boy," Annie said, her face filled with love and regret. "I didn't want to leave you. I didn't even know something happened until I saw your grandpa smiling at me."

Next to her stood a man Mateo had never met. "This is your grandpa Pedro," Annie said, introducing the man beside her.

Mateo was still upset with Annie for leaving him, but he had always wanted to meet any of his other family members. He greeted his grandpa Pedro with *man nginge'* and said, "*Ñot.*"

"*Dioste ayudi*, boy. I'm very happy to finally meet you," Pedro said with a huge smile. "I know this is all a big shock to you and your grandma here. But we cannot know God's plan. Please don't blame your grandma."

Annie rubbed Pedro's arm in understanding. Then she looked at Mateo, "We love you, Mateo."

"You should get back to *Tan* Chai. I need to steal your grandma away for now." Pedro smiled and wrapped an arm around Annie as they turned to walk away.

Mateo took a moment to compose himself as he watched his grandparents fade away after just a few steps. The whole interaction was a lot to take in, as this was the first time he actually spoke to a spirit. It was also the first time he met his grandfather. He let it all sink in before he went back into the room with *Tan* Chai.

Tan Chai and Father Tony had finished praying when Mateo walked back in. They could see that something had changed in just the little time since he had stepped out. He was more frustrated than lost and depressed like he was just moments ago. But Father Tony had to get back to the Church, so he said his goodbyes and left.

"Mateo, are you okay?" *Tan* Chai asked as she placed a hand on his shoulder. "What happened, my boy?"

Mateo wasn't so worried anymore about *Tan* Chai knowing his secret. He was more worried about how his life was going to have to change with Annie now gone.

"I saw her, *Tan* Chai. I saw my grandma Annie," Mateo said with his head hanging a little low.

"Just now?" *Tan* Chai asked.

"Yeah. Actually, I saw her and my grandpa Pedro." He looked at *Tan* Chai and continued, "I even talked to them, just like I'm talking to you now."

Tan Chai seemed a little taken aback, as though she couldn't believe it was true. But her expression quickly changed to worry for Annie and for Mateo. "How were they? How did they look?" She had never seen a spirit. Her only references to how spirits looked were from movies and television shows. She remembered him saying that he could see spirits, but she had never asked him more about it.

"They were fine." Mateo paused to think a little more about what *Tan* Chai was asking. His brows raised as he questioned her, "Do you mean if they looked scary... like ghosts?"

Tan Chai nodded reluctantly. "Yes, that. But did your grandma seem scared or worried?"

"They looked normal. My grandma actually looked happier... not as tired as she normally looks." But he was still frustrated. "*Tan* Chai! What am I supposed to do? My grandma didn't even seem worried about leaving me all by myself."

"Don't blame your grandma, my boy. She was very important to us, even more important to you. It's only natural to feel lost and alone after losing someone like that in your life."

Mateo looked over at Annie's body. "My grandpa Pedro said not to blame her, too."

"Well, it's true. It wasn't her choice. It was just her time. We have to trust that God has a reason for letting things like this happen."

"Hmm. My grandpa even said something like that."

Tan Chai hugged Mateo from the side. "I know it's easy for us to say things like that even though we're not going through the same things that you are. But we do understand. And it is very important to remember that you are not alone. You are going to feel like you're alone, and you're going to feel that way a lot for some time. But you still have people here who love and care about you. And your grandma will always just be a memory away."

Mateo listened but was clearly still feeling lost and worried. "So, what am I supposed to do next? Where am

I supposed to go?"

"For tonight, how about we just get you home and I stay with you there? You don't need to think about anything past that for now."

Mateo agreed. That night, they returned home together, the weight of loss heavy but softened by the enduring strength of family. Mateo said a quiet goodbye to Annie in his heart, carrying her love with him as he prepared to face an uncertain future.

Chapter 15

The Broken Boundary

Mateo stood in the doorway of his home, hesitating before stepping inside. The air outside was still and humid, the way it often was in the evenings, but as soon as he crossed the threshold, a chill swept over him. It wasn't just a drop in temperature, it felt unnatural, the kind of cold that seemed to settle into his bones no matter how much he rubbed his arms or moved around.

He paused just inside the doorway, his hand lingering on the frame. The house had always been his sanctuary, a place of comfort and warmth. But now, it felt different - wrong. The lightbulb in the entryway flickered weakly, casting the room in uneven shadows. Mateo frowned and tapped the switch a few times, but the flickering continued. He made a mental note to replace the bulb, though deep down, he couldn't shake the feeling that the issue wasn't electrical.

"Just tired," he muttered to himself, shaking his head as he walked further into the house. The sound of his voice in the empty space did little to comfort him. His words fell flat, swallowed up by the quiet that had settled over the house like a heavy blanket.

He dropped his bag on the dining table and took a deep breath, forcing himself to focus on the familiar scenery. The faint scent of Annie's lavender soap still lingered in the air, mingling with the smell of wood polish. It was the same as always. And yet, Mateo couldn't shake the sense that something was off, as if the house were holding its breath, waiting for something to happen.

As he walked to the kitchen to grab a glass of water, a faint creaking sound stopped him in his tracks. It came from the living room, just beyond the doorway. Mateo froze, his ears straining to catch the sound again. The creak repeated, slow and deliberate, like the weight of someone shifting in an old chair.

His heart thudded in his chest as he moved cautiously toward the sound. The living room was empty, the furniture exactly where it had always been. The armchair in the corner - the one Annie used to sit in - looked untouched, its cushion slightly indented from years of use. But as Mateo stepped closer, he swore he saw the cushion rise slightly, as though the weight of an invisible presence had just lifted.

He stood there for a moment, his breathing shallow, staring at the chair. The room was silent except for the faint hum of the refrigerator in the kitchen. Finally, he shook his head and turned away, trying to dismiss the thought. He had been under a lot of stress lately, grief could play tricks on the mind, after all.

Later that night, Mateo found himself in the bathroom, splashing cold water on his face in an attempt to shake off the unease that had settled over him. The water was refreshing, grounding him for a moment as he braced his hands against the sink and stared at his reflection in the mirror.

Dark circles shadowed his eyes, a testament to the sleepless nights he'd had since Annie's passing. His hair was a mess, sticking up at odd angles where he'd run his fingers through it one too many times. He barely recognized himself.

As he reached for the towel hanging on the rack, a soft crack echoed through the room. He froze, the towel slipping from his grasp. Slowly, his gaze shifted back to the mirror. At first, he didn't see anything unusual. But then he noticed a thin line running diagonally across the glass, splitting his reflection in two.

The crack grew wider, spreading slowly like a living thing. Mateo could only watch as the glass fractured further, each new split accompanied by a faint popping sound. His own fragmented reflection stared back at him, his wide eyes and slackened jaw distorted by the jagged lines.

A sudden chill swept through the room, and the small hairs on Mateo's arms stood on end. The temperature had dropped sharply, enough that he could see his breath misting in front of him. His heart raced as he stepped back from the sink, his eyes darting around the room for any sign of an explanation.

There was no logical reason for the mirror to crack like that, not without some kind of force. But the bathroom was empty, the only sound the faint drip of water from the faucet.

Mateo backed out of the room, his chest tightening with every step. The moment he crossed the threshold, the suffocating pressure that had been building in his chest released. He turned and hurried down the hallway, not daring to look back.

*****

Mateo found it harder to go about his daily routine without being interrupted by the odd occurrences. It wasn't just the flickering lights or the occasional cold spots anymore; the events were becoming deliberate, undeniable.

One afternoon, as he sat at the dining table sorting through a stack of newspapers, the sound of shattering glass echoed from the kitchen. Mateo bolted upright, his chair scraping loudly against the wooden floor. His heart raced as he approached the kitchen, his footsteps hesitant.

He found the source almost immediately; a glass he had left drying on the counter was now in pieces, scattered across the floor as though it had been hurled against the wall. The shards gleamed under the harsh fluorescent light, each one a sharp reminder that this wasn't normal. He crouched to pick up the larger pieces, careful not to cut himself, but the air around him felt oppressive, heavy with an energy that prickled at his skin.

As he stood, something caught his attention out of the corner of his eye. The refrigerator door was ajar, though he was certain he hadn't touched it. Slowly, he pushed it shut, the seal making a soft suction sound. The moment it clicked into place, a low creak came from the cupboard behind him.

Mateo spun around, his pulse thundering in his ears. The cupboard door, which he distinctly remembered closing earlier, was now wide open, its contents perfectly still. A wave of nausea swept over him as he stepped toward the door, his body screaming at him to leave, to get out of the house. But he couldn't bring himself to go. This was his home, his safe space. He wouldn't be driven out by something he didn't even understand. However, he couldn't shake the feeling of being watched. It was as though a thousand unseen eyes were trained on him, waiting for him to falter.

The tipping point came later that evening, when Mateo ventured into Annie's room. He hadn't been inside since her passing a week before, the grief of her absence too raw to face. But something drew him there right then, an inexplicable pull he couldn't ignore.

The room was exactly as she had left it. Her favorite shawl was draped over the back of the chair by the window, and the faint scent of her perfume lingered in the air. Mateo stood in the doorway for a long moment, his hand gripping the frame so tightly his knuckles turned white.

Finally, he stepped inside, his movements slow and deliberate. He ran his fingers over the edge of her dresser, tracing the grain of the wood. Everything felt so painfully familiar, yet distant, as though the room existed in a different time.

As he moved to sit on the edge of the bed, his foot nudged something on the floor. Looking down, he saw the corner of a book peeking out from beneath the bed frame. He crouched and pulled it out, the cover dusty but intact.

It was a journal. Mateo turned it over in his hands, his thumb brushing against the worn leather. The initials "C. B." were engraved on the front, Annie's grandmother's initials. He opened it carefully, the pages brittle with age, and began to skim the entries.

The handwriting was neat but hurried, the words written in CHamoru interspersed with occasional English phrases. Mateo's heart sank as he read the passages, each one recounting encounters with spirits that sounded eerily similar to what he was experiencing now. The descriptions of shadows that moved of their own accord, objects breaking without cause, and an overwhelming cold felt all too familiar.

One entry in particular stood out. Annie's grandmother had written about a malevolent presence that grew stronger the more fear it was fed. The words sent a chill down Mateo's spine:

They prey on our doubts, our guilt. The more you fear them, the more power they have over you.

Mateo closed the journal and held it against his chest, his mind racing. This wasn't just grief or coincidence. The spirits weren't random; they were deliberate. And now, they were targeting him.

*****

The reality of the situation became undeniable when the spirits shifted their attention to the people Mateo cared about. Jesse, his best friend and closest confidant, was the first to experience their wrath.

They had been sitting in the living room one evening, laughing over old photos and trying to lighten the mood. Jesse leaned back on the couch, mid-laugh, when he suddenly stopped, his expression twisting in pain.

"Jesse? You okay?" Mateo asked, his voice tinged with concern.

Jesse didn't respond. His hand clutched his chest as his breathing grew shallow. Mateo moved closer, panic setting in. "What's wrong?"

"I - I don't know," Jesse gasped. His face was pale, beads of sweat forming on his forehead. Suddenly, his body convulsed, and he collapsed onto the floor. Mateo knelt beside him, his hands trembling as he tried to help.

Bruises began to bloom on Jesse's arms and neck, appearing out of nowhere like invisible hands were gripping him. Mateo's stomach churned as he watched, helpless. After what felt like an eternity, the attack stopped. Jesse lay still, his breathing ragged but steady.

Mateo called for an ambulance, but by the time the paramedics arrived, Jesse's bruises had faded, leaving no trace of what had happened. He couldn't bring himself to explain. *How could he? Who would believe him?*

Mateo sat alone that night, his head in his hands. The spirits weren't just tormenting him; they were going after the people he loved. Jesse's attack was proof of that. His heart ached with guilt as he thought about what his friend had endured, all because of him.

But the guilt was quickly replaced by anger. He couldn't let this continue. He wouldn't let the spirits take anything else from him.

Yet, despite his resolve, the question lingered: *How do you fight something you can't see?*

The answer seemed just out of reach, hidden in the fragments of Annie's journal and the memories of what he'd been taught as a child. If he was going to protect himself - and the people he cared about - he would need to face the spirits head-on, no matter how terrifying the prospect.

Just past midnight, the house grew unnaturally quiet. Mateo lay in bed, staring at the ceiling when he heard it, a low, guttural voice calling his name. The sound was faint at first, but it grew louder, more insistent. He sat up, his heart pounding.

"Mateo..." the voice rasped, echoing through the room.

He turned toward the corner where the shadows always seemed to gather. This time, there was no mistaking it. A figure stood there, barely visible but undeniably present. Its outline shimmered like heat waves on asphalt, and its eyes glowed faintly in the darkness.

"You cannot stop this," it whispered, its voice chilling and final. "You will lose everyone."

Before Mateo could react, the figure disappeared, leaving behind a suffocating silence and a bitter coldness that seeped into his bones. He sat frozen, the warning replaying in his mind. His thoughts were racing, but one thing was clear: The boundary between the physical and the spiritual world was no longer intact.

The spirits had crossed over, and their intentions were anything but peaceful.

Chapter 16

In the Shadows

Annie's passing had left a hole in Mateo's world that no amount of sympathy could fill. The Santa Barbara Parish office, with its quiet efficiency, had helped *Tan* Chai with the arrangements. They had worked with Father Tony to organize the funeral and rosary, and it had been a simple, heartfelt ceremony. Annie had been clear about her wishes in her will, naming Father Tony as the executor. That had made handling the legal matters straightforward, but it didn't ease the emotional burden.

Mateo remembered that day clearly. The funeral day had been bright, almost too bright. The glare of the sun contrasting sharply with the somber mood of the small congregation gathered at the church. Mateo had sat silently near the front, his hands clasped tightly in his lap. His white shirt, paired with black slacks and a neatly knotted black tie, felt stiff and too warm against his skin. A black ribbon wrapped around his upper arm as a mark of mourning. Despite the discomfort, he didn't move.

The priest's voice had echoed in the quiet church as he spoke about Annie's kindness and her dedication to the community. Mateo had heard the words but couldn't absorb them. His eyes had stayed fixed on the casket, his heart aching with every passing second. When it was time to lower the casket into the ground, Mateo had felt a sudden weight settle on his chest. However, a familiar presence materialized beside him. Annie, her form translucent, pressed her nose against his cheek in a silent gesture of love. It was a bittersweet moment, a final farewell from the woman who had been more than just his grandmother - a mother in every way that mattered. Mateo closed his eyes, savoring the fleeting connection, before Annie faded, leaving him alone with his sorrow.

The school had excused Mateo from attending the final weeks of classes, given the circumstances. He had been set to graduate, but the thought of standing among his peers, wearing a cap and gown, was unbearable. Instead, he went to the school office alone a few weeks later. The secretary handed him his diploma and yearbook with a gentle smile. "She would have been so proud of you," she said softly.

Mateo nodded, muttered a quick "thank you," and

left. The yearbook felt heavy in his hands, but he didn't open it. Instead, he tucked it into his bag and returned home.

Jesse, as always, was there to make sure Mateo wasn't entirely alone. He came over frequently, bringing snacks or just sitting with Mateo in companionable silence. Sometimes they played video games on the old console Jesse had brought over, their laughter a rare sound in the quiet house.

"You've got to get out of this funk, man," Jesse said one evening, stretching out on the couch. "You're too young to be this serious all the time."

Mateo shrugged. "I'm just trying to figure things out."

At eighteen, Mateo was legally an adult and didn't need *Tan* Chai to stay with him, but he felt anything but ready for the responsibility that came with being an adult. However, he couldn't afford to stay in the unit that he and Annie had been renting because it was now too expensive to keep. The landlord was kind, offering Mateo extra time to figure out his next steps, but Mateo knew he couldn't stay there much longer.

He considered asking Jesse to move in with him. "We could split the rent," he suggested one afternoon while they were walking to the store.

Jesse hesitated. "I wish I could, man. But I can't leave my grandma alone. She needs me around."

Mateo nodded, trying to hide his disappointment. It wasn't Jesse's fault, but the thought of living alone made him uneasy. He didn't want to move in with *Tan* Chai either. Her house bordered the jungle, and Mateo was still very much afraid to go near it.

After a lot of thought, he decided to use the rental income from Annie's house on Wusstig Road to cover a small apartment. It wasn't much - a studio with beige walls and an ancient air conditioner - but it was affordable and close to the church and *Tan* Chai's house, and he really liked it.

Jesse helped him move in. They spent hours setting up the space, arranging furniture, and arguing about the best place for the TV. By the end of the day, they were sprawled on the floor, eating pizza from the box and laughing over nothing in particular.

"This place isn't bad," Jesse said, looking around. "It's got potential."

Mateo smiled faintly. "It'll do."

*****

As Mateo adjusted to his new reality and apartment, Jesse and he would almost regularly hang out after work. Mateo even bought a Nintendo console that the two of them would spend hours playing.

To pay the bills, Mateo found a job with the Department of Parks and Recreation. The work was physical: trimming grass, clearing debris, and maintaining public bathrooms, but it kept him busy. His coworkers were mostly older men who had been with the department for years. They were kind to Mateo, offering tips and sharing jokes to pass the time.

Mateo appreciated the praise but kept his focus on the task at hand. The parks were beautiful, but many of them bordered the jungle. Mateo made a point to stay near the open spaces, his eyes flicking toward the tree line more often than he liked to admit.

Mateo didn't have many expenses, so he decided to just keep building the savings account he had. Annie had left a monetary inheritance as well as her house in Wusstig Road. She had designated the inheritance to be used only for educational purposes. So, the house rental income was able to constantly provide Mateo with some monthly cash flow.

Father Rogelio then helped Mateo get the necessary paperwork completed so he could have a business license. With this, he would be able to continue renting the house out as the new landlord. It felt strange walking into the bank where Annie had worked for years, however, the folks at the bank were always happy to see him when he came to make deposits, as most of them knew Annie and missed her dearly.

Later that summer, Jesse and Mateo had made plans to watch an outdoor laser light show. It was a very big deal since this would be the first of its kind on the island. It was part of the grand opening festivities for the new Sterling Department Store that just completed construction in Dededo. But the two arrived just a little late that evening and all the good parking spaces had already been taken. The street was already filled with people driving around, looking for parking to watch the show.

"Dude! I told you we were going to be late," Mateo said.

"Whatever! You're the one who took so long getting ready, like this was a date or something," Jesse quipped.

Mateo punched Jesse in the shoulder lightly as he said, "Shut up!"

"Dude! I'm driving!" exclaimed Jesse as they both laughed.

They drove past the new store looking for a way into the parking lot, but all entries had been blocked. The parking lot had a lot of equipment and loudspeakers setup. It looked like parking for the show was meant to be across the street. A large portion of the jungle had been cleared just for temporary parking. It was getting pretty dark out already.

"Looks like that's where we have to park," Jesse gestured with his head toward the clearing.

"Hurry! Let's get a spot in the middle so we get a good view." Mateo didn't actually know if being in the middle would give them a better view. He just didn't want to be close to the jungle. But he didn't want Jesse to know that.

They found a decent spot to park in and got settled. The music started up as the lights in the store parking lot went dark. The show was pretty cool with laser lights flashing through smoke from smoke machines. The images weren't so great, but the show was still very otherworldly.

But a few minutes into the show, Mateo started getting uncomfortable. It was now very dark, and the show was captivating, so Jesse didn't really notice. Mateo's skin started to crawl as a painful chill slowly crept up from between his shoulder blades up to his neck. It felt like something was slowly getting closer as the sensation intensified. Mateo felt like he was being watched. He kept looking over his shoulders, but all he saw were the laser lights reflecting off of all the other windshields and lighting up the faces inside the cars.

Pressure started building in his ears to the point where the loud music seemed muffled. Suddenly, all of the chills and the feeling of being watched seemed to be coming from one specific spot to his left. Mateo turned to Jesse, who was on his left, then started to focus his sight on the edge of the jungle that was visible beyond Jesse. It was dark, but the shape was clear and horrible in the flashing lights. The menacing black dog had found Mateo again. Thankfully, cars started to move. The light show was over. Mateo's hearing rushed back, and he couldn't see the dog anymore. Even so, he hurried Jesse to get going.

"Let's go. Let's go, man." Mateo said suddenly, tugging Jesse's arm.

Jesse was annoyed. "I'm going, Matt. Jeez! Where's the fire?"

"I need the bathroom, man. It might get ugly in here if we don't move," Mateo joked.

"Not in my truck, Matt! Besides, I can't make all this traffic just magically clear up."

"I know. Hey! Let's go eat at King's. We can avoid all of this traffic trying to get back home."

"Ooh! I won't say no to King's." Jesse faked slurping up drool.

They both liked the food at King's Restaurant. It was located in the village of Tamuning, a more commercially developed village with lots of shops and restaurants. But the main reason Mateo recommended King's was that there were no jungles around.

The two boys made it to the restaurant and took their time having dinner. There was no rush to get home. Mateo never mentioned a thing to Jesse about the dog. In fact, he never spoke about any of his spiritual encounters and hoped they would remain a secret.

Only Annie, *Tan* Chai, Kiko, and Fathers Tony and Rogelio knew of Mateo's background and of the demon dog that seemed to be following him. Jesse and other classmates knew that Mateo used to help *Tan* Chai because a couple of their parents were her patients. But that was all Mateo was comfortable with anyone knowing.

*****

Mateo still kept in contact with Kiko Aguon and would call on him every once in a while. After the night of the laser light show, Mateo asked Kiko for fresh charms. Kiko tried to make sure Mateo always had something newly made at least a few times a year. This time, Mateo asked to pick them up from Kiko as soon as they were ready.

"Are you okay, Mateo?" Kiko asked. "You usually wait for me to bring these to you. Did something happen?"

"Uh... yeah," Mateo replied very reluctantly. "I saw it again. The dog."

"The *ga'lågu*? It's been a while since you've seen it. Was it still keeping its distance?" Kiko asked.

"Yeah."

"Ok. That's good." Kiko tried to reassure Mateo... and maybe himself, too. "As long as it doesn't get closer to you. You can come by the shop tomorrow any time after lunch. I'll have some things ready for you by then."

"Thanks, *Tun* Kiko."

Mateo wanted to make sure he had new charms with him, especially for when he was at work. There were two parks in particular that always worried him when they had to clean them because they were surrounded by jungle. The first was Two Lovers' Point and the second was Tanguisson Beach. Two Lovers' Point Park was a clearing at the top of a cliff overlooking the ocean. Tanguisson Beach was a beach park surrounded by jungle and cliffs. Both were beautiful parks. But lately, to Mateo, they felt more like traps with something hiding in the shadows just waiting for him to step in.

****

Mateo's call and urgency got Kiko thinking. He started pondering about Mateo's history. The black dog seemed to keep popping up, and it was not attempting to get to Mateo. It just seemed to be watching him, almost making sure to keep reminding him that he had not been forgotten. But why would Mateo be remembered? He hadn't been involved in anything serious with any *taotaomo'na* except...

No. It couldn't be! Kiko remembered the old sayings that spirits were patient because time made no difference to them. Kiko also remembered the one and only time when Mateo had a serious encounter with a *taotaomo'na*: during his birth. *Was this the same taotaomo'na? Was it still after him? After all this time?* Kiko wanted to do some research to try to figure out what they might be dealing with. Until he got some answers, he didn't want to alert anyone.

Maybe it was because of the charms from Kiko or maybe it was because Mateo was always respectful in asking the *taotaomo'na* for permission before entering and working in the parks. But he never saw the demon dog again. Every once in a while, he would get some spine tingling, like the demon was close by somewhere, watching him. But it never felt close enough to scare him. When he started feeling safe enough again near the jungle, he figured he could try visiting *Tan* Chai some time at her house. After all, he did miss spending time with her.

So, Mateo started visiting *Tan* Chai about once or twice a month and helped her with chores around her house. And it was just like when he cleaned the parks. He never saw the dog, even if he did slightly feel its presence.

Tan Chai didn't have as many plants anymore. Mateo blamed himself, thinking it was because he wasn't there all the time to help her like he used to. He still worked full-time and still assisted regularly with mass at the Church. He was no longer an altar server. Instead, he was now a Eucharistic Minister. He also helped to train the newer altar servers. He didn't have much time to help *Tan* Chai with making *åmot* and *palai* like he used to. But she was just happy to have him coming around again anyway.

Chapter 17

A Friend in Need

Mateo had started working at the Guam International Airport, a significant shift from the unpredictable, intense days out in the sun and too close to the jungle for comfort. His job was simple but fulfilling. Each day, he worked on polishing concrete floors until they gleamed, wiping down expansive glass walls until they were spotless, and cleaning aluminum counters and conveyor belts that lined the bustling terminal. The environment was cool and comfortable, a welcome contrast to the humid, sweltering air of the public parks.

Jesse had been instrumental in helping Mateo secure the position. Working at the ticket counter of one of the airlines, Jesse had informed him about the job opening.

The two friends appreciated the opportunity to see each other during lunch breaks, catching up over plates of fried chicken or sandwiches at the employee cafeteria. Occasionally, after work, they'd sit together at the Micronesia Mall food court, sharing laughter and stories about their day.

It was now about two years since Annie had passed away and Mateo had graduated from high school. He had learned to navigate life without her presence, becoming more independent in the process. Marie from the parish office continued to offer personal advice to Mateo about things like health insurance and other work benefits. She made sure he understood that health insurance was a major consideration when looking for a job.

"Mateo," she would remind him, "you're on your own now. You need to make sure you're covered, especially for emergencies." When Mateo landed the airport job, with its better pay and benefits, Marie couldn't hide her relief. "This is a good start," she had said with a smile.

Meanwhile, the Gulf War was dominating headlines, bringing changes to the island. The Naval Base Guam was busier than ever, with ships coming and going regularly, and the Andersen Air Force Base saw an influx of jets, bombers, and the personnel needed to maintain them. The island seemed to hum with heightened activity. Military families arrived daily, filling up base housing and spilling into nearby villages.

Mateo didn't realize it, but Genevieve was among the

many who arrived. She had married an Air Force Senior Airman, Bill Fielding, who was part of the support crew maintaining the aircraft that was now bustling with activity. Genevieve was pregnant with her first child, and the military build-up was a good opportunity for her to move back to Guam where she had her immediate family to help and support her through the pregnancy.

With all of the new personnel on the island, base housing was hard to come by. So, Genevieve and her husband found a house just minutes away from the Andersen AFB main gate. However, much of the housing was along roads that scattered through the jungle. The home was a spacious single-story, painted a crisp white, with a neat lawn bordered by hedges. Its backyard, however, opened into the dense jungle. She waited until she was all settled in before she invited her parents over.

Genevieve's brothers had both enlisted in the U.S. Army after high school. They had both wanted to do their part, especially since their father was a Vietnam combat veteran. Only Genevieve's parents, Mark and Rosemarie Ninete, were on the island when she arrived. Bill was still very busy and was not there when Genevieve's parents first visited their house.

"It's good that there are more houses around here now," Genevieve's mom commented. "We hardly ever drive up this way. I think the last time we were here, the Machananao subdivision was still under construction."

"Yeah. Only the front half was done," Genevieve's dad added.

"It's good that Bill's housing allowance is more than enough to cover the rent. Plus, this place is close to the base, so it doesn't take him long to get in for emergencies." Genevieve brought over a couple of soft drinks for her parents as they sat in her living room. "So how are my brothers? Have you heard from them? We were so busy getting ready for the move here that I haven't had time to check in with them."

Her mom answered, "Well, Peter is supposed to be heading to Fort Bliss. I don't fully understand what his job is, but he's working with the Patriot missiles that are being used for the war. He said he may be deployed soon."

Her dad added, "I think it's something with the guidance systems. He must be smarter than his grades ever showed when he was in school here." They all laughed. "Even David. He's training to be a Communications Specialist. He might be deployed right after he finishes his MOS training."

"Yeah. This war has all of our kids involved," Genevieve's mom added. She was very proud, but also very worried. So, she changed the subject. "Anyway, when are you getting this house blessed?"

"Bill and I haven't talked about it yet."

"You shouldn't wait too long," her mom quickly warned. "We also noticed on the drive in that there's a big rubber tree in the jungle just behind your lot. You might want to think about cutting that down."

"What's wrong with the rubber tree?" Genevieve

asked.

"*Taotaomo'na*, Gen," came her mother' reply.

"I thought they were only in banyan trees?"

Rosemarie shook her head. "They can reside in any tree, actually. But trees like the banyan and rubber trees are almost always inhabited. They are both very large, magnificent trees with aerial roots that eventually grow to make up the ever-growing tree trunk. Some legends say that the *taotaomo'na* can capture people and entangle them in all the roots where their bodies and souls become part of the tree."

"Okay. I get it. But I don't think we can cut it down since we're just renting." Genevieve tried to dismiss her mother.

"Probably not. But I wouldn't want one of those trees so close if I was pregnant. Anyway, at least get the house blessed," her mom insisted.

"Alright. I will, Mom." Genevieve agreed, just so that she could appease her mother, but in truth, she didn't think it was necessary. Bill didn't believe in the island's superstitions, and Genevieve herself had always considered them exaggerations. However, about the third week after moving in, things began to change.

Bill was hardly home. So, he was never there to see or hear the things that Genevieve did when she was home alone. She knew the local superstitions. It all began with noises at night; small, almost imperceptible sounds that seemed to come from the jungle. At first, Genevieve attributed them to animals, but soon the noises grew more distinct. One evening, as she sat alone in the living room, she heard the unmistakable sound of baby rattles. The soft, rhythmic shaking sent a chill down her spine.

Another night, she could have sworn that she heard tapping on the sliding door to their back patio. Her heart pounded as she crept toward the door. When she turned on the patio light, she froze. There, on the concrete outside, were tiny, muddy footprints, as clear as day. That was the last straw. It was all really starting to scare her. Terrified, Genevieve confided in her mother, who repeated her plea. "You need to get the house blessed, Gen. This isn't something to ignore."

The following morning, over breakfast, Genevieve brought it up with Bill.

"Hon? I'd like to get us registered with the church today," she said cautiously as Bill ate his breakfast.

"Mmmm," Bill acknowledged, then swallowed his food. "That's so a priest can come out to bless the place, right?"

"Yeah. Is that okay?" she asked.

"We don't have to actually go to church, right?"

"I don't think so. We just need to be registered as part of the parish. There's a fee for the blessing, but my mom says it's customary to donate a little more." Genevieve replied.

"Sure. I'm fine with paying the fees and getting registered. Especially if it will help you feel safer when I'm not home. I'm just sorry I can't be here that much." Bill did feel bad that he was working long hours with last-minute schedule changes. But they both knew that was the way the military worked.

Bill was more concerned about Genevieve's state of mind and her safety. So, he was happy that she was going to get the house blessed. He didn't believe in it, but she did. As far as cutting down the large rubber tree was concerned, that wasn't going to happen. First of all, they were renting. Secondly, the tree was not on the property and thirdly, the tree was huge. Besides, Bill didn't understand what the big deal with the tree was anyway.

Because their house was in the village of Yigo, the closest parish was Our Lady of Lourdes. Genevieve was able to get registered and scheduled to have their house blessed. But the next available date for the blessing was not for another two weeks. Genevieve expressed her concerns about having just moved into a new house and her being pregnant. The parish office recommended that she visit the gift shop at the Dulce Nombre de Maria Cathedral Basilica in the village of Hagatña. They would have some holy water and blessed crucifixes that she could buy to place throughout her home.

Genevieve decided to make it a mother–daughter outing. So, she asked to borrow the phone in the parish office and called Rosemarie.

"Hello. Ninete residence," her mom answered.

"Mom. It's your favorite daughter." Genevieve giggled as she knew the woman behind the counter could hear her.

Rosemarie laughed, too. "Hi, Gen. What are you up

to?"

"Hi, mom. I'm at the Our Lady of Lourdes parish office. I just registered and got scheduled to have my house blessed."

"That's great! When?"

"Not for a couple of weeks. But they recommended that I go to the gift shop at the Cathedral Basilica to get some things for the house in the meantime."

"Okay. You know, I've never been there."

"I was just going to ask if you could go with me. I don't even remember there being a gift shop."

"I've seen it. They sectioned off a part of the Cathedral Basilica and turned it into the gift shop."

"Do you have time to go today? I can head over to your house now."

"Sure, my girl. Come over. We'll eat first. Your dad made some smoked pork yesterday."

Genevieve laughed. "Ooooh! I haven't had that in forever. I'll be there in ten minutes. Save me a plate!" She hung up, feeling a small sense of relief. Maybe the blessed items would help. At least, she hoped they would.

*****

After a quick lunch, Genevieve and her mom drove to the Cathedral Basilica. Genevieve bought a crucifix for each bedroom and one for the living room. She also bought small bottles of holy water to place at each window of the house and a couple of blessed palm leaves that were woven into crosses to place over the front door and over the patio sliding door. Everything they bought was blessed, so Genevieve felt safer being home alone.

The days didn't worry her because she could always visit her mom, or her mom could visit her. It was the nights that really had her concerned. But now, she felt like she had a spiritual security system installed.

Things seemed to calm down after Genevieve surrounded herself with the religious items. The strange noises had stopped, and she was sure that things would only get better once the house was blessed.

A couple of days before the house blessing, Bill and some friends had a rare evening off. So, he invited them over for some pizza and beer on the back patio. Genevieve was happy he was home, but she wouldn't be joining them.

"I'll take some pizza, but I can't join you out back," Genevieve said.

"Why not?" Bill asked.

"I'm six months pregnant and I shouldn't be hanging outside at night."

"Are you sure, Hon? They won't be staying long. Maybe they'll be here for just a couple of hours."

"I'm sure. Sorry. It's actually getting close to my usual bedtime anyway," Genevieve explained.

"Really? It's not even nine o'clock yet," Bill said, surprised.

"Yes sir." Genevieve giggled as she explained, "I'm

resting for two, remember?"

"Okay. I know." With a hand on her shoulder, Bill kissed her on the forehead. "We'll keep it down."

"Thanks, hon. I love you."

"I love you, too. I'll grab some pizza for you."

Bill and his friends were fairly quiet. Genevieve could still hear them laughing from the bedroom, but she was able to fall asleep. She woke up around one o'clock in the morning to get some water. Bill and his friends were just wrapping up. Bill came into the house and kissed Genevieve as he walked his friends out through the front door.

After he locked up, Bill hugged Genevieve from behind. "Thanks for letting me have them over, Hon."

She smiled and patted his arm. "We should have a barbeque next time, during the day, so I can join you."

"Absolutely! A barbeque sounds great!" He hugged her a little tighter and kissed her on the cheek. "Let's get to bed."

Later that morning Genevieve wasn't feeling well. By the afternoon, she was running a fever, so she took it easy for the day. Bill got her some soup but had to go to work that evening. Before he left, they called Genevieve's mom to let her know what was going on. Genevieve's parents decided to come over to keep an eye on her since the fever was not going down. Bill had to leave for work before they arrived, so Genevieve answered the door.

"Hi, Mom. Hi, Dad. Thanks for coming."

"Of course, my girl. Do you want anything? Your dad

can go get whatever you need." Genevieve's mom rubbed her back as they followed her in.

"That's okay. I don't have much of an appetite."

Genevieve's mom walked her back to her bedroom. "What happened, Gen? Do you remember being close to anyone who was sick?"

"No. I don't think so." Genevieve got in bed, but she sat up leaning against her headboard. "I was fine yesterday. The only people I was exposed to were Bill's coworkers. They came by last night, but none of them seemed sick."

"Did they keep you up?" her mom asked.

"No. They hung out on the patio to have some beer and pizza, and they weren't too loud."

"How late did they stay?"

"I got up around one o'clock and they were just leaving."

Her mom seemed curious and concerned. "Did anyone touch you when they came in from the patio?"

"No. Bill just walked them from the patio to the front door and they left."

"That's good."

"Why did you ask if someone touched me?"

"There's another superstition regarding the *taotaomo'na* with expectant women. It says that when someone comes indoors after being outdoors near a jungle, they have to wait for at least fifteen minutes before touching you. If they don't, then they might give you what they call *minaipen chalan*."

"What's that?"

"It's a *taotaomo'na* illness. The *taotaomo'na* outside of the house can piggyback on someone walking in, but only for a little bit. If that person touches you within that time, they can make you sick."

"Yeah. Nobody came close. They just walked past while I was in the kitchen getting some water." But then Genevieve paused. A worried look rushed across her face. "Wait! Bill kissed me." She looked straight at her mom. "Bill came straight in and kissed me as he walked everyone else out."

Her mom shared her worry. But her dad said, "Okay. Let's not worry too much just yet. Let's just see how this goes. Hopefully this will just pass." Genevieve's mom agreed.

But as the night dragged on, Genevieve's fever was still not going down. When her temperature hit 104 degrees, her mom called Bill and let him know that they were taking her to the emergency room.

By the time Bill got to the hospital, Genevieve had ice packs under her neck and in her underarms. They were able to bring her fever down a little, but it just kept going back up. The doctors couldn't figure out what was going on and her blood tests didn't reveal anything. She also didn't have any injuries or other symptoms.

When things didn't improve after a couple of days, Genevieve's parents were really starting to think the doctors wouldn't be able to help. It had to be *taotaomo'na* illness. But it wasn't their choice to call someone in. They figured their daughter would be open to a visit from a *suruhåna. But would Bill agree?*

"Gen? Bill?" Genevieve's mom called their attention. "Your dad and I would like you to consider having a *suruhåna* or *suruhånu* visit." They didn't want Bill to get defensive, so they weren't going to bring up how the *taotaomo'na* illness might have been passed to Gen through him.

Genevieve's dad continued, "When a woman is pregnant and lives near the jungle, there is always a chance that they can get *taotaomo'na* illness somehow. We usually suspect that someone has *taotaomo'na* illness when they have something that should be simple to cure, but the doctors can't figure it out."

Bill didn't believe in the *taotaomo'na* and didn't know about any of the superstitions. But he did understand that Genevieve's parents only had her best interests at heart. As long as they weren't being unreasonable, it wouldn't hurt to listen to them.

Her mom continued, "We're not saying to stop what they're doing here. But we would like you to consider letting us invite a traditional CHamoru healer in to help. As long as they don't interfere with each other, maybe taking both approaches might be good. What do you think?"

Bill was truly worried about Genevieve and their baby. He turned to his wife and said, "The sooner you get back to normal, the better. I don't care what works as long as it works." He gently rubbed her forearm as she lay exhausted in the hospital bed. "Did you want to see a saru... saru..." He turned to his in-laws for the correct word.

"*Suruhånu*," Genevieve's dad filled in.

"Yes. *Suruhånu*. Thanks, Dad." Bill nodded in appreciation to his father-in-law before turning back toward Genevieve. "I'm okay with it if that's what you want. I don't think it would hurt."

Genevieve nodded with a smile and answered in a very weak voice, "Yes, please."

"We know there's a *suruhåna* in Dededo. Gen, didn't you have a classmate who lived with her?" her mother asked. "He used to be an altar server with your brothers."

"Mateo Leon Guerrero." Genevieve answered.

"That's the one. We still see him active at Santa Barbara, so we'll check with him to ask," her mother said as she turned to Genevieve's dad who concurred.

"We can also just check with the parish office to get ahold of him," Genevieve's dad added.

Genevieve nodded and squeezed Bill's hand.

"That sounds good. Thanks," Bill replied.

"Okay. We'll get going then," Genevieve's dad said as he stood up. He helped his wife up and grabbed her purse. They both kissed Genevieve on her forehead and then left for the parish office.

When Mr. and Mrs. Ninete got to the Santa Barbara Parish office, Marie informed them that Mateo was still at work, though she offered to call him for them later that evening. That's when Rosemarie Ninete explained their urgency.

"Marie, maybe you can help us. We're actually looking for Mateo because we need a *suruhåna*. I don't remember if he lived with her or was related to her, but we remember he was close with *Tan* Chai."

Marie understood. "Don't worry, Rosemarie. I'm not busy right now, so I'll try to reach him at the airport."

"Thank you, Marie. We really appreciate that," Rosemarie said.

*****

Marie was able to track down the phone number for Facilities at the airport and left a message for Mateo to call her back. He was still out, working on the floor somewhere, so they would have to wait for him to check back in at the office.

Marie explained to Mark and Rosemarie that she wasn't sure how long it might take before Mateo called them back, however, they were welcome to hang around and wait or they could call her later. They decided to grab some food and head back to the hospital and let Marie know that they would call her from the hospital to check in.

About an hour later, Mark Ninete called Marie from the hospital.

"Hi, Marie. Did Mateo happen to call back?" he asked.

"Hey, Mark. Yes. He called. He said *Tan* Chai doesn't help with *taotaomo'na* illness."

"Really?"

"Yeah. But he said he knows a *suruhånu* who should be able to help."

"That's good. Did he give you a phone number?"

"No. He said he would call the *suruhånu* and ask him to meet at the hospital."

"Okay. Thanks so much for your help, Marie! We really appreciate it."

"Good luck, Mark. Tell Rosemarie I'm praying for Genevieve and her baby."

They hung up and Mark walked back to his daughter's room. He updated everyone, and they waited for Mateo to arrive.

Bill didn't know any of the people his father-in-law mentioned, though he remembered them being mentioned earlier. "So, who are these people? These... Marie, Mateo, and other man? And how are they supposed to help?"

Mr. Ninete responded, "Marie works in the Santa Barbara Parish office. We went there to find Mateo's contact information. Mateo lived with a *suruhåna* in Dededo, so we thought he would be able to help us contact her. The boy has always been very active with the church, so Marie was our best chance at getting a hold of Mateo."

"Okay. So, this other man must be the *suruhåna*?" Bill asked.

"*Suruhånu*," Mr. Ninete corrected him. "*Suruhåna* is for a female. It seems that the *suruhåna* that Mateo lived with can't help with *taotaomo'na* illness. So, Mateo called a *suruhånu* that he knows and who can definitely help us."

"How do you guys know this Mateo? He seems to really be going out of his way to help," Bill asked.

Mrs. Ninete answered, "He was an altar server for years with our sons. He also was Genevieve's classmate in middle school and high school. We don't know much more about him other than the fact that he has always been active with the church that we go to."

"He always seemed like such a nice boy. It doesn't surprise me that he wants to help," Mr. Ninete added.

Bill couldn't help the little voice in the back of his mind that started identifying dots to connect. *So, this is some guy who was Gen's classmate and is going out of his way to help her even though she's been off the island for years? He must have really liked her.* But he kept the thoughts to himself. They didn't matter. Besides, he was not insecure in his marriage, and at the moment, Mateo was just someone helping, so that's all that mattered.

Around seven o'clock that evening, a nurse came into the room to let them know there were visitors asking to come in. It was Mateo and the *suruhånu*. Mr. Ninete stepped out to bring them in. Genevieve was asleep. Surprisingly, the noise of people talking didn't wake her. Nonetheless, they all spoke just a little softer than normal.

Mateo walked into the room first. "Hi Mr. and Mrs. Ninete." He greeted them with *man nginge'*. First to Mark, "*Ñot*". Then to Rosemarie, "*Ñora*".

"*Dioste ayudi*" they both said.

"Mr. and Mrs. Ninete, this is Kiko Aguon. He's a *suruhånu*. He can try to help Genevieve." Mateo began.

"Thank you, Mateo. Thank you so much for coming, Kiko," Rosemarie said.

"It's okay. I can already tell that this young lady has *taotaomo'na* illness," Kiko said as he got straight to business. "Can someone tell me what happened?"

Mrs. Ninete answered, "We think it's *minaipen chalan*." She looked at her husband as she said it to confirm that he agreed. They were worried that they would have to point out that Bill was the one who unintentionally made her sick.

Kiko held one of Genevieve's forearms for a couple of seconds, then proceeded to feel her head and neck with the back of his hand. "From what Mateo told me, I assume you two are Mr. and Mrs. Ninete... Genevieve's parents."

Mrs. Ninete acknowledged, "Yes." Then she gestured toward Bill and said, "And this is her husband, Bill."

Kiko greeted Bill with a nod. "*Minaipen chalan*, huh? Was someone doing work outside or was there a party?"

"Yes. Just a small get-together, but it was outdoors and at night." Mrs. Ninete answered.

Bill was just a little lost in the discussion.

Kiko pulled out a couple of things from a small bag that he had brought with him.

Bill had to jump in at this point because nobody was explaining anything to him. "Wait. What's he doing? And what's *minaipen chalan*?"

Since Kiko was busy preparing, and Genevieve's parents were watching him, Mateo answered. "*Minaipen chalan*. It's an illness caused by *taotaomo'na*."

Bill didn't like that Mateo answered, but at least he was getting answers. "I thought *taotaomo'na* only made you sick if you made them mad. My wife didn't do anything to make any *taotaomo'na* mad."

Mateo explained, "You're partially right. It's true that they will make you sick if you make them mad. But some *taotaomo'na* are attracted to pregnant women as well as babies and young children."

"Yeah. Gen told me that she's not supposed to go to new places or be outdoors at night while she's pregnant. That's why she stayed inside that night. She never went out."

"That's good. But, if this is *minaipen chalan*, then she wasn't the one who was outside." Mateo noticed Bill was getting a little defensive.

"How does that work? How can she get sick but not be the person who was actually outside?" Bill asked, trying to understand.

"Well... *taotaomo'na* can cling to someone, and they can do that without making the carrier sick. When they pick someone to cling to and that person goes indoors, they can hang on for a few minutes, especially if the house has not been blessed. So, that's how they can reach someone inside the house. All it takes is some kind of physical contact with the child or pregnant woman, and then they will get sick. Nobody even knows it has happened until someone is already sick," Mateo clarified.

Bill remembered everything about that night, including the fact that he kissed Genevieve almost as soon as he came in. Then he realized that his in-laws must have already thought it was him if they were suspecting it was *minaipen chalan. Were they blaming him?* If they weren't, he was already beginning to blame himself anyway.

Bill looked at them, feeling guilty. His in-laws had both heard Mateo explaining things to Bill, and they figured he would be blaming himself.

Mrs. Ninete was quick to say, "Bill, nobody's placing any blame on you for this."

"But you guys were already thinking I did this."

His mother-in-law tried again to reassure him. "Bill, this isn't your fault. We didn't say anything because we didn't want you to feel guilty. This is a *taotaomo'na* illness. Gen stayed inside. And all you did was to be a normal, loving, affectionate husband. The *taotaomo'na* did this, not you."

Kiko chimed in, "The guilt and the blame are with the *taotaomo'na* that is after this baby. Right now, we just need to help this mother and her baby. Mateo, can you put the *palai* on her arms and neck while I work with the charms?"

Mateo was caught off-guard. "Me? I haven't done this in years."

"I know, Mateo. But you know your hands are good for this, and I need your help. Besides, I know you can tell more than I can that this *taotaomo'na* doesn't have a very strong hold here."

Mateo acknowledged that Kiko was right. He grabbed the bottle of *palai* from Kiko and started massaging it into Genevieve's arms. Kiko then brushed a bundle of dried plant material around Genevieve and also asked that Genevieve's family follow him in prayer. Genevieve was so exhausted that she slept through the whole thing.

The treatment didn't involve Genevieve ingesting anything and Kiko explained that the *palai* ingredients were mainly salt mixed in coconut oil so that it wouldn't come off easily. So, there were no medical issues with what he was doing. Bill didn't understand any of it, so he asked how it was all supposed to help.

Kiko explained, "The salt serves as a deterrent. The coconut oil helps to make the salt stick to her skin longer. The mix of plants and roots that I used are also deterrents. The *taotaomo'na* don't like the smell. Lastly, the prayers are a deterrent too. So, we are basically attacking the *taotaomo'na* to drive it out. We are working toward making it so uncomfortable that it decides to leave."

Kiko and Mateo continued for about an hour. After that, they were only saying prayers. Kiko packed up his things and suggested that they continue praying through the night. Bill and his in-laws thanked Kiko and Mateo for their help, and Mateo said he would check in on them the next day after work.

It was an overcast evening and there seemed to be no breeze at all as Kiko and Mateo walked out into the parking lot of the hospital. They had met up at the hospital, so they were leaving in separate cars. Mateo was parked a little farther away from the entrance because the parking lot was more crowded when he arrived. Now, there were only a couple of cars remaining in the area where Mateo had parked. Kiko had been lucky enough to find a closer parking spot because someone had been leaving when he arrived.

As Kiko drove past Mateo in the parking lot, Mateo waved and thanked him. However, as soon as Kiko's taillights disappeared around the corner, Mateo got hit with that terrible chill. He already knew what it was. The parking lot lights started flickering for a second or two, then shut off altogether. Mateo rushed into his car and fumbled to get the key into the ignition in the dark. He looked down to try to see where he was inserting the key and started the car quickly. As he sat back up, the *ga'lågu* was right outside his window. The hound from hell looked like it had blood mixed with its filthy black fur. It stood with its ears folded back and its lips curled to bare its huge fang-like teeth. It had never been this close before.

The monster then let out a very deep, guttural growl as it stared right at Mateo with its cataract-filled eyes. Mateo was a man now, but suddenly finding this monster just inches away from his face made him feel like a little kid wanting to pull his blanket over his head to hide. But there was nowhere to hide.

The smell of sulfur was absolutely nauseating. He was going to try to just ignore it and leave. But then it started barking at him ferociously and clawing at the glass. Its paws were the size of fists with frightening two-inch claws that gave a horrible screech as they scraped against the window and car door. *Could it see him with its eyes like that?* He wondered, but that didn't matter. To Mateo, it felt like the monster was looking straight into his soul as it clawed frantically trying to get in the car.

The demon stood on its hind legs, reaching up to seven feet in height as it pushed at the car, shaking it violently. It felt like it might even be strong enough to turn the car over, and the barking was so intense that Mateo's body convulsed uncontrollably in fear. It shook him from the inside out, almost vibrating through his bones. It also felt like his heart was being squeezed with each bark.

Mateo struggled, but not to find a way to escape. There was no escape. Instead, he struggled to pray. It took all his effort to even make a sound. He kept trying until he was able to squeeze in one word... then another.

"Uh... uh... ou... our... F... F... Fa... Fath... ther... who... who art in H... Heav... v... v... ven," he struggled. He focused so hard that the sound of the barking slowly started to dull. The words came easier and easier as he went on and kept his eyes closed as he proceeded to pray the rosary.

When breathing was easier, he noticed the barking had stopped. He opened his eyes and looked around. The parking lot lights were back on, and he couldn't see the dog anywhere. He was scared to look in the rearview mirror. But he didn't hear or feel the dog around anymore. He took a couple of deep breaths, then backed out of his parking spot, though he continued on praying as he rushed home.

As he arrived at home, he knew this wasn't over. The *taotaomo'na's* grip on him was far from broken. He thought back to the words of one of the nuns who had taught him in middle school. The words had always stuck in his head. She had said that *when things go bad, don't swear or cuss... pray. If you're about to die, make God's name be the last thing you say. Cuss words can't save you... but God can.* Her words might have just saved his life.

Chapter 18

Spirits Grow Bolder

That night at the hospital stuck with Mateo. He couldn't shake the feeling that the demon dog - the *ga'lågu* - was more than just a coincidence. It wasn't the first time he'd encountered it, but this was different. It had been deliberate, chasing him, trying to get to him. He felt it in his bones. It wasn't just an accident. This thing was following him, hunting him. The fear weighed heavy on his chest, making him feel like he couldn't breathe.

The next day, he was too shaken up to go to work, so he stayed home. It wasn't something he often did, Mateo prided himself on his dependability, but this felt different. Every time he thought about going to work, he felt the dog's presence again. He kept thinking about those cataract-filled eyes and sharp teeth. He tried to pray, but even that felt hollow that day. He wasn't sure what was wrong with him.

Still, he couldn't stop himself from calling the hospital. He wanted to check on Genevieve, so he left a message for a family member to call him back. When her father, Mr. Ninete, returned his call, Mateo braced himself for bad news, but the man's voice was calm and even joyful.

"Mateo," Mr. Ninete said warmly, "I wanted to thank you for what you did. Genevieve is awake and her fever has gone down. She's recovering well."

Mateo let out a breath he didn't realize he was holding. "That's great to hear," he said, his voice steady but his heart pounding.

"We owe you so much," Mr. Ninete continued. "You and Kiko. Genevieve wouldn't have made it without you two."

Mateo swallowed hard. He didn't feel like a hero. All he'd done was call for help, and the real work had been Kiko's. "I'm glad she's okay," Mateo said simply.

"Will you come visit her?" Mr. Ninete asked.

Mateo hesitated. The thought of going back to the hospital made his stomach churn. He remembered the dog again, the way it had lunged at his car, its claws scraping against the window. "I... I don't think I can," he said quietly. "But thank you for letting me know she's alright."

Mr. Ninete didn't push. "Alright, Mateo. Thank you again, from all of us. We'll never forget what you did."

After the call, Mateo sat alone in his small apartment. He didn't feel like a savior or a hero. He felt scared and uncertain. He couldn't shake the memory of the *ga'lågu*.

*****

A few days later, Mateo forced himself to go to mass at Santa Barbara. It was his routine, and he thought that maybe being in church would help him feel less haunted. The familiar sights and sounds of the service did comfort him a little - the glow of the candles, the gentle hum of the choir - but he still felt uneasy. He prayed harder than usual, asking for strength, for clarity, for some kind of guidance.

Genevieve, her parents, and Bill had planned to surprise Mateo after mass at Santa Barbara, so they attended and waited in a pew where Mateo would notice them. After the service ended, as Mateo was preparing to leave, he noticed their familiar faces in the crowd. Genevieve waved enthusiastically.

"Mateo!" she called out, her voice bright and cheerful.

Her parents, Mr. and Mrs. Ninete, smiled warmly as Mateo approached. Always respectful, Mateo first greeted his elders with *man nginge'*. Then Bill stepped forward to shake Mateo's hand, followed by Genevieve extending her hand, gesturing for Mateo's hand to hold.

Genevieve was first to speak. "You didn't come back

to the hospital, so we didn't get to fully thank you. That's why we're here."

Bill added as he wrapped an arm around his wife, "Yeah. You and Kiko probably saved the lives of Gen and our baby. We got to thank Kiko when he came by to check on Gen at the hospital, and we wanted to make sure we thanked you, too."

Mateo waved his hands and sat in the pew next to them saying, "No need to thank me. Genevieve was always a friend to me throughout school, so I was happy to help. Besides, all I did was call *Tun* Kiko to help. He's the *suruhånu*."

Mrs. Ninete was quick to reply, "It's nice that you're so modest, Mateo. But don't sell yourself short. If God gives you a gift, it's only right to use that gift in His name."

Mateo responded with an uneasy smile. He was never comfortable accepting praise. "Okay. I know. Thank you, Mrs. Ninete."

Bill chimed in, "Please don't be a stranger. We're having the baby's christening soon, and we'd love for you to come. It would mean a lot to us."

"Okay," Mateo answered. "Thanks. I'd love to be there. I can give you my phone number if you happen to have something to write on."

Mrs. Ninete pulled out a pen and a piece of paper from her purse. "Here you go."

Mateo wrote down his phone number and handed the paper and pen back to Mrs. Ninete. "I have an answering machine and am usually home from work around six o'clock in the evening. But if there's something urgent, you can leave a message for me with the Facilities office at the airport."

Bill then stood up and looked at Genevieve. "Well, we really should get this mother-to-be back home to rest." Genevieve nodded in agreement as Bill helped her to stand up.

They all said their goodbyes and left the church. However, Mrs. Ninete's words really struck a chord with Mateo. *Tan* Chai and Kiko had always talked about how special he was. They had always marveled over the things he had been able to do with traditional medicine and the massages. They'd also been amazed by his ability to hear the *taotaomo'na* and also see dead people.

He had always downplayed it, dismissing it as flattery, but he wouldn't disagree that hearing these things made him feel special. He remembered how good it always felt when he helped *Tan* Chai heal people. Thinking back on all of it, he did start to feel that maybe God did intend for him to be a *suruhånu*. It did seem to be a natural fit for him.

At the same time, he couldn't ignore the darker side of his gift. Seeing spirits wasn't always a good thing for Mateo. The *ga'lågu* was definitely one of the things he wished he could never see again. After it tried to attack him at the hospital, Mateo really needed answers, and he needed them fast.

So, he asked Kiko and *Tan* Chai if they could meet

him and have a serious talk about his recent events, hinting that the talk would be about the *ga'lågu*. They agreed without hesitation, sensing the urgency in his voice. The threat to Mateo had become much more urgent, so he arranged for the meeting to be at his apartment the next morning.

*****

Mateo's dining table was small and round, but just big enough for the three of them. Mateo had some rosketti cookies out on a plate and some freshly brewed coffee. He had gotten the rosketti from one of his coworkers who had stopped by the Chodes store on his way into work a couple of days before. The store was famous for its local baked goods. The coworker had bought enough for the whole Facilities crew to celebrate his recent promotion to supervisor, and Mateo was happy to share the gift with *Tan* Chai and Kiko.

Tan Chai was first to ask, "Where did you get these? These are the good ones!" She hadn't had any rosketti in months, so she was excited to be having some.

"They're from Chodes," Mateo said. "A coworker got some for everyone."

"Mmmm!" Kiko said as he caught some crumbs that were trying to get away as he took a bite. "That's a very good coworker."

They all shared a laugh, but Mateo wanted to get past the pleasantries. He took a deep breath before starting.

"*Tan* Chai. *Tun* Kiko. I need your help."

Tan Chai and Kiko both took a quick peek at each other, then focused on Mateo.

"Shoot, boy. Anything you need." Kiko answered.

"I saw that demon dog again... the *ga'lågu*." He turned to Kiko, "Remember that night at the hospital when we helped my former classmate?"

Tan Chai shot Kiko a dirty look. "You made him help? I bet that's how the *ga'lågu* found him."

"Maybe not, *Tan* Chai." Mateo continued, "I've seen it even when I wasn't doing any *suruhånu* work, remember?" He was especially thinking about that day when he fell asleep on *Tan* Chai's living room floor and woke up to see the dog across the street. After that day, there had been other times, too.

"You're right. I remember," *Tan* Chai reluctantly agreed. "So, what happened this time?"

Mateo tilted his head and looked down at the plate of rosketti. "This time, it chased me to my car and was trying to break through the window."

Tan Chai sat straight up in her chair and turned to Kiko. She was scared for Mateo, and she felt very helpless.

"It is definitely following me, and I don't know why."

"Right outside your car window?" Kiko asked.

"Yeah. It stared and growled at me first. Then, when I was going to try to back out from my parking spot and leave, it went crazy."

Kiko leaned back in his chair. *Tan* Chai reached out

and held Mateo's hand. Neither of them knew what to say.

Kiko asked, "So, what happened? You're here. So, that means you got away. How?"

"I was able to start praying. It was shaking the car and scratching at the window and door like crazy. I thought it was going to get in. I couldn't move because I was so scared and because of all the shaking, and I could barely breathe. However, I was able to close my eyes and start praying. It was so hard, but I eventually was able to start forming one word after another until full prayers started coming out. Then the *ga'lågu* disappeared."

Kiko started trying to put the pieces together. "So, you have been seeing this dog on and off ever since you were a kid, right?"

"Yeah."

"So as far as you know, it could have been following you for your whole life," Kiko added.

"I guess. That's how it seems."

Kiko looked at *Tan* Chai first, then slowly turned to Mateo as he leaned to rest his elbows on the table. "Remember when you called me for new charms, and you asked to pick them up from me instead of the way I usually bring them to you?"

"Yeah," Mateo replied

"That's when I started to think that this might be the same spirit that you see every time. I think maybe it has been following you since before you were born," Kiko said.

The room went silent as the weight of Kiko's words sank in.

Tan Chai was stunned. "No."

Kiko continued, "Think about it. None of us can see it. Only Mateo can. And as far as he knows, it always takes the same form. We both know that there was a very strong, mean *taotaomo'na* that took hold of Mateo's mom. What if this is the same *taotaomo'na*?"

Tan Chai didn't want to believe it, but what Kiko said made sense. It could very well be the same *taotaomo'na*. It had wanted to take Mateo back then and had patiently been waiting for an opportunity to try again. *Tan* Chai didn't want to accept this because if that was the case, then this *taotaomo'na* was never going to stop going after Mateo.

Mateo was a little confused and a little frustrated. So, he asked, "Didn't you guys try to help my mom?"

"Yes, we did," *Tan* Chai assured.

"Then what happened? We have helped other people. Why couldn't anybody save my mom?" Mateo thought a little more after saying this then asked, "Wait. Did this thing take my mom because it was trying to get to me?"

Tan Chai and Kiko knew they couldn't explain things away anymore to try to spare Mateo's feelings. Mateo already knew enough to be able to see through any rosy picture they tried to paint for him. He knew that the *taotaomo'na* were attracted to babies and young children. So, the *taotaomo'na* that took his mother had to have been going after him.

"So why weren't you able to help my mother?" he asked again.

Kiko was the more no-nonsense straight shooter. He usually felt that was the best approach. "You know that all the prayers and rosaries and statues in the world can't help you if you don't believe in them, right?"

"Yeah. I know."

"Well, your mom never believed the superstitions about the *taotaomo'na*. Your grandma Annie said she ignored them. She also said that your mom wouldn't go to church, and she didn't believe in praying."

Tan Chai wanted to qualify what Kiko said and try to soften the blow of the harsh news. "Your mom wasn't a bad person. She was just going through some bad times. Your grandpa, her dad, died. Then her best friend moved away. Then she ended up with your dad, who we think was abusive to her. So, she was already in a vulnerable state while she was pregnant with you."

Kiko summed things up. "She was pregnant, she was vulnerable, she was exposed, and she didn't believe. If you add in the fact that the *taotaomo'na* she was exposed to was one mean and tough son of a bitch, then you end up with all the cards stacked against her. By the time your grandma noticed anything was wrong, it was already too late."

This was all difficult for Mateo to accept. This was his mother they were talking about. But he also knew that *Tan* Chai and Kiko would have done their best for her. He was hurt that they couldn't save her. But he did understand. "So, if you couldn't save her, how did you save me?"

"I don't know if *we did* save you," Kiko said.

Tan Chai looked straight at Mateo and nodded in agreement.

Kiko continued, "To me, it felt like *you* were the one stopping the *taotaomo'na*. It felt like you were stronger than it was. We did what we could to help deter it and make it feel uncomfortable. But I think you were able to keep it away on your own, and you weren't even born yet."

Tan Chai felt herself filled with a sense of urgency. "Mateo, I'm afraid for you. I think Kiko is right. I think the *taotaomo'na* has been following you because of your special abilities. You have a strong connection to the spirit world. I think that's why this *taotaomo'na* has been so interested in you. I'm afraid that it will always be interested in you."

Mateo was worried. But he was finally getting some answers.

Tan Chai added, "Mateo, you have a very powerful gift. From what we have seen, that gift is meant for helping people. That's why you have been so good at it. You can help people feel calm. You are great with growing, making, and applying traditional medicines."

Kiko also had to add, "Maybe you haven't realized it yet, but it also appears that your gifts come from God. You were baptized. This normally separates people from the spiritual world to help keep them safe from bad spirits. But your baptism did not separate you from the spiritual world. That means that God wanted you to keep your gifts. He wanted you to use them."

Mateo shook his head in disagreement. "But this *ga'lågu* already scares the crap out of me. How am I supposed to deal with that? And what if there are worse things out there than that dog?"

"You're right to worry, Mateo. We need to figure out how you can deal with this, and maybe even move past it." Kiko started taking stock of things. "Let's look at the facts that we know. This dog only appears near jungle areas. Praying seems to chase it away. But why couldn't it get into your car? This thing should be able to go through walls if it wanted to."

Mateo realized why the dog couldn't get into the car. "Father Rogelio blessed the car." He smiled as he remembered. "Yeah. This was back when I first started driving it."

"Really?" *Tan* Chai was surprised. She chuckled a little as she said, "That sounds like something Father Rogelio would do. But I've never heard of them blessing a car."

"Mm-hmm." Mateo smiled as he continued. "Me too. I drove it to serve mass one weekend. He saw me park, and he walked over. He smiled and helped himself into the passenger side. Before I knew it, he started praying and sprinkling holy water all around. Father Rogelio said he just wanted me to have an extra layer of protection."

Mateo then picked up his arm to show the wooden rosary bracelet that he was wearing. "Father Tony actually gave me this for the same reason. He said not to hang a rosary from the rearview mirror like some people do because it's not supposed to be used as decoration. It's better to wear it and use it. He didn't say, but I'm pretty sure he blessed it too."

Kiko seemed surprised. "Wow! These people really love you, boy. Honestly, I think you just need to keep doing what you've been doing. It's all been working. Your faith has been protecting you. If anything, you just need more faith in yourself."

"What do you mean, 'I need more faith in myself'?"

"Think about it, boy." Kiko seemed more confident in what he was saying now. "You were able to keep this powerful *taotaomo'na* away before you were even born. You already had the power to protect yourself before you learned to fear. I don't know how, but I think if you can control your fear, then you don't have anything to worry about."

Tan Chai grabbed Mateo's hand again and seemed a little frustrated with herself. "We've never met anyone like you before. So, we don't have a lot of answers for you. There are legends about how some of our ancestors had the same kind of abilities. If they became healers, they were called *makåna*. They were like *suruhånu*, but they also had knowledge of spiritual healing, and they were able to see and speak to spirits. But their knowledge was never passed down. Back then, the church thought they were sorcerers or witches and killed them all."

Kiko started waving his finger at *Tan* Chai, pointing at her as he recalled what he was taught. "Yes. *Makåna.* I remember my grandpa telling me about them."

Tan Chai continued, "It was just after you were born, Mateo. Me and your grandma Annie took you to see *Tan* Paro in Umatac. *Tan* Paro told us that you reminded her of the legends of the *makåna.* She also told us about the *kakahna.* The *Kakahna* were evil *makåna* and were very bad people. They were the reason the church thought the old teachings were all evil sorcery and witchcraft. They used their power to cause harm. It was believed that evil *taotaomo'na* could possess a *makåna* and turn them evil. That is how they would become a *kakahna.* The *taotaomo'na* used them as a vessel to gain more power in the physical world."

"That makes sense," Kiko said. "This evil *taotaomo'na* seems to want to take Mateo as its vessel because of his gifts." He then turned to Mateo and added, "Now that gives us an idea of why this dog has been following you. But it doesn't change what I was saying about how to deal with it. Faith in God... and faith in yourself."

This was a lot to take in for Mateo. He had to come to grips with the idea that he had been, was, and always would be a target for this evil *taotaomo'na* that wanted to possess him. He thought to himself, *how does someone live with that? And the way I'm supposed to deal with this is basically... don't be scared? Really?*

Tan Chai and Kiko could see that Mateo was a bit overwhelmed. But there wasn't much more that they could do for him.

"You're not alone in this, Mateo. We will always do what we can to help you." *Tan* Chai let him know.

"I know, *Tan* Chai. I know."

Kiko noted, "It's really good that you are active with the church. Don't change that. If anything, I might need to give you the recipes for my charms and *palai*. It would be good for you to learn how to make your own in case you can't get a hold of me."

"Come to think of it," *Tan* Chai added, "maybe you should train with both of us to become a *suruhånu*. It will keep you in practice, and you will always have the charms and other deterrents that you need. Besides, you will get to help people." She was really feeling that training as a *suruhånu* might be a great option for Mateo.

Kiko was nodding his head, eager to add, "I think that this is the exact reason why God gave you this gift. I think God also made sure that you had all the right people around you, doing all the right things at all the right times to keep you protected."

"But, why does it have to be me?" Mateo knew it was useless, but he asked anyway out of frustration.

Tan Chai tapped Mateo's arm as she struggled to remember something. "I remember Mother Teresa saying something." She paused a moment longer. "Okay.

I got it. I remember her saying something once like... God can help you accomplish great things as long as you believe in Him much more than you believe in your own weakness."

With that, all three of them fell silent for a minute. The words seemed to hit home for all three of them, but maybe a bit more so for Mateo.

"Wow, *Tan* Chai! You got me deep with that one." Kiko laughed a little but was serious when he said, "I couldn't have said it better." Then he reached toward the center of the table and said, "That makes me want to eat another rosketti."

They all laughed and grabbed another cookie for themselves. They were in agreement on what Mateo should do. But they weren't going to pressure him into any timelines. It was his life, and he was dealing with things that were really on a level beyond the abilities of *Tan* Chai and Kiko. Mateo had some serious thinking to do about how ready he was to embrace what was looking more and more like something he was destined for.

Chapter 19

The Bond of Friendship

The afternoon sunlight streamed through the living room window of *Tan* Chai's home, casting a warm glow on the room. Mateo sat across from Mrs. Iriarte, carefully massaging *palai* into her hands and elbows. The fragrant herbal mixture filled the air, mingling with the faint smell of freshly brewed lemongrass tea from the stove.

"*Tan* Chai, your boy here is really good," Mrs. Iriarte said with a satisfied smile as she flexed her fingers slightly to test their range of motion. She looked over at *Tan* Chai, who was busy at the sink, rinsing out a handful of leaves for the *åmot*.

"I agree with you... one hundred percent," *Tan* Chai replied, her tone filled with pride as she continued to prepare another batch of *åmot* in the kitchen. "But don't tell him too much, or it'll go to his head." She winked at Mateo, who chuckled quietly. Though she wasn't one to openly boast, her heart swelled with pride whenever she heard someone complimenting Mateo, coupled with the fact that he had taken to the practice so naturally. Not that she would take any credit for his talents, she was just proud to be a part of his life.

Mateo gave a modest shrug, his hands continuing their careful movements across the older woman's joints. She had been coming to Mateo and *Tan* Chai for a couple of years now for her arthritis. Hearing the compliments, Mateo smiled, "I'm just happy to help, Mrs. Iriarte," he said sincerely. There was a calm satisfaction in his voice.

He could understand why *Tan* Chai had served as a *suruhåna* for this long. Helping others through traditional healing made him feel deeply connected to the community and the values he had grown up with. It wasn't about recognition or praise; it was about making a difference. He felt that he was able to contribute and that made him proud of his work.

Jesse, who was sitting at the dining table, watched the scene unfold. He had tagged along with his grandmother, as he often did during her regular visits to *Tan* Chai for her treatment. After a moment, Jesse leaned forward slightly and asked, "Why don't you guys charge for all this? It's a lot of work, isn't it? I mean, preparing the medicine, taking the time - it must add up." The question was directed both to *Tan* Chai and Mateo.

Tan Chai had been asked that question many times over the years, so she was ready with an answer. She dried her hands and turned toward him, her expression thoughtful.

"It's not that we haven't been asked this before," she began, "But it is part of an old tradition. In our culture, we believe in helping one another without expecting anything in return. It's called reciprocal aid. If someone needs help, you help. Later, if you need help, someone will do the same for you. It's not about money; it's about community."

Jesse raised an eyebrow. "But what about the stuff you need to make the medicine? That costs money, doesn't it?"

"It does," *Tan* Chai acknowledged, walking over to stand near the table. "However, a lot of the people I help know that I don't get around as much as I used to. So, they bring me things like eggs from their chickens or fish that they have caught. And they all know that I love young mango, so I always get more than I need when it's mango season."

Mrs. Iriarte nodded in agreement. "That's right. In the old days, farmers would share their crops with the village, and fishermen would work together with huge nets, splitting the catch with everyone. Nobody kept score, but everyone contributed what they could."

"Okay. I get it," Jesse responded, leaning back in his chair, processing everything. He then turned to his grandma. "So, it's kind of like how *Tun* Ben from Agat brings us land crab when he catches some and we bring him avocados from our tree when we harvest."

"Yes, boy. That's right." Then she tilted her head slightly, ready to make a point. "But here's the thing; you've probably noticed that even when we don't have avocados to share, *Tun* Ben still brings us land crabs"

Jesse thought for a moment and then nodded. "Yeah, I guess that's true." He also remembered how his grandma would have him give Mateo avocado bags every once in a while, to bring to *Tan* Chai.

Mrs. Iriarte gave him a small, knowing smile. "We all help as much as we can and it's not because we expect something back. Sometimes typhoons wipe out the avocados and we have nothing to give *Tun* Ben. But that doesn't stop him from giving anyway. It's about the spirit of giving." Mrs. Iriarte looked at *Tan* Chai as her expression changed more to that of concern. "It's sad that people are starting to forget our CHamoru values."

Tan Chai's expression turned more somber. "Yes, it is. It's good that they're starting to teach CHamoru in some schools now, though. That's a step in the right direction."

Tan Chai then halted what she was busy with in the kitchen and moved closer to Mateo, who was still massaging Mrs. Iriarte. "But you know, I also learned something from working with Mateo. He seems more in-tune with the energies between and within people and things. When he intently focuses, he can sense the energy as it transfers between people while they interact.

"Another thing you should know, money carries a lot of negative energy. People stress about earning it, they stress about sharing it, they stress about saving it, and they also stress about getting value in return for it. Therefore, I have always felt bad about taking money for what I do. So, when Mateo explained the energies to me, it made sense why I had been feeling that way. Money brings negative energy, and we need positive energy for healing. So, that's why it's better not to involve money."

Jesse snickered a little and said, "Man, Mateo. I didn't know you were such a sensitive guy."

Mateo laughed, shaking his head. "I knew that was coming."

Jesse's grandma gave him an irritated side-eye look, but she knew it was just friendly banter.

"Okay, Mrs. Iriarte," Mateo said, gently patting her hands to signal the end of the session and grabbing the hand towel on his lap to wipe the *palai* from his hands. "You're all set."

"Thank you, boy. Thank you, *Tan* Chai." Mrs. Iriarte said as she stood up and stretched her arms forward. She then twisted her wrists around and a warm smile spread across her face. "This feels so much better."

As they walked to the door, Mrs. Iriarte and *Tan* Chai exchanged a few words about scheduling her next visit.

Tan Chai then held the door open for them. "You're very welcome. It's always good to see you. Same time next week?"

"Yes, *Tan* Chai. We'll see you then," came Mrs. Iriarte's reply.

After some goodbyes, Jesse and Mateo agreed to meet up later that evening to hang out.

*****

That evening, Jesse met Mateo at his apartment, and the two friends took one car from there and headed to a nearby pool hall. They had begun going to the pool hall after they had both turned twenty-one years old and were old enough to drink, but neither of them was interested in actually getting drunk. They would only have a beer, and they'd try to make it last for about three games of pool before they would head off to dinner somewhere. However, recently they were starting to get the hang of shooting pool. They liked going early though, before the crowds showed up, so they could play in peace and avoid the haze of cigarette smoke that usually filled the room later in the night.

As usual, they were the first customers there. The pool hall was fairly dark with almost a dozen pool tables to choose from. The two friends liked the table farthest from the entrance so that they could avoid the foot traffic as people began to arrive. Jesse racked the balls, and Mateo prepared to break for their first game. Jesse, leaning casually on his own cue, brought up the earlier conversation. "Dude. I get why you guys don't charge for the *suruhånu* stuff. But the bills still have to be paid. I know that you can pay your bills because you work full time, but how does *Tan* Chai manage? I mean, she doesn't work anymore, right?"

Mateo started to think about it but put the thought on hold so that he could concentrate. Jesse would have to wait until after he broke to begin the game. The crack of the cue ball breaking the rack echoed through the hall, and Mateo seemed pleased with the break. He usually didn't get good contact on the cue ball on a break, but this time it was a solid one.

He had actually gotten the striped ball to drop in the side pocket. "Yes!" Mateo exclaimed. Now he had time to answer Jesse's question. "I remember my grandma telling me that *Tan* Chai was a retired teacher. So, there's that. I never met her husband, but if you saw the pictures in her house, she has a picture of him in a police uniform. I think I remember *Tan* Chai saying he was a retired police sergeant. So, she likely gets a pension too. I don't know what her numbers are, but it seems like she's covered financially." Mateo sank three more balls before missing.

"Okay. That makes sense." Jesse said, stepping up for his turn. He took a shot but missed. He then turned to Mateo and said, "So, we just need to find ourselves some girlfriends with pensions, huh?"

"You're so dumb, man" Mateo said as they both

laughed. Mateo finally sank the 8 ball to win the game.

Jesse walked to the head of the table to prepare to break while Mateo racked the balls. His tone got just a little more serious as he asked, "Hey, Matt. Have you had to help anyone with a *taotaomo'na* illness?"

Mateo nodded, taking his shot. "A few times. It's not that common, but it happens."

"What was that like?" Jesse was curious. He had never seen anyone with *taotaomo'na* illness and quite frankly, he didn't know much about it.

"It's... intense," Mateo said, pausing to find the right words. "I can usually feel if someone's been touched by a *taotaomo'na*. When they arrive, I try to figure out what the *taotaomo'na* did to them and why. That usually means I have to try to figure out what that person did to hurt or anger the *taotaomo'na*. We can try to treat their symptoms, but they won't really get better until they go back to the *taotaomo'na* that they upset and ask for forgiveness."

Jesse leaned on his cue stick, listening intently. "So... so when you say you can feel if someone's been touched by a *taotaomo'na*, what does that mean? What does it feel like?"

"The *taotaomo'na* give off different energies depending on their mood. The cold, spine tingling that you usually feel just means that a spirit is around. You are in range of their energy field. If they are happy with you, you will then get a warm feeling and may even smell flowers of some kind. If they are upset, then their energy feels more like a prickling static. The more upset they are, the more it starts to feel like pins and needles. That, and the spine tingling gets colder and soaks deeper inside you. But I think that's just me. I think I'm the only one who feels them like that." Mateo said.

Jesse's eyes widened. He was still curious but was also a bit concerned about Mateo. "Man, that's wild. So, what's the worst that you've had to deal with?"

It was Mateo's shot. He took aim with the cue stick as he replied, "Nothing bad. Just people with strange fevers, rash, or bruises. The illnesses were usually just because the person forgot to ask for permission in the jungle or maybe they were just too loud near the jungle."

The ball sank, but Mateo paused and looked straight at Jesse. He was trying to gauge how prepared Jesse might be for what he was about to say. Or maybe he was more scared of what Jesse would think of him. Mateo dropped the butt of the cue stick to the floor as he held the stick vertically. "I've actually been haunted by a *taotaomo'na* for as long as I can remember."

"What?" Jesse was surprised and nearly dropped his cue. "Are you serious? How do you know?"

Mateo nodded. "I've seen it."

Jesse stared at him, his expression a mix of disbelief and concern. "No way! Are you kidding me?"

"I can see spirits, Jess." Mateo placed all his cards on the table. This was his best friend. He was putting himself out there, hoping his best friend would not leave him hanging.

Jesse lowered his voice just a little as he quickly scanned the room to make sure nobody would hear him. "What the hell, Matt? Are you serious?"

Mateo nodded.

"Dude! Doesn't that scare you?" Jesse asked.

"Absolutely!" Mateo admitted.

"Oh, man! That's nuts, Matt. I'm freaking out. Are you okay? Wait. Of course, you're okay. And you've been dealing with this alone? Holy crap, this is nuts!" It was slowly sinking in for Jesse. "How come you never told me before?"

Mateo was relieved that his friend was still his friend. Jesse believed him and was genuinely concerned about what his best friend had had to deal with.

So, Mateo was comfortable continuing. "Well first, I didn't believe it. Then, when I realized what was happening, I was afraid to tell anyone. Just imagine what you would have thought if I told you this when we were still in middle school."

"Crap! You're right. I wouldn't have believed you." Jesse felt guilty just thinking about it. "I'm sorry, Matt."

"Yeah. But you believe me now. That's what matters."

The two friends took a seat on the bench near their pool table.

"So... so what do they look like?" Jesse asked.

"Spirits?"

"Yeah."

"To me, they look just like normal people. I can't tell the difference just by looking at them. I was still an altar boy when I figured out that I was seeing dead people. I would see them in their casket at their funeral. Then, I would see them walking around at the cemetery when they were getting buried. That's when I would see them walk off and disappear into a crowd of people."

"Whoa! Okay. Well, that's not too scary. I mean I'd be scared. But I guess it's not so bad if they're nice to you. What about the *taotaomo'na*? The one that's been haunting you?"

"At first, I didn't know it was a *taotaomo'na*. I thought it was just a big, ugly, scary black dog. But then I noticed that I always got a bad *taotaomo'na* feeling whenever I saw the dog. I told *Tan* Chai and another *suruhånu* about it. That's when they told me that *taotaomo'na* can take different forms. The one that has always followed me takes the form of a *ga'lågu*. It's like a demon dog." Mateo paused for a bit before admitting, "That thing scares the crap out of me!"

"Man, Matt! I wish I knew. I wish I could help." Jesse said.

"You were there a couple of times. You did help."

"What? When? How?"

"Have you ever noticed that I don't like being near the jungle? And whenever we are near a jungle, I'm pushing you to hurry up and leave?" Mateo asked him.

"Actually, yeah. Now that you mention it. I remember the Sterling laser light show. You made a big stink about how you were going to make a *big stink* in my truck if we didn't hurry up and get out of there." He turned his eyes to Mateo to let him know he was trying to joke around even though he was still freaking out.

"Yup! That's one of those times," Mateo admitted.

"Dude! You know what? This place is too dark right now. We need to get out of here. Plus, this is all a lot to take in. Forget King's. I need fried rice from Shirley's Coffee Shop in me right now!"

"Shirley's it is, my friend," Mateo said with a slight chuckle.

Jesse turned to his friend with the sincerest look Mateo had ever seen from him.

"Seriously, Matt. I don't know jack about these things. But I'm here if there's ever anything I can do to help. You know that, right?" He stood up and started walking around the table. "I still can't believe you've been dealing with this the whole time. I can't even imagine." He was shaking his head. As they walked toward the door, he shoved Mateo and added in a more joking tone, "But I'm serious, man. Whenever you need me. I'm for reals, bro. From the bottom of my heart."

"Shut up," Mateo said as they both laughed.

Jesse meant every word, though. He was happy to be Mateo's friend. But learning about this whole other side of Mateo made him respect his friend more than he already did. He truly felt honored that Mateo had trusted him with his secret.

Chapter 20
Taken

It had been a few years now since the Fieldings had their brush with *taotaomo'na* illness. They had proceeded to get their house blessed after the incident, and they had not experienced any issues with the *taotaomo'na* afterward, their lives settling into a comfortable routine. However, the large rubber tree in the jungle behind their house was still there, looming as an unspoken reminder of their supernatural encounter.

While Genevieve and her husband would both get chills when they were in their backyard near the tree, they just made it a point not to be out there at night but during the day - it was easy to forget about the tree altogether. They simply treated it as part of the backdrop of their lives, and for years, that seemed like enough of a precaution.

Sometimes during the day, Genevieve would let their daughter Emily play in the backyard while she hung clothes to dry or just sat on their patio to read a book. Their small yard had a swing set and a colorful little playhouse with a cute matching picnic table, and Emily would spend hours out there, her giggles floating through the air. There were only a couple of other children in the neighborhood, but they didn't come by to play with Emily too often. So, she often played by herself or with an imaginary friend that she called Maiana.

Genevieve didn't think much about Maiana. It wasn't uncommon for kids to invent imaginary friends, and Emily seemed happy. She would chatter away as if someone was right beside her. Genevieve would smile and let her daughter's imagination run wild.

*****

The Cruz family lived next door. They were the only neighbors in the area with children. Emily was five years old now. Jennifer Cruz was seven years old, and her younger brother James was four years old. Their parents, Mary and George Cruz, were always fine with their children playing with Emily, and Genevieve always felt a sense of relief when the kids came over because she thought it was good for Emily to have friends.

One warm, late Saturday morning, Jennifer and James saw that Emily was playing outside. They came over and asked Genevieve if they could play with Emily. Genevieve was thrilled and allowed them into the yard. She preferred Emily playing with other kids instead of playing on her own. So, it was nice that the Cruz kids had come over. She stayed nearby, watching the children laugh and run around. The Cruz kids had been over a few times before, and they all seemed to be having fun running around as usual.

About thirty minutes had passed before Genevieve noticed that the children had grown quiet. They were sitting at Emily's small picnic table. Genevieve thought it was a little strange, but didn't think anything more of it. A few minutes after that, Jennifer and James stood up abruptly and left the backyard, walking quickly toward their house. Genevieve barely had a chance to ask if something was wrong before they were gone. She assumed Mary or George Cruz had called them home for lunch. Shrugging it off, she returned to her chores.

Later that week, Genevieve was outside, as usual, with her daughter Emily. It was quite a warm afternoon, so Genevieve decided to head into the kitchen to get some lemonade for Emily. She stood at the kitchen sink, rinsing cups while keeping an eye on Emily through the sliding door. From the corner of her eye, Genevieve saw another child running with Emily along the edge of the jungle. The two girls were laughing, playing a lively game of tag. Genevieve assumed it was Jennifer Cruz, Emily's occasional playmate from next door, and the sight brought her comfort.

Genevieve turned back to finish washing the cups. By the time she dried her hands and stepped onto the patio, the backyard was eerily silent. She looked around but didn't see Emily or the other child anywhere. Frowning, she called out her daughter's name. "Emily! Emily, where are you?" The only response was the rustling of leaves in the distance.

Genevieve's concern grew quickly. She walked across the yard, scanning the swing set, the playhouse, and the area near the jungle, but there was no sign of the children. Fear began to creep into her chest. She rushed to the Cruz house, hoping that perhaps Jennifer had taken Emily over there to play. But the Cruz driveway was empty. Their car wasn't home.

Did they just leave? Was Jenny really the girl in the yard with Emily? Did she go somewhere with them without telling me? Mary and George wouldn't just leave with Emily without checking with me first. Would they? Genevieve's mind was now racing wildly.

Genevieve ran back to her house and searched the rooms frantically. She checked every closet, under the beds, and behind doors. Still, Emily was nowhere to be found. Her breaths came faster, panic taking over. She rushed to her phone and called her mother. She had to talk to someone to help her try to stay calm.

"Ninete residence - " Mrs. Ninete barely had enough

time to say that before Genevieve interrupted.

"Mom! I need you! I need help! I can't find Emily!" Genevieve's voice was shaky.

"Gen, calm down. What happened?" Mrs. Ninete's voice was steady, trying to ground her daughter.

She was in the backyard! I saw her playing with another kid, and now they're gone. I've looked everywhere. Can you please come over? Maybe everything's okay. I don't know. I just need you here!"

"Yeah, yeah, my girl. We'll be right there." Her mother replied firmly before hanging up.

While she waited for her parents to arrive, Genevieve looked all through the house calling out for Emily. She then went outside again, shouting Emily's name. The backyard felt unusually still, almost oppressive. She also walked around the Cruz house yelling Emily's name as she tried to peer into their windows.

The Cruz family drove up as Genevieve was walking back from their driveway. She turned and walked to their car as they drove up and parked.

"Is Emily with you?" Genevieve asked, upset as she looked into their car.

"No, Gen. We've been gone all day." Mary and George Cruz both answered and looked at each other, Mary's face twisting in confusion.

Genevieve was frantic and ran back to her driveway where her parents just happened to be driving up. Mary followed while George took their kids into their home. She ran toward her mother, tears already staining her face.

"Mom! I can't find her!" She said, her voice full of emotion.

Mrs. Ninete hugged Genevieve. "What happened?"

"I don't know. We were in the backyard. I went in to get some lemonade. I swear I saw a little girl playing with her. Then they were gone when I got back outside. I was only gone for a minute!" By this time, Gen was loudly wailing.

"Shhh... Don't fret my girl, we'll help you look for her." Genevieve's mom said.

"I already looked all around my house... inside and out."

Mrs. Cruz said, "We'll check our house first. Then, we'll head back here to help." She rushed back home to let her husband know what was happening.

"Thank you," Genevieve's mom said. Then she turned her attention back to Genevieve.

"Let's call Bill. He will want to help, too."

Genevieve nodded in agreement as she and her mom walked into her house. Even if Emily was just hiding, Bill had to know what was going on. They called him as soon as they got inside the house, and he promised to get home right away.

Genevieve's dad immediately searched around the house again and checked the yard and the area near the jungle once more, looking for any signs of what might have happened. All he found was Emily's notepad on the picnic table and a box of crayons. He saw the whole Cruz family walking over, so he signaled for them to come in with him from the patio.

"We all came to help," said Mary Cruz.

Mr. Ninete proposed, "I think we should check with the other neighbors... and probably check in the jungle. But we'll need to get help to check the jungle."

Mary offered, "I can help with making calls to the Police and Fire Department."

George turned to Genevieve's dad and said, "How about you and I split up to check with the neighbors first. Then we'll meet back here if we need to start looking in the jungle."

"Let's do it." Mr. Ninete was already thinking that the police would want to know if they had already checked with the neighbors. So, this was a good first step.

"Hon." He called out to his wife to show her the notebook that he found outside. "This was still out on the picnic table." He placed the notebook on the coffee table in the living room where his wife and daughter were sitting. "Maybe we'll check the neighbors first before calling the police. There aren't many houses here. We'll be right back."

The women nodded as the men rushed out through the front door to begin canvassing the area.

"I hope it's okay that I brought my kids over. They're concerned about Emily, too." Mary really did want to help but couldn't leave her kids home alone. She thought it best that they all be with Genevieve.

Genevieve replied, "Yes. Yes. Thank you." She was

still bothered, though. She could have sworn it was Jenny who she had seen with Emily in the yard.

"Mary..." she started, but then just let out a heavy sigh.

"What is it, Gen?"

"Well... never mind." Genevieve's mind was still jumping all around. "It's just... I know you guys were gone. But I could have sworn that I saw Jenny playing with Emily earlier. And there are no other kids around here."

"I'm sorry, Gen. We were at my sister's place for a birthday party." Mary assured her. Then she remembered something. "Actually, James and Jenny said the other day that they were scared of Emily."

The children had been listening in. Jenny jumped in to correct her mother. "Not Emily, Mommy. Her friend, Maiana."

The name caught Genevieve's attention. She looked up sharply, "What? Who were you afraid of?" She didn't realize she was squeezing her mom's hand tighter as if she was bracing herself.

"Maiana... and her dog," Jenny answered.

"What happened that scared you?" Genevieve prompted Jenny to continue.

Genevieve's mom was confused. She whispered to her, "Gen. Who's Maiana?" The whisper was loud enough for Mary to hear, and she wanted to know the answer, too.

"Emily's imaginary friend," Genevieve answered.

James was slowly shaking his head at his older sister. It didn't seem that he wanted to keep it a secret as much as it was that he just didn't want anyone to bring it up again. He seemed scared of just the thought. But the big sister in Jenny wanted to protect her brother, so she had to tell.

"Maiana didn't like us being there with Emily."

"How do you know she didn't like you being there? Is that why you guys left so fast the other day?" Genevieve was starting to connect some dots but didn't like the picture she was getting at.

"I don't know. First, Emily said Maiana was friendly, even though she looked a little creepy. However, Maiana wasn't as Em had described her to us. She was scary and really mean to us. She said, 'Emily, I don't like your friends. Tell them to go away.'

"So, I asked her why? And that we had been Emily's friends first, and we hadn't done anything wrong. That's when Maiana's face got really scary, and her voice changed. She sounded like a man when she told us to look in the jungle by the big tree. There was a big, black, scary dog growling at us. She said that if we didn't leave Emily alone, she was going to make her dog eat us."

Tears streamed down Genevieve's face as she turned to her mother. Her eyes were begging for some kind of reassurance that this wasn't really happening.

Mary was now upset. "Emily said that to you?"

"No, Mommy. It was Maiana." Jenny said.

"Maiana's not real, Jenny," her mom argued.

"She is, Mommy. But she's like a ghost," Jenny said.

"Yeah." James added. "She can disappear like a ghost. I don't like her, Mommy."

The more Jenny and James talked, the colder Genevieve felt.

Curious, Genevieve's mom picked up Emily's notebook and started flipping through the pages. She stopped suddenly on a page and looked up at Genevieve. Her face was full of panic, almost as if she had just seen a ghost. "Gen! I think we need to call Mateo."

"Mateo? Why?" Genevieve knew the answer as soon as she asked the question.

Her mother reached out and held her hand tightly. "Gen," she whispered, "this might be the *taotaomo'na*."

Genevieve shook her head in denial. "No! No! We had the house blessed years ago. We haven't had any problems since then. Why would this happen now?"

But her mother's expression didn't change. She looked worried, her lips pressed tightly together. Genevieve's mind raced. *Could this really be happening again? Could Maiana, Emily's so-called friend, be connected to the jungle spirits?*

Mary was confused. "What are you talking about? What's going on?"

Genevieve's mom placed the notebook on the coffee table. She flipped it open to the page she found so that Mary could see. It had a drawing of two girls holding hands and a big, black dog next to them. One of the girls in the picture looked normal. But the other one had big black eyes that were white in the middle. The dog had the same kind of eyes.

Jenny was quick to point out, "That's Maiana and her dog."

"Oh, my God!" Mary was really scared, now. "Are you saying that's real?"

Just then, Bill, George Cruz, and Mark Ninete all walked in the front door together. Bill had seen them in the street and met them in the driveway. The men explained that they had no luck with the canvassing. They were going to check in with the ladies before calling the police.

Mr. Ninete was first to speak. "We checked up and down the street. Nobody's seen Emily. It's time to call the police. We need to start getting ready to check the jungle, too."

The women were all very quiet. They didn't react very quickly to the announcement. They seemed distracted.

Bill asked, "What's going on?"

The women shook off the shock of thinking that *taotaomo'na* might be involved.

Mrs. Ninete broke the awkward silence. "Mary, George. Maybe you should take your kids back home before the police get here."

"Yeah. You're right." Mary called her kids. "Jenny, James, let's go." Then she whispered to her husband as she got up. "I'll tell you what happened at home."

As soon as the Cruz family left, Bill and his father-in-law looked at their wives for an update.

"We need to call the police now, but I think we also need to call Mateo." Rosemarie reached her hand out to her husband. She pointed at the drawing on the coffee table. "The Cruz kids said this is Emily's imaginary friend Maiana... and her dog."

The men took a look at the creepy drawing.

"They said Maiana was like a ghost. They're scared of her. They also said that Maiana threatened them to stay away from Emily or else she would have her dog kill them."

"Is this true, Hon?" Bill asked his wife.

"I... I don't know. It seems to be. But I don't know how." Gen answered back.

Rosemarie continued, "This might be the *taotaomo'na*. We'll call the police, of course. But just in case, we should bring in Mateo."

Bill was irritated by the talk about *taotaomo'na*. But he wanted his daughter found as soon as possible. "You can do what you want. I'm calling the police now."

So, Bill called the police. Because Emily was very young, the police considered her more at risk. They arranged with the fire department to begin a search. They arrived at the Fielding house about an hour after Bill's call. There were only a few hours of daylight left. The police canvassed the neighborhood again while the fire department began organizing for a search of the jungle. Just in case, they prepared for a search that may go well into the night.

Mrs. Ninete left a message for Mateo at the airport's

Facilities office. He was still at work. So, they stayed by the phone until he finally called. When Mateo learned what was happening, he got cleared to leave work. He had plans with Jesse after work, so he told him he had to cancel. Jesse asked for the address so that he could stop by after work to help. Then, Mateo called Kiko and *Tan* Chai. Mateo was going to pick up *Tan* Chai, then they would all meet at the Andersen Air Force Base visitor center so that Kiko could follow Mateo to the Fielding house.

The Police and Fire Department had already begun the search through the jungle. All Genevieve and her mom could do was wait. Genevieve's mom started looking through Emily's notebook again. There were some drawings of Maiana and a couple with the dog.

But then she came across a drawing that truly scared her. On one page, there was a giant scary man standing in the jungle. He had a hole in his side with a plant sticking out of it. He had big pointy teeth and long fingernails.

"Gen. Do you know about the different forms that *taotaomo'na* can take?" Rosemarie asked her daughter.

"Not really, Mom. Why?"

"They say that *taotaomo'na* can take the form of children… to lure other children into the jungle. They can also take the form of animals. The *ga'lågu* is the dog form."

"Mom. Why are you doing this?" Genevieve was starting to feel like her mother was attacking her. "Are you trying to make me more scared than I already am?"

"No, Gen. I'm not." Her mother was trembling as she continued. "But there is something in this notebook that is worse than what I've just told you."

Genevieve held her hands up over her mouth. "No, Mom. How can things be any worse?"

She was shaking her head. She didn't want to hear any more.

"Okay. Okay. We'll wait for Mateo and *Tan* Chai to get here."

About thirty minutes later, Mateo, *Tan* Chai, and Kiko arrived.

As they parked, Mateo said he could already feel it. The *ga'lågu* that had been following him was there... somewhere.

"*Tan* Chai. We need to get moving. That *ga'lågu* is here. I think it took the little girl, *Tan* Chai."

They all went inside to see Genevieve and her mom. There was a police officer in the house with them and several more outside with some firefighters.

Mateo didn't waste any time. He greeted Mrs. Ninete with *man nginge"*, then turned to Genevieve. Mateo knelt on one knee beside Genevieve and placed his hands over hers. He looked straight at her until she met his gaze. Her expression went from frantic and lost to just worried. Without saying a word, Mateo seemed to have reassured her that he would do everything in his power to get her daughter back. Mrs. Ninete had felt it too.

Mateo and Kiko headed out through the sliding door and grabbed a couple of flashlights. They still had a couple of hours left of daylight, but they didn't know how long they might be out in the jungle. They asked a couple of firemen to go with them. One of the firemen recognized Mateo and *Tan* Chai and knew that they were *suruhånos*. Their chief wanted most of his men following their protocols, but he also understood that they shouldn't ignore a lead from the *suruhånos*. Mateo was walking fast and with purpose across the yard and toward the jungle. Kiko and the firemen kept pace with him. *Did he know where he was going?* Kiko wondered.

Chapter 21

Mateo Falls

At the edge of the dense jungle, the group stood in silence. Kiko, the seasoned *suruhånu* that he was, clasped his hands together, and his voice broke the quiet. His words were respectful and purposeful, directed toward the spirits of the land.

"*Guella yan guello, pot fabot dispensa ham. In espipiha y påtgon palaoan ni makoni. Dispensa ham pot fabot ben fan maloffan gi tano' mu,*" Kiko said out loud.

He had explained to the group earlier that this was the traditional way to ask the spirits for permission to enter sacred land and search for the missing girl.

295

Disturbing them could lead to dire consequences, so showing respect was very important.

Mateo, standing beside him, added his own plea. His voice was soft but earnest. "We are sorry to disturb you. And we ask for your help with finding the girl."

The two men waited; their heads bowed slightly. Mateo's connection to the spiritual world was growing stronger, and he tried to sense if their request was granted. Kiko lifted his gaze to meet Mateo's, and they paused again for a few more minutes to try and sense once again if their requests had been granted or denied. They both nodded their heads with raised eyebrows.

"Feels good to me. You?" Kiko asked.

Mateo nodded. "Yes, *Tun* Kiko. I don't feel any resistance. I do feel something... pulling me in that direction." He was pointing to the area just past the big rubber tree.

Kiko turned to the two firemen joining them. "Okay. We're good to go. We're following Mateo, here."

The search party moved into the dense jungle, with Mateo leading the way. His steps were firm but cautious. To him, it felt like he was being guided by *taotaomo'na*. But he couldn't tell yet if they were good or bad. They were either being unclear intentionally, or there was a mix of those with good and bad intentions. But it didn't matter. They needed to find the girl. If it was a trap of some kind, he had Kiko with him. They would deal with whatever came their way. Besides, he trusted his instincts. He also trusted Kiko, knowing the older *suruhånu* would have his back if things went wrong.

*****

Back at the Fielding house, Rosemarie quietly slipped away from the rest of the family. She held Emily's notebook tightly as she approached *Tan* Chai, who was sitting quietly on the patio.

"*Tan* Chai," Rosemarie said softly, "can you help me make some tea?"

The older woman raised an eyebrow but nodded, sensing Rosemarie wanted to talk privately. Genevieve also noticed, but said nothing because she didn't want to be part of the discussion. Together, Rosemarie and *Tan* Chai walked into the kitchen. Rosemarie set the notebook on the counter and opened it, flipping through the pages.

"What's going on?" *Tan* Chai asked.

Rosemarie's hands trembled slightly as she turned to a page showing a childlike drawing of a girl and her dog. "I'm really scared, *Tan* Chai. It's my girl's drawings. This is Emily's imaginary friend Maiana... and this is Maiana's dog. They look like... *taotaomo'na*, don't they?"

Tan Chai's eyes widened as she studied the sketches. "Oh, my goodness. Yes, they do." *Tan* Chai remembered that Mateo mentioned something about the *ga'lågu* being involved, but she still found herself in disbelief.

Rosemarie continued flipping through the notebook.

"The Cruz kids next door say that they saw Maiana and the dog, and they look just like the drawings. Also, they said Maiana told them to stay away from Emily."

Tan Chai's face grew serious. "It's good that you called Mateo. This does seem like something… unnatural. A *taotaomo'na* may have been after your granddaughter and may possibly have grabbed her." She paused. "Kiko and Mateo are the right people to help. We just need to pray. Pray for Emily, for Mateo, and for everyone searching for her."

Rosemarie nodded that she understood. However, as she continued to flip through the notebook pages, her heart sank further. There was something else. Something more serious than what she had already shown *Tan* Chai. She stopped on a page and pointed at the drawing as she turned the notebook toward *Tan* Chai. "Is that what I think it is?"

Tan Chai held a hand up to her mouth as she gasped. "Oh, God help us!" *Tan* Chai recognized the drawing right away. She was trying not to show her worry earlier… trying to be strong for the family. But there was no chance of that now. The fear she was feeling was too much to hide. "Your girl drew that?"

"Yes, *Tan* Chai. How could she draw that unless she saw it?"

She was talking about the drawing of the giant scary man with claw-like hands and a huge hole in his side. Many of the CHamoru legends referred to spirits in general, and there were only a handful that referred to specific spirits by name. One of the most notorious and menacing of the ancient CHamoru spirits was known as Anufat, and the drawing that Rosemarie and *Tan* Chai had laying before them fit the description of Anufat.

Tan Chai was afraid and confused. "Why would Anufat be involved? Why would he be interested in this little girl? This doesn't make sense." She turned around to lean back against the counter. "But if Anufat is involved, we need to pray. We need to pray for your girl... and for everybody who is out there looking for her," *Tan* Chai said once again.

The women sat back down in the living room and started to pray the rosary. Rosemarie stepped away a couple of times to make some calls. She reached out to other relatives and friends and asked them to pray. They didn't have to come by. They could simply pray from where they were. They wanted to get as many people as they could to help pray for Emily and for the people searching.

*****

The sun had just slipped past the horizon and darkness was quickly creeping in. The firemen couldn't keep track of where they were going as they followed Mateo and Kiko through the jungle, who were moving with determination. They just dropped glow sticks on their path as they rushed through the dense foliage, just in case they needed help to find their way back.

After a little over thirty minutes of hiking, Mateo and his search party arrived at a clearing. Strangely, stepping into the clearing felt almost like they were slipping into a vacuum-sealed bubble with no wind and no sound inside. The whole clearing was filled with an uneasy stillness. It felt like they were being engulfed by the silence.

Mateo paused, sensing something was wrong.

"Does anyone else feel that?" one of the firefighters asked, looking around nervously.

The men spotted Emily at the other end of the clearing. She appeared to be wrapped in what looked like a shroud of dark smoke and was in some kind of trance. She was just standing still in front of another huge rubber tree similar to the one near the Fielding's house.

As the men got closer, they found that the girl was not standing but was instead floating a few inches off the ground. From what they could see, her eyes were white, and she was not blinking. One of the firemen radioed in their general position as best as he could and reported that they had found the girl.

Mateo and Kiko then began asking the *taotaomo'na* for permission to get the girl. As they wrapped up, the firemen then tried to retrieve her.

"Emily!" one of the firemen called out, rushing forward.

Mateo raised a hand to stop him. "Wait!"

But it was too late. As the fireman approached, Mateo's vision sharpened, and he saw it - the *ga'lågu*.

Just then, it stepped into the clearing. It was massive, with its cataract-filled eyes and sharp fangs. However, only Mateo could see it.

In a blur, Mateo saw it lunge at one of the firemen, its jaws clamping around his arm. The man screamed in agony as he felt the attack by an invisible force. His arm was mangled as he was thrown across the clearing. The other fireman panicked, trying to pull his colleague to safety, but the *ga'lågu* attacked again, targeting the other man. This time, the *ga'lågu* grabbed the other fireman by the leg and shook him violently from side to side. His cries were quickly silenced when the beast slammed him to the ground.

The *ga'lågu* kept its distance from Mateo. Though Kiko couldn't see the demon dog, he could feel its cold, oppressive presence. Just as heat radiates from a fire, there was a terrible chill that radiated from the *ga'lågu*, making it easier for Kiko to feel it moving around him. He also noticed the shadow of the large rubber tree moving. Part of the shadow moved like an arm that was reaching out to Mateo.

"Mateo!" Kiko shouted.

But the shouting was in vain because Mateo was already in trouble. The shadowy arm grabbed him by the throat and lifted him off the ground, choking him.

By now, Kiko could feel that the *ga'lågu* had circled behind him. Kiko began praying loudly and sprinkling holy water everywhere, but nothing seemed to happen. That is until the holy water finally hit the *ga'lågu*. That's when it showed itself.

Kiko couldn't have imagined just how big the monster was. Standing on all four feet, its head stood at Kiko's shoulder height. It slowly stepped closer to him as it continued to walk around. The sulfur smell was incredibly strong. Kiko tried his best to maintain his composure because Mateo needed him. He kept praying and splashing holy water on and around Mateo who was being choked by the shadowy arm. By now, it was carrying Mateo three feet off of the ground. The chills Kiko felt made his arms and legs weak as the *ga'lågu* stood behind him.

However, the *ga'lågu* was just a distraction.

Suddenly, another shadowy arm struck Kiko, flinging him across the clearing. The impact launched him into the air. He was hurled ten feet across the clearing, and when he rolled to a stop, he landed face-down in the underbrush. It felt as though he was hit by a truck and was slowly losing consciousness. Before everything went black, the last thing he saw was Mateo still in the grips of the shadowy force. *I'm sorry, Mateo*, was his last thought.

Just a few minutes later, the other searchers arrived at the clearing. They had heard the screams and rushed to where the cries had come from. They found Emily just sitting on the grass in the clearing with the injured men scattered around her, their injuries severe but not life-threatening. She was staring at the big rubber tree along the clearing, almost oblivious to the people rushing around her. She was still in a daze, and it seemed as though she didn't know where she was or what was going on around her. She didn't appear to have any injuries, though. They also found Mateo, lying unconscious next to Emily. He had terrible bruising around his throat and on his arms, but he was breathing and had no other visible injuries.

The search team brought Emily and the men back to the house. The police sealed off the clearing to secure it as a crime scene. They needed to determine what actually happened and if a crime had been committed. But nobody was going to get any answers that night. All of the men who were at the site were unconscious, and Emily was dazed and lethargic.

Everyone back at the house heard the report that Emily had been found. Bill and Mr. Ninete had already circled back to the house by then. After the word came in, Emily's parents and grandparents were all waiting anxiously on the patio. They swarmed around her as she was carried onto a gurney. A paramedic on the site had to squeeze his way through to perform an assessment before they transported Emily to the hospital for a full evaluation and observation.

"Is she okay?" Genevieve asked the paramedics.

"She seems physically fine, but she's not responsive," one replied.

"Thank you, God! Thank you, God!" Genevieve pushed her way through to hug her daughter. "My baby! Are you okay?" Emily didn't respond, so Genevieve asked the people who brought her in. "What's the extent of her injuries? Is she badly hurt? Where did you find her? Why isn't she saying anything?"

"I'm sorry, ma'am. We'll have to take a look at your daughter to know more," the paramedic replied, passing his little flashlight in front of Emily's eyes as he checked her pulse on her wrist.

Bill squeezed in to hug his wife and daughter. He also noticed the injured men being brought in. "What happened?"

"We're not sure. We just found them this way," one of the firemen said.

"Who did this? Did someone do this?" Bill was thinking that someone tried to take Emily and attacked Mateo and his search party when they found them.

"There was nobody else there. And, uh…" the fireman paused as they carried in the two injured firemen. "Well, these injuries don't look like something any person could do. And not in the short amount of time between when they called us and when we found them."

Tan Chai saw that Emily was okay. But her attention was more on the injured men being brought in behind Emily. She had a very bad feeling that something terrible had happened to Mateo and Kiko. Her heart sank as she saw them being carried onto stretchers in the yard. *Oh, God. Please let them be okay. Tan* Chai prayed in her head as she walked up to the stretchers.

"Are they okay?" she asked one of the firemen helping to move the men to the ambulances parked at the front of the house. "Are they alive?"

"Yes, ma'am. They're alive. But they need to be evaluated at the hospital."

"What happened?"

"Nobody knows, ma'am. They reported that they found the girl. A few minutes later, they were all found injured and unconscious."

Mr. Ninete stayed behind to lock up the house after the search crews had packed up and left. Genevieve, Bill, and Mrs. Ninete followed Emily's ambulance to the hospital. *Tan* Chai was heading for the hospital, too, for Mateo and Kiko. But she planned to make a stop at the Santa Barbara Church on the way. She needed to let the priests know what happened. She was worried that Mateo would need their help.

*****

The next morning, *Tan* Chai came across Rosemarie in the hallway at the hospital. She asked her how Emily was.

"Hi, Rosemarie. How's our little girl doing?"

"Much better, *Tan* Chai. I thank God for you and the other two *suruhånos*."

"That's so good to hear."

"We know Mateo, so we knew he would help. But we really appreciate that you and Kiko were also very willing to do what you could."

"We always try to help each other out. And with

305

something like this, it's always safer not to work alone. I'm happy that the three of us have each other to rely on."

Rosemarie's expression changed from a very thankful smile to something more serious. "*Tan* Chai. Emily is talking again."

Tan Chai leaned in. "That's good! That's so good. What is she saying?"

"*Tan* Chai. She remembers. She remembers what happened. But I don't think the police believe her." Rosemarie held *Tan* Chai's hand and continued. "They were *taotaomo'na, Tan* Chai."

"What did she say?"

"She said Maiana took her into the jungle. Maiana told her that the scary man was coming, so they had to hide. Maiana also said her mean dog was going to help protect them from the scary man. But Maiana lied. She led Emily straight to him... straight to the scary man."

Tan Chai's face paled. "Oh my! She's so young. That would have scared me to death. Is she still shaken up?"

"Yes. I don't think she will be going near the jungle for a long time."

"I'm so glad they found her. I still don't understand what Anufat wanted with her."

Rosemarie knew. She chose to delay telling *Tan* Chai for just a little longer. She dreaded telling *Tan* Chai because she herself was still having trouble believing it. She hesitated before asking, "How are Kiko and Mateo doing?"

"Oh. Kiko will be okay. He has some broken ribs and a dislocated shoulder and collar bone." *Tan* Chai had a hard time saying how Mateo was because that would mean accepting that it was true. But she had to. She had to accept it. "Mateo... is in a coma."

Rosemarie started shaking her head. She felt so bad about what she had to tell *Tan* Chai next. But it was better to let her know. "*Tan* Chai... Emily said the scary man told her she was going to be okay." She took a deep breath before continuing, "He told her they were waiting for someone else."

"Mateo!" *Tan* Chai's heart sank. This is what she was so afraid of. "Anufat was waiting for Mateo."

"She didn't say. The scary man didn't give a name. I thought it would be either Kiko or Mateo."

"It has to be Mateo."

"But why Mateo?" Rosemarie was confused. *Kiko and Mateo were both suruhånos. Why was Tan Chai so sure that it was Mateo... and why would such a terrible taotaomo'na be after him?*

"Mateo has talents that I have never seen before. He can do everything we can do and usually does it better than us. He operates on a different level than we do. He has a very strong connection to the spiritual world. And because of that, he has been followed by *taotaomo'na* his whole life." *Tan* Chai was feeling so helpless again and it showed. "That boy has been through so much."

"He saved my granddaughter. He deserves all the prayers we can pray for him, and that's just what he will get."

"That's about all any of us can do for him. But every prayer makes a difference. So, thank you! Please. *Please* pray for him." *Tan* Chai wiped away some tears that started to trickle down her cheeks. Mateo was strong. He was in a coma because he was stopping Anufat from taking control. *It's just like before he was born. Outside the room, I can feel Anufat's horrible energy. But inside the room, it's not so strong. Mateo is resisting. God, please give him strength, Tan* Chai thought.

In the days that followed, the Fielding family, the *suruhånos*, the community, and even strangers came together to pray for Mateo, Emily, and all those affected by the terrible events in the jungle.

Chapter 22

Mateo Sleeps

The sun rose gently over the land, but its warmth didn't reach the cold halls of the hospital where Emily remained under observation. Her parents sat beside her bed, thankful for her miraculous recovery, though their nerves were still frayed.

Emily seemed to be back to her normal self the next morning, as if the ordeal in the jungle had been a bad dream. The doctors wanted to keep her just for another day for observation, but the police did not want her returning home until they could figure out what had happened. She couldn't explain what had happened to her, and the questions from the police had left her feeling confused and overwhelmed. The only clear memories she had were of fear and the terrible darkness chasing her.

The police seriously needed to interview the men who found her. Kiko was the first to regain consciousness. The police questioned him, asking for details about how they found Emily and who attacked them. The story he told was just as unfathomable as the one Emily told them earlier. But parts of their stories did match up. They both implicated what could be described as evil spirits that fit descriptions of *taotaomo'na*. Neither Emily nor Kiko mentioned the involvement of any other people.

The extent and severity of the injuries sustained by the men who found her were unbelievable and could not be attributed to any known animal that existed on Guam. They also could not have been caused by any human. The police preferred to get at least one more account of that night from one of the other men present before concluding that there was no foul play involved. At this point, things seemed more like a child getting lost in the jungle and a large, wild animal attack on the men who found her.

The two firemen who were injured had survived their attacks. But they both had long recoveries ahead of them. Both had to have their injured limbs amputated because the damage was too severe. They were placed in induced comas until after the amputations in order to protect them from the excruciating pain that awaited them. The police had hoped their statements might shed light on what had happened, but the injuries alone were baffling enough to hold back any conclusions. At the time, the official explanation was a wild animal attack. However, privately, even the investigators doubted their own theory. *What kind of animal could be so large, so violent, yet leave no trace?*

Three days after that horrible night, the firemen woke up. Pain coursed through their bodies as they adjusted to the loss of their limbs, but when questioned about the events of that night, to the dismay of the police, their stories matched Kiko's account of that night. This only served to deepen the mystery. However, the men had not seen the monstrous dog like Kiko had. They did describe being attacked by what felt like a huge animal. All they could say was that it was an invisible force of incredible strength and violence.

"It wasn't an animal," one of them insisted, his voice trembling as he recounted the events. "It was... something else. I didn't see it, but I felt it. It threw me like I was nothing."

The other nodded in agreement. "It was strong. Too strong. I've faced wild boars, wild dogs, but this... This wasn't natural. We couldn't see it, couldn't fight it."

When asked about Emily, they confirmed finding her alone in the clearing. But they both added a strange detail; one that sent chills down the investigators' spines.

"She wasn't just lying there," one of the men said.

"She was floating. Like... something was holding her up."

The second fireman nodded. "She wasn't awake, but it was like something had her. Something we couldn't see."

Ultimately, with no evidence of foul play and no clear answers from anyone involved, the investigators concluded that Emily's disappearance was a mystery and the case was closed. So, she was allowed to return home with her parents. The official report also concluded that the injuries sustained by the men were caused by an unknown wild animal that could not be seen in the dark of night. But in the hearts of everyone involved, the truth remained far more terrifying.

*****

Since the night of the disappearance, *Tan* Chai was spending most of her time at the hospital, barely leaving Mateo's side. She would usually pray for him in his room, burning herbs to purify the air and muttering chants to keep the spirits at bay. Despite her efforts, she couldn't shake the heavy energy that lingered around him. Something dark was still attached to Mateo, and she could feel its presence.

On some days, she would also check-in on Kiko to see how he was doing. One day when Kiko was well enough to talk, she visited him in his room. He was bandaged and tired, but his mind was sharp, and he seemed eager to talk. *Tan* Chai asked about the night they found Emily.

"Kiko," she said gently, sitting beside his bed. "I need you to tell me what happened that night. All of it."

Kiko hesitated, the memories still raw and frightening. "We found Emily," he began, his voice low. "But before we could get her out of there, something came for us. A *ga'lågu* - the same spirit dog. It wasn't normal. It was watching us, stalking us. And then... there was something worse."

Tan Chai leaned in, her expression serious. "What did you see?"

"A spirit," Kiko whispered. "A man... but not a man. He grabbed Mateo. He was... huge, dark like a shadow. I've never seen anything like it."

He noticed that *Tan* Chai didn't seem too surprised, though her face had gone pale.

"Kiko," he said slowly, "I saw the girl's drawings in her notebook. They were *taotaomo'na*. The *ga'lågu* was there. But she drew something else... something far worse." Kiko saw the worry in *Tan* Chai's eyes as she shared.

"There was a drawing of... Anufat, Kiko." *Tan* Chai added, hesitating before saying the name.

Kiko felt his blood run cold. "Anufat?" he repeated. However, he made the connection. Anufat had to have been the spirit that they ran into that night. *But why would Anufat want the girl?* When he looked up at *Tan* Chai, he saw that she was waiting for him to make another connection.

"I don't think Anufat was really after the girl, Kiko." *Tan* Chai tilted her head a little, hinting for Kiko to make that last connection.

The realization hit Kiko like a punch to the gut. He stared at her, his mind racing.

"No way! That was a setup? Anufat used the girl to get to Mateo?" Kiko couldn't believe it. But it made sense. The *ga'lågu* was spying on Mateo all these years for Anufat. *But how could that be? Could a spirit actually set such a trap?* The more it sank in, the more amazing... and unnerving the realizations were becoming.

"*Tan* Chai. I... I think it's worse than we might think." Kiko added.

"How can it be worse than Mateo being attacked by Anufat?" *Tan* Chai asked.

"You know how some *taotaomo'na* give off different energies? They feel different when you are exposed to them?"

Tan Chai nodded. "Yeah."

"Well, I could swear that the energy I felt that night coming from that spirit was the same that I felt when we were trying to help Mateo's mom all those years ago. And now... I feel it here. In this hospital."

Horror filled *Tan* Chai's eyes as she now understood.

"Anufat has been waiting all these years for an opportunity to try to get Mateo again," Kiko continued.

Tan Chai now had her hands over her mouth. "Oh, my God. And now he has Mateo."

"I don't think so. Yes, he's in a coma. But I still feel Mateo. Don't you?"

Tan Chai had been so consumed with worry that she had forgotten she had already noticed. It was just like when Mateo was born. He was fighting.

*****

Mateo's consciousness flickered in and out like a weak flame. He felt disconnected from his body, as though he were floating in an endless void. When he finally opened his eyes, he found himself in a dense jungle, the air thick and suffocating. Shadows danced between the trees, and the smell of decay filled his nostrils.

For a moment, though he had his eyes open, he could neither see nor move. The last thing he remembered was being in the clearing where they had found Emily. Then out of nowhere, an enormous shadow figure appeared before him with angry, hypnotic eyes. Mateo remembered the being grabbing him by the throat, and that's when everything went pitch black.

It took a minute, but he started to get his bearings. He realized that he couldn't move because his arms and legs were bound by the thick aerial roots of the rubber tree, twisting around him like snakes. Straining against them only made them tighten. Panic rose in his chest as he looked around, trying to make sense of his surroundings.

From somewhere behind the massive tree he was tied to, he heard heavy footsteps approaching. The ground trembled with each step, and a low, raspy chuckle echoed through the air, followed by deep evil snickering.

A figure emerged from the shadows, towering over Mateo. It was the same shadow figure he had seen before losing consciousness, and as it stepped fully into his view, it began to take shape.

With a bellowing, raspy, monstrous voice, it started speaking in CHamoru, "*Kao makåna hao. Kao un tungo hayi yu?*"

The creature leaned closer, its rancid breath making him gag.

Mateo couldn't respond. He was confused and afraid. He didn't understand what the spirit was saying, but he could feel the malice behind its words. Mateo had never actually learned to speak CHamoru. He was only familiar with words *Tan* Chai used in her practice as a *suruhåna*.

Mateo also could not look at the spirit directly. He couldn't stand the sight of it. In the form of a man, it stood about ten feet tall. Its skin looked like some kind of thin tree bark that was peeling away in some areas, revealing decrepit bones beneath, and leaking black smoke from the openings. Thin, wood-like vines wrapped all around its body, leading to a gaping hole in its side. Ferns were growing out of the hole that exposed a rib cage and emitted what smelled like putrid, decaying tissue. Its face had cheek and jaw bones exposed, surrounded by a mane of wild, unkempt black wavy hair.

It had strange, inhuman fangs for teeth and a gaping hole where its nose should be. But its eyes were more unsettling. Somehow floating in its eye sockets, its eyes were bloodshot and seemed filled with cataracts. If Mateo tried to look at its eyes, they seemed to know. They seemed to move of their own accord and behaved as though they were trying to capture Mateo... to lock him in its gaze. They were like a cat pacing around a bird in a cage, waiting for the bird to get close enough so that it could snatch it quickly and dig its claws deep into the bird's flesh.

"*Mudoru hao!* Stupid boy," the spirit scoffed in frustration. "Ignorant," the spirit continued to speak, taking long deep breaths intermittently. "Ignorant... but it doesn't matter." The spirit leaned closer, with its face just inches from Mateo's. The stench made Mateo extremely nauseous.

"I am Anufat," it growled. It then leaned back and continued to pace in front of Mateo. "I have been watching you, boy. Watching you." It took another deep breath as it turned to face Mateo again. "You have power... power, yes. But you do not know... how to use it."

Mateo could only look at the spirit's feet, clenching his jaw and refusing to meet its gaze. Its feet looked like tree roots with tendrils that would dig into the ground with each step. *The spirit said it had been watching him.*

Was it... "Are you the *ga'lågu* that has been following me?"

Anufat let out a horrible chuckle. "Not me. But the *ga'lågu*... they watch for me, yes. They watch."

"They? There's more than one?" Mateo was shocked.

"Enough!" Anufat shouted. "Enough of your... ignorance. Yes, enough." He ducked down to try to get Mateo to look at his face. "You are a *suruhånu*. They... teach you... to be a *suruhånu*. But they... do not know... your power. They... they cannot teach you."

Mateo squirmed and closed his eyes to avoid contact with Anufat.

Anufat stepped back and stood up straight. "You... will have power... power over others, yes. Power over spirits... and power... over men." As he continued, he seemed to grow another five feet taller. His voice seemed to bellow even louder as he proudly proclaimed, "I am... Anufat. I... will teach you, yes. I will share... my power with... you."

"I don't want your power. I don't even want my power," Mateo said. In actuality, he was extremely afraid, but Kiko had to be around there somewhere. Kiko could get Emily away while Mateo kept Anufat busy. Anufat wasn't hurting him at the moment. Mateo realized that Anufat wanted him. But it seemed like Anufat could not just take him. The monster was trying its best to entice Mateo.

Anufat chuckled, a sound like cracking bones. "Oh, but you will. You will... learn. I will teach you. You are mine." The spirit repeated. "We have time... time, yes." He turned away to leave but turned his head to glance back at Mateo. "*Iyo-ku hao på'go.* You are mine, now."

"I'll never be yours," Mateo shot back, his voice trembling but defiant.

The spirit straightened, its skeletal face twisting into a grotesque grin. "You already are," it said. "You do not know it yet. But you will see."

With that, it turned and disappeared into the shadows, leaving Mateo alone and entangled in the tree.

The jungle grew quiet again, but Mateo's heart was still racing. He realized that he was in the spirit world. He didn't know where exactly Anufat had gone to, but there was some sort of calm at the moment. He could hear voices in the distance, but it sounded like he was underwater. He couldn't see anyone, and he didn't want to try calling out because he had no plans of alerting Anufat about his true intentions.

Mateo also realized that Anufat hadn't really hurt him extensively. Well, Anufat did hurt him, but the spirit did not seem interested in killing him. It seemed like he wanted to use Mateo. Mateo started to recall his talk with *Tan* Chai and Kiko. Kiko had pointed out that even before he was born, Mateo was strong enough to hold back the powerful *taotaomo'na* that had held his mother and was after him. *I need to believe in God. I need to believe in myself. I need to believe in God... more than I believe in my own weakness*, Mateo thought.

He closed his eyes and began to pray silently. *God. I*

wish I knew a prayer that fit my situation better. The ones I know seem so generic. I want to ask for the strength and courage to remember you when I am so scared that I can't even think straight. I want to ask for some direction so that I can find my way to You when I am lost in darkness. I am in the presence of evil, God. Please hear my prayer. He proceeded to pray the rosary.

He didn't realize it right away, but the tree's grip slowly loosened as he prayed. He eventually wiggled free and tried to follow the voices that he had heard. As he circled around the tree that held him, he saw something glowing among the brush. Framed between some smaller trees, he found what looked like a screen of some kind.

There was a scene being projected on the screen, but it was very blurred, matching the voices. They were garbled, like they were underwater, but he could make out snippets of the words. It seemed like a hospital room with a few people surrounding someone in a hospital bed. He could make out the words better. *Is that me in a hospital bed?* He wondered.

Mateo tried to touch the image, hoping he could somehow slip through to return to the physical world. But the image just wrapped around his hand like smoke, refusing to let him through. *I can't touch it,* he noticed. He tried to walk into it but just ended up getting spun around looking at the same image.

"Where have you... run off to?" Anufat's voice rumbled through the air. "You will stay... with me, yes.

You are mine. You... do not know how... to leave."

Mateo's heart sank. Anufat was right.

Mateo didn't have a clue as to what he was doing or how he was going to get out of the spirit world. He had managed to free himself from the tree, but he had no next step. However, he refused to give up. He would keep fighting. He would find a way.

For now, all he could do was try to hide and pray, hoping he didn't fall back into Anufat's clutches.

Chapter 23

The Awakening

Three long weeks had passed, and Mateo remained in a coma. Each day felt endless, especially for *Tan* Chai and Kiko, who refused to leave Mateo alone for even a moment. They worked out a system, taking turns at his bedside to ensure someone was always there. Even when one was not physically present, the other would sit vigil, praying silently or simply watching over him. They believed in their hearts that Mateo was fighting something they couldn't see, something dark and powerful, and they didn't want him to feel like he was alone in that fight.

In their own way, they imagined the kind of battle

Mateo must have been waging. They couldn't truly understand it, but they knew Mateo was special, marked by gifts and burdens none of them could fully grasp. If he was struggling somewhere in the unseen world, as they suspected, then the least they could do was stay physically present for him in the one they shared. Leaving him, even briefly, felt like betrayal.

Word spread quickly about Mateo's condition, especially within the close-knit community. Rosemarie and Mark Ninete came by regularly. They were now friends of the family, and though they didn't fully understand what had happened to Mateo, they knew he needed their prayers. They brought fresh flowers to brighten the room and left rosaries near his bedside, hanging them gently on the corner of the bed frame.

Father Tony and Father Rogelio both visited daily. They alternated their schedules to make sure Mateo had constant spiritual support. Father Rogelio would sometimes lead prayers, his voice soft but firm as he asked for Mateo's healing. Father Tony, on the other hand, often sat quietly, holding Mateo's hand and praying silently. Neither man needed to say much; their presence spoke volumes.

Marie from the Santa Barbara Parish office even made it a point to visit. She'd bring simple snacks for *Tan* Chai and Kiko, knowing they rarely left Mateo's side and were unlikely to take proper care of themselves. Sometimes she'd sit quietly in the corner, thumbing through her own rosary, adding her prayers to the growing chorus of support.

The room became a revolving door of visitors, each bringing their unique form of care. Some prayed, others simply sat and offered quiet company. But there was one noticeable absence: Jesse.

He hadn't shown up. Not at first. Days turned into a week, and then two. *Tan* Chai had quietly wondered why Mateo's best friend hadn't come. But she didn't push the matter. She knew Jesse well enough to guess that he was probably struggling with his own feelings about what had happened.

And she was right. Jesse was overwhelmed with guilt. He thought about Mateo constantly, replaying the events that had led up to his coma. Jesse remembered vividly the last time he and Mateo had spoken. Mateo had told him about Genevieve's missing daughter and the spirits that seemed to be involved. Jesse had promised to help. But when the time came, he wasn't there.

His grandmother had fallen at home, and Jesse had been needed to help her. That was the excuse he gave himself. But deep down, Jesse knew the truth: He had been afraid. Mateo had shared things with him - dark, terrifying truths about spirits, *taotaomo'na*, and powers that Jesse had only heard about in legends. Jesse had believed him, but believing didn't make it easier to accept.

The fear had been paralyzing. *What if something happened to him? What if he got hurt - or worse -*

because of the supernatural things Mateo dealt with? These thoughts consumed him, keeping him away from the hospital even as guilt gnawed at him.

It wasn't until the middle of the third week that Jesse finally worked up the courage to visit. As he walked into the hospital, his stomach churned with anxiety. *What would he say? What could he possibly do?* He felt useless, but staying away any longer felt even worse.

When Jesse entered Mateo's room, *Tan* Chai was there. She was sitting in the chair closest to the bed, her hands moving methodically as she prayed the rosary. Her lips moved silently, her focus so intense that she didn't notice Jesse at first.

"Hi, boy," she said softly when she finally looked up. Her voice was warm, almost motherly. "Thank you for coming."

"*Ñora*," Jesse replied, greeting her with *man nginge'*, his voice barely above a whisper. He gave her a respectful nod, then turned his attention to Mateo. The sight of his best friend lying motionless in the hospital bed was worse than Jesse had imagined. Mateo's face was pale, his neck bruised and discolored. Tubes and wires connected him to machines that beeped rhythmically, keeping him alive. Jesse's breath hitched as he stepped closer, his heart breaking.

He reached out, gripping the bed rail tightly as tears began to fall. One landed on his hand, then another. His chest felt heavy, his guilt bubbling to the surface.

Tan Chai noticed his tears and put her rosary down.

"It's okay, boy," she said gently. "Let it out."

Jesse shook his head, his voice trembling as he finally spoke. "I should've been there for him. I promised him I'd help, and I wasn't there."

"You're here now," she said simply.

Jesse turned to her, his face full of pain. "I wasn't there because I was afraid," he admitted. "He told me everything. About the spirits. About what he can do. I didn't know what to do with it. And then, when he needed me, I wasn't there."

Tan Chai looked at him thoughtfully. "So, he told you his secrets?"

Jesse nodded.

"Then he trusts you," she said firmly. "Do you know how rare that is, boy? Mateo doesn't trust just anyone. He told you because he believes in you."

"But I'm not brave like him," Jesse said, his voice breaking again. "I'm just... me. I don't have powers. I don't know how to fight spirits or any of this stuff."

"Mateo doesn't need you to fight spirits with him," she said, her voice steady. "He doesn't need you to be brave. He needs you to be his friend. That's why he told you his secrets - because he needed someone to remind him that he's still human. That he's still loved."

Jesse wiped his eyes, her words slowly sinking in.

Tan Chai smiled gently. "Do you know what Mateo would hate more than anything? If you got hurt because of him. He'd never forgive himself. That's the kind of boy he is. He doesn't need you to be like him. He just needs you to be you."

Jesse nodded slowly. "Okay," he said softly. "I'll try."

From that day on, Jesse began visiting Mateo every evening after work. He'd sit beside the bed, sometimes praying, sometimes talking to Mateo as though he could hear him. He still didn't fully understand the world Mateo was part of, but he decided he didn't need to. All he needed to do was be there.

One day, as Jesse sat beside Mateo, he remembered something *Tan* Chai had told him earlier. "Do small things with great love," she had said, quoting Mother Teresa. At the time, Jesse had thought it was just a nice sentiment. But now, sitting beside his best friend, it meant something more.

Jesse realized that he didn't need to do anything extraordinary. He didn't need to fight spirits or be brave. All he needed to do was care - and show that he cared.

So, he poured his energy into praying for Mateo. Every word he spoke came from his heart. He prayed at work, he prayed at home, and he prayed by Mateo's side. It wasn't much, but it was what he could do.

And for Mateo, though still trapped in his spiritual battle, those prayers meant everything.

*****

The days stretched into weeks, and Mateo's condition remained unchanged. By the fourth week, Jesse had settled into a routine of visiting Mateo every evening. He would sit by his friend's side, sometimes talking to him, sometimes simply keeping him company in silence. It was comforting, in its own way, to be there, even if Mateo couldn't respond.

One evening, Jesse arrived at the hospital at his usual time. The room was dimly lit, the soft glow of the bedside monitor casting shadows on the walls. He stepped inside and saw *Tan* Chai sitting in her usual spot beside Mateo's bed. Her rosary was resting in her lap, her head slightly tilted forward as if she had fallen asleep mid-prayer.

"*Tan* Chai," Jesse called gently, not wanting to startle her.

She didn't respond.

Jesse moved closer, thinking she must be in a deep sleep. "*Tan* Chai?" he said again, a little louder this time. Still, there was no reaction.

A knot of worry formed in his stomach. He leaned down and gently touched her shoulder. "*Tan* Chai?" he tried again, his voice now trembling.

She didn't stir.

Jesse's heart began to race. He crouched down to get a better look at her face, his eyes scanning for any sign of movement. Her breathing was absent. Her usually warm complexion had taken on an unsettling pallor. Panic surged through him.

He bolted out of the room and down the hallway, yelling for help. "Nurse! Somebody, please! Help!"

The nurses at the station immediately jumped into

action. Two of them followed Jesse back to the room, moving quickly but with calm precision. They approached *Tan* Chai and checked for a pulse. One nurse gently tilted her head back and listened for breathing.

"She's unresponsive," one of the nurses murmured grimly.

The other nurse moved closer, noticing something Jesse hadn't seen. "Her leg..." she said quietly.

Jesse's eyes followed the nurse's gaze. *Tan* Chai's left leg, usually hidden beneath her long skirt, was swollen and purple. It was a shocking sight. The nurse's face was solemn as she called for a doctor.

The doctor arrived minutes later, examining *Tan* Chai and confirming what Jesse already feared. "It looks like she suffered a pulmonary embolism," the doctor said softly. "Likely caused by deep vein thrombosis - probably from sitting for too long."

The words hit Jesse like a punch to the gut. He stood frozen as the medical team carefully prepared to move her body. They handled her with respect, gently lifting her onto a gurney and covering her with a white sheet.

Jesse couldn't bring himself to move. He stood rooted in place as the gurney was wheeled out of the room. The nurses offered him sympathetic glances, but no one explained much to him. He wasn't family, after all.

As the door closed behind them, Jesse looked back at Mateo. The sight of his best friend lying there, still unconscious, now without *Tan* Chai's comforting presence, filled him with a profound sense of dread. The room felt emptier than it had ever been.

*****

Jesse slowly pulled up a chair and sat down beside Mateo's bed. His mind was spinning, his chest tight with grief. He stared at Mateo, his still, lifeless form illuminated by the soft glow of the machines.

"Hey, Matt," Jesse said softly, his voice cracking. He paused, his eyes filling with tears. "It's me, Jess."

He swallowed hard, trying to steady himself. "I don't know if you can hear me, man, but... *Tan* Chai's gone. She's gone."

Saying the words out loud made it feel more real, and the weight of it crashed down on him. Jesse rubbed his hands over his face, trying to hold back the tears threatening to spill over.

"I don't know what to do," he continued, his voice barely above a whisper. "I don't know how to help you. I feel so... useless."

He leaned back in the chair, his eyes moving to the ceiling as he tried to collect his thoughts. "*Tan* Chai always knew what to say," he said, a faint, bitter smile flickering across his face. "She always had the right words, you know? Even when I was a mess, she'd say something that made it all feel... manageable."

His gaze returned to Mateo. "She reminded me once that I don't have to do big, brave things to be your friend.

She told me it's enough to do small things with love. I don't know if that's true, Matt. But I hope it is."

Jesse reached out and gently touched Mateo's hand. It was cool to the touch, a stark contrast to the warmth of *Tan* Chai's reassuring presence. "Because you're my best friend, Matt. My only friend. And if all I can do is sit here and pray, then that's what I'm gonna do. I'm gonna pray harder than I ever have. For you, and for her."

As the night wore on, Jesse's thoughts drifted to memories of *Tan* Chai. He thought about the way she always carried her rosary, the way her lips would move silently as she prayed. He remembered her calm presence, the way she could fill a room with warmth even when she wasn't speaking.

She had been like a second mother to Mateo - and, in many ways, to him too. She had always been patient, always willing to listen. Jesse realized now just how much she had held them all together, how her steady faith and quiet strength had been a source of comfort for everyone.

He thought about the sacrifices she had made over the past few weeks, sitting by Mateo's bedside for hours on end. She had barely taken care of herself, too focused on being there for him. And now, she was gone.

The guilt crept in again, sharper this time. Jesse wondered if there was something he could have done. *Could I have convinced her to take better care of herself? Could I have spent more time at the hospital so she didn't feel the need to stay so long?* The thoughts swirled in his mind, each one more painful than the last.

But deep down, he knew that *Tan* Chai wouldn't want him to dwell on guilt. She had lived her life with purpose, guided by faith and love. She wouldn't want her death to weigh him down.

Jesse wiped his face and sat up straighter. He looked at Mateo, his heart heavy but resolute. "I don't know how to do this, Matt," he said quietly. "But I'm gonna try, for you."

He reached for the rosary that *Tan* Chai had left behind, its beads warm from being held so often. Jesse wrapped it around his fingers, feeling a strange sense of comfort in its weight.

"I'm not good at this, you know," he said, letting out a shaky laugh. "Praying, I mean. I never really understood it. But *Tan* Chai believed in it. She believed it could help you. So, I'm gonna believe it too."

Jesse closed his eyes and began to pray. The words didn't come easily at first, but he kept going, whispering each line with as much sincerity as he could muster. For the first time, he felt like he was doing something that mattered.

The room was silent except for the hum of the machines and the faint sound of Jesse's voice as he prayed. It wasn't much, but it was something.

And for Mateo, still trapped in his coma, those prayers carried a weight that neither of them could fully understand yet.

*****

Mateo was trapped in a world of endless darkness, a dense jungle that seemed to stretch infinitely in every direction. The air was thick, making it hard to breathe, and the shadows shifted constantly, as if alive. For what felt like days - or maybe weeks - Mateo had been running. He didn't know where he was or how he had gotten there. All he knew was that something terrible was hunting him.

Anufat.

The spirit's name sent chills down Mateo's spine. Anufat was more than just a spirit; it was a presence, a monstrous entity that could feel Mateo's fear and thrive on it. Every time he thought he'd found a safe place, the heavy sound of Anufat's footsteps or its guttural growl would echo through the jungle, forcing him to flee again.

Now, utterly exhausted, Mateo had taken refuge in a small cave. It was damp and cold, but it was the first place he'd found where the oppressive energy of Anufat didn't seem to reach. His chest heaved as he tried to catch his breath, his body trembling from both fear and exhaustion. He pulled his knees to his chest, wrapping his arms around them in a futile attempt to feel safe.

"Jesse," Mateo whispered to himself. "Kiko. *Tan Chai.* Somebody, please help me."

He closed his eyes, and in the silence of the cave, he thought he heard Jesse's voice.

"Mateo."

The sound was faint but unmistakable. His heart skipped a beat. *Was it real? Or was his mind playing tricks on him?*

"Mateo!"

This time, the voice was clearer. He turned sharply, his senses on high alert. But instead of seeing Jesse, he saw a figure slowly emerging from the shadows of the cave. Mateo scrambled to his feet, his body tensing for another confrontation.

"Who's there?" he demanded, his voice shaking.

The figure stepped closer, and as it came into the faint light filtering into the cave, Mateo froze. His breath caught in his throat.

"*Tan* Chai?"

Standing before him was *Tan* Chai, her kind, familiar face glowing softly in the dim light. She wore the same clothes she always wore, her rosary dangling gently from her hand. Her smile was warm and reassuring, just as it had always been.

"Yes, my boy. It's me," she said, her voice as gentle as a mother's touch.

Mateo's eyes filled with tears. "You… you're gone."

She nodded, her expression calm. "It was my time, Mateo. But that doesn't mean I'm not here for you."

Mateo's knees buckled, and he sank to the ground, overwhelmed by grief and relief all at once. "I'm scared, *Tan* Chai," he admitted, his voice breaking. "I've been running for so long. Anufat doesn't just want to kill me. He wants to control me. He's trying to break me, to make me give in, and I don't know what to do. I don't even know how I got here."

Tan Chai crouched down in front of him, her smile unwavering. "You're here because Anufat wants you to believe you're alone," she said. "This place feeds on your fear, Mateo. It's not just a jungle - it's a reflection of what's inside you. Anufat knows your doubts, your insecurities, and he's using them against you."

Mateo clenched his fists, frustration boiling up inside him. "That's easy for you to say," he snapped. "You're not the one being hunted. He's a monster, and I'm just... me."

Tan Chai's expression hardened, her eyes narrowing slightly. She reached out and poked his shoulder, just hard enough to make him flinch. "No, Mateo. You're not *just you*. You're stronger than you think. You're surrounded by love, my boy. Look around you."

At first, Mateo didn't understand. He looked around the cave, but all he saw were the same dark, damp walls. "What are you talking about?" he asked, confused.

"Focus," *Tan* Chai urged. "Open your eyes, Mateo. Really open them."

Taking a deep breath, Mateo tried to concentrate. Slowly, the cave walls began to shift and change. The darkness faded, replaced by a warm, golden light. Faces started to appear in the walls - dozens of them, maybe hundreds. Mateo gasped, his eyes widening as he recognized some of them.

"Grandma Annie," he whispered, his voice trembling.

"Grandpa Pedro…"

The faces of his ancestors surrounded him, their expressions kind and protective. Their eyes glowed softly, filled with a love that seemed to radiate warmth. Mateo could feel their presence, their strength.

"We've always been here," *Tan* Chai explained, her voice steady. "Your ancestors have been watching over you since the day you were born. They've protected you, not because of your powers, but because they love you."

Mateo's chest tightened as a wave of emotion washed over him. He had always felt alone, like his ability to see and communicate with spirits had set him apart from everyone else. But now, for the first time, he understood that he had never been truly alone.

Tears streamed down his face as he looked at the faces surrounding him. "Why didn't I see this before?" he asked, his voice breaking.

"Because you let fear blind you," *Tan* Chai said gently. "Anufat thrives on fear. It's his greatest weapon. But love, Mateo - that's your weapon. Love is what gives you strength. It's what connects you to your ancestors, to your friends, to the people who care about you."

Mateo wiped his tears, his heart swelling with a newfound sense of determination. "But how do I fight him? How do I stop Anufat?"

Tan Chai stood, her expression firm. "You don't fight him, Mateo. That's what he wants. He wants you to believe that this is a battle you have to win. But the truth is, Anufat only has power over you if you give it to him.

The more you fear him, the stronger he becomes."

"But I don't know how to stop being afraid," Mateo admitted. "He's so powerful."

"Then start small," *Tan* Chai said. "Take one step at a time. Remember what I always told you - do small things with great love. Start by remembering who you are and where you come from."

Mateo looked around the cave again, his eyes lingering on the faces of his ancestors. He could feel their love, their strength, their unwavering support. It was like a protective shield, wrapping around him and keeping the darkness at bay.

"Okay," he said quietly, more to himself than to *Tan* Chai. "I'll try."

"That's all you need to do, Mateo," *Tan* Chai said, her smile returning. "And remember, you're not alone. You never were."

Before Mateo could respond, the golden light surrounding the cave grew brighter, enveloping everything in its warmth. *Tan* Chai's figure began to fade, her voice echoing one last time.

"We're always with you, Mateo. Always."

As the light consumed the darkness, Mateo felt a surge of strength and clarity. He wasn't sure what lay ahead, but he knew one thing for certain: He wasn't running anymore.

*****

Anufat's voice boomed through the jungle like a thunderclap, shaking the very ground Mateo stood on. The oppressive darkness seemed to close in tighter around him, the air heavy with malice.

"Boy! I smell you!" the spirit snarled, its tone laced with cruel amusement. "And... someone else. Yes, I smell them. Who dares defy me?"

Mateo's heart raced, but for the first time since entering this otherworldly jungle, he didn't shrink in fear. His ancestors' presence surrounded him, their love and strength like an impenetrable barrier between him and Anufat's darkness. Mateo straightened his posture, taking a deep breath.

"You have no power over me, Anufat," he said firmly, his voice echoing in the unnatural silence that followed the spirit's taunt.

A guttural growl ripped through the jungle, followed by a low, menacing laugh. "No power?" Anufat hissed. "Foolish boy. I am power. I am fear. You cannot stand against me!"

From the shadows, Anufat emerged, his form more monstrous than Mateo had ever seen. He stood at least twice Mateo's height, his body cloaked in writhing shadows. His face was a grotesque mix of sharp, jagged features and hollow, glowing eyes that radiated malevolence. Clawed hands twitched with anticipation, as if they itched to tear something apart.

Despite the terrifying sight, Mateo didn't falter. He felt the strength of his ancestors at his back, their whispers of encouragement steadying his resolve.

"You're wrong, Anufat," Mateo said, his voice steady. "Your power comes from fear. And I'm not afraid of you anymore."

Anufat roared, the sound so loud it made the ground quake. Without warning, the spirit lunged at Mateo, moving faster than anything that large should have been able to. Mateo braced himself, but the sheer force of Anufat's attack sent him flying backward.

Pain exploded in Mateo's chest as the spirit's claws raked across him. The sensation was so intense it felt like his entire body was on fire. In the physical world, Mateo's body convulsed violently on the hospital bed. Alarms blared, and nurses rushed into the room, working frantically to stabilize him.

Jesse, who had been sitting by Mateo's side, jumped to his feet in a panic. "What's happening?!" he shouted, his voice cracking with fear.

"We're doing everything we can," a nurse said, her tone urgent but professional. "Please step back!"

Jesse pressed himself against the wall, his heart pounding as he watched Mateo's body writhe uncontrollably. He clenched his fists, helpless to do anything but pray.

Back in the spirit realm, Mateo lay on the ground, gasping for breath. Anufat loomed over him, a cruel smile twisting its monstrous features.

"You are nothing," the spirit spat. "A weak, pathetic child who thinks he can defy me. I will break you, boy.

And when I'm done, you'll beg for my mercy."

Mateo struggled to his feet, every movement sending waves of pain through his body. Despite the agony, he met Anufat's gaze, his jaw set in determination.

"You're wrong," Mateo said through gritted teeth. "I'm not alone."

As if in response to his words, the golden light of his ancestors flared brighter, illuminating the darkness of the jungle. Their faces appeared again, surrounding him in a protective circle. Anufat hissed, recoiling slightly from the light.

"You think they can save you?" Anufat sneered. "They're nothing but ghosts, clinging to a boy who's already mine!"

"They're not just ghosts," Mateo retorted. "They're my family. And they love me. That's something you'll never understand."

Anufat let out an enraged roar, charging at Mateo again. This time, Mateo stood his ground. When the spirit's claws swiped at him, they met the golden barrier formed by his ancestors' light. Anufat howled in frustration as the light burned through his shadowy form.

"You can't control me!" Mateo shouted, his voice ringing with conviction. "You can't break me. You can't take what's not yours!"

The golden light grew brighter, forcing Anufat to stumble back. Mateo felt the strength of his ancestors flowing through him, their love filling him with an unshakable sense of purpose.

"Serve... me!" Anufat screamed.

With one final surge of defiance, Mateo shouted, "NO!"

The light erupted in a blinding flash, consuming everything in its path. Anufat's screams echoed through the jungle as his form disintegrated, the darkness retreating before the overwhelming power of the light.

When the light faded, the jungle was gone. Mateo stood alone in a vast, open space filled with warmth and peace. He could still feel his ancestors' presence, but Anufat was gone.

Meanwhile, in the hospital room, Mateo's body stilled. The alarms stopped blaring, and the nurses paused, their eyes fixed on the monitors.

"He's stabilizing," one of them said, her tone incredulous.

Jesse, who had been holding his breath, let out a choked sob. "Mateo?" he whispered, stepping closer to the bed.

Mateo's eyes fluttered open, his chest rising and falling with shallow breaths. His gaze was unfocused at first, but then it landed on Jesse.

"Matt!" Jesse shouted, a wide grin spreading across his face. "You're awake!"

Mateo tried to speak, but his throat was dry, and his body felt like it had been run over by a truck. He managed a weak smile, his lips forming the word "Jesse."

The nurses quickly swarmed around him, checking his vitals and making sure he was stable. Jesse stepped back, his heart pounding with relief and joy. He watched as they worked, unable to stop smiling despite the tears streaming down his face.

Later, after the nurses had finished their checks and Mateo was resting, Jesse stepped into the hallway to find Kiko waiting for him.

"Well?" Kiko asked, his voice filled with both hope and fear.

"He's awake," Jesse said, his voice cracking. "He's gonna be okay."

Kiko let out a sigh of relief, his shoulders sagging as the tension left his body. He smiled softly, his eyes glistening with unshed tears.

"Maybe *Tan* Chai kicked Anufat's butt in the afterlife," he said with a small chuckle.

Jesse laughed, the sound genuine and full of gratitude. "Yeah," he said, nodding. "She probably did."

The two of them stood in silence for a moment, their shared grief for *Tan* Chai tempered by the joy of Mateo's recovery.

"Come on," Kiko said finally. "Let's go see *Tan* Chai. We owe her everything."

Together, they walked to the room where *Tan* Chai's body rested. As they entered, the atmosphere was heavy with both sadness and reverence. Jesse and Kiko stood by her side, silently paying their respects to the woman who had been a pillar of strength in all their lives.

"Thank you, *Tan* Chai," Jesse whispered, his voice thick with emotion. "For everything."

Kiko placed a hand on Jesse's shoulder, and together, they promised to honor *Tan* Chai's memory by taking care of Mateo and each other.

Back in the hospital room, Mateo lay quietly, his body weak but his spirit stronger than ever. He closed his eyes, feeling the presence of his ancestors and *Tan* Chai's love lingering around him.

For the first time in a long time, he felt at peace.

Chapter 24

A New Light

For the first few days after waking up from his coma, Mateo felt disoriented. His mind floated in and out of focus, and everything around him seemed like a blur. He could hear voices - familiar ones like Jesse's, *Tun* Kiko's, and even Father Rogelio's - but it was like they were far away, muffled. His whole body felt heavy, and the pain was numbed by the strong medication the doctors had him on.

As the fog in his mind started to lift, Mateo slowly became more aware of his surroundings. The sterile smell of the hospital, the steady beeping of machines monitoring his vitals, and the soft hum of fluorescent lights above him all started to register. On the third morning, he opened his eyes fully and blinked, adjusting to the brightness in the room. His head felt like it was stuffed with cotton, but he could make out a figure sitting in the chair beside his bed.

"Jess?" Mateo called out weakly, his voice hoarse and barely audible.

The figure jolted upright, and soon, Jesse's familiar face came into focus. His best friend smiled widely, his eyes brimming with relief. "Matt! Hey! Glad to see you awake, man," Jesse said, scooting his chair closer to the bed. "How are you feeling?"

Mateo tried to sit up but winced at the sharp pain shooting through his body. "I'm good," he replied, though his voice was strained. "Everything hurts. But I'm alive, right?" He managed a weak smile.

"You sure are," Jesse said. "We were starting to think you were going to sleep forever. You were in a coma for four weeks. And even after you woke up, they kept you sedated for another two days because of the pain."

Mateo's eyes widened in shock. "Four weeks? Really? It only felt like a couple of days to me."

"Well, time moves differently when you're in a coma, I guess," Jesse said with a shrug. "A lot's happened while you were out. People are going to have a ton of questions for you when you're feeling better."

Mateo's mind immediately went to the events before his coma. He remembered the jungle, the *taotaomo'na*, and Emily's terrified face. "What about Emily? Is she okay? What happened to everyone else that night?" he asked, his voice filled with concern.

Jesse hesitated for a moment, scratching the back of his neck. "First, I need to say sorry for not being there that night. My grandma had a fall, and I had to stay home to help her."

Mateo shook his head. "Dude, don't apologize. It's a good thing you weren't there. That was the worst *taotaomo'na* experience I've ever had. But... I don't know what happened to everyone else."

"Emily's fine," Jesse reassured him quickly. "She was in shock for about a day, but she bounced back really fast. As for *Tun* Kiko and the firefighters who went with you... it's a different story." Jesse's tone became more serious. "They were attacked. Badly. *Tun* Kiko said the *ga'lågu* - those spirit dogs - went after the firefighters. One of them lost an arm, and the other lost a leg. They're still alive, though. From what I hear, they're grateful they were able to help save the girl, even if it cost them."

Mateo's heart sank. He felt a pang of guilt for what had happened to the men who had come to help. "What about *Tun* Kiko? Is he okay?"

"He's tough as nails," Jesse said with a small smile. "He had some broken bones, but he's been coming by to pray for you. He and *Tan* Chai talked a lot about what happened, and they think Anufat was using Emily as a pawn to lure you into the jungle."

Mateo nodded grimly. "That's exactly what happened. Anufat knew how to get to me. He wanted me alone."

Jesse leaned forward, curiosity written all over his face. "How did you get away? *Tun* Kiko joked that when *Tan* Chai passed, she went and kicked Anufat's butt for messing with you."

Mateo chuckled but quickly winced as pain shot through his ribs. "Don't make me laugh, man. It still hurts." Despite the discomfort, he smiled, picturing *Tan* Chai scolding Anufat in the afterlife. "I did see her, though. She said it was her time to go. Does *Tun* Kiko still come by?"

"Yeah. He should be here soon, actually," Jesse said. "He and I have been taking turns since *Tan* Chai passed. We didn't want you to be alone."

"Good," Mateo said, his voice soft with gratitude. "Stick around for a bit after he gets here, okay? There's a lot to tell, and it'd be better to share it with both of you at the same time."

"Of course, man. I want to hear everything. You know, things got pretty freaky here, too, just before you woke up."

Mateo raised an eyebrow. "What do you mean?"

Jesse leaned back in his chair, his expression serious. "Dude, it was like something out of *The Exorcist*. You were convulsing, coughing up blood, and it looked like your whole body was being squeezed by an invisible hand. We could hear bones cracking. It scared the crap out of me - and the nurses."

Mateo blinked, stunned by the description. "What?"

Jesse nodded. "Oh, and here's the kicker. A patch of your hair turned white."

"What?" Mateo repeated, his voice rising slightly. He looked around the room, searching for a mirror, but couldn't see one.

"It's true. You've got a streak now," Jesse said, smirking. "It's not like a cool Mr. Fantastic look, though. It's more like the *Bride of Frankenstein*. But if you style it right, it could be a racing stripe."

Mateo groaned, half-annoyed and half-amused. "You're ridiculous."

"Hey, I've been saving that one," Jesse said, laughing. "But seriously, man, hurry up and get better. We've got chicken fried rice at Shirley's with our names on it."

Mateo laughed though it hurt. For the first time in a while, he felt like things might be okay.

*****

Once Mateo was strong enough, he shared his experience with *Tun* Kiko and Jesse. He also told Fathers Tony and Rogelio when they came by to visit. They were amazed at what he had lived through. He recounted every detail - the terror of facing Anufat, the love and strength he felt from his ancestors, and *Tan* Chai's comforting presence in the spirit world. They listened intently, their faces a mix of awe and reverence.

"What you went through..." Father Rogelio began, his voice thick with emotion. "It's a testament to the power of faith and love. You've shown us that even in the darkest places, God's light is there."

Mateo felt a deep sense of peace as he listened to their words. He realized he had changed. He wasn't just surviving anymore - he was living with purpose. The fear and doubt that once weighed him down were gone, replaced by a quiet confidence. He felt called to embrace his role as a *suruhånu*, a traditional healer, fully.

When Mateo was discharged from the hospital, he moved into *Tan* Chai's house. The space felt sacred, filled with memories of the woman who had been like a second mother to him. Her shelves were lined with jars of herbs, oils, and tinctures. Her notes and recipes were carefully organized, a treasure trove of knowledge passed down through generations. Mateo vowed to honor her memory by continuing her work.

He had been learning from Kiko as well. Because *Tan* Chai's own son had been killed in Vietnam, she had no other relatives besides Mateo. So, she named him as the sole beneficiary in her last will. Now that he didn't have rent to pay, he could live off of his rental income from Annie's old house as well as from the inheritance left for him by Annie and *Tan* Chai.

Of course, Jesse played an important role in this new chapter of Mateo's life. Together, they began documenting everything Mateo learned - traditional remedies, spiritual practices, and healing stories. Mateo wanted people to understand that healing wasn't about special powers; it was about faith, love, and pure intention.

"Anyone can be a healer," Mateo told Jesse one evening as they worked on their notes. "It's not about what I can do. It's about what we're willing to do for each other."

Jesse nodded. "Still, not everyone can pull off a *Bride of Frankenstein* streak like you."

Mateo groaned. "I hate you."

Mateo kept finding himself reflecting on how *Tan Chai* would quote Mother Teresa. "Do small things to help others but do them with great faith and love. And when times are at their darkest and you feel abandoned or alone, put more faith in God than in your own fear. Have faith that God will do what's best for you, even if it's not what you want, and know that if you're ever called home to God, loved ones who have gone before you will be waiting, for they are always there and always will be."

*****

One Sunday after mass, Father Rogelio approached Mateo as he was leaving the church.

"Mateo, my son, I need your help," the priest said, his tone serious.

"Of course, Father. What's going on?"

Father Rogelio explained that he had tried to bless an abandoned house with a banyan tree on the property. The new owners believed the place was haunted, and strange incidents had occurred during the restoration. "I tried to perform a blessing," the priest admitted, "but... my presence was not welcome."

He rolled up his sleeve, revealing dark bruises on his arm. "The spirit, or spirits, physically resisted me. I need someone with your gifts to help."

Mateo agreed immediately. "I'll help."

As they walked to discuss the plan, Father Rogelio chuckled. "When I left the property, I thought, 'Who are you going to call?' And I realized - it's you."

Mateo laughed, shaking his head. "Really, Father? Even you?"

"Hey, if the shoe fits," Father Rogelio said with a grin.

Together, they prepared to face whatever awaited them. Mateo knew this was just the beginning of his journey as a *suruhånu*, but he felt ready. Whatever challenges lay ahead, he would meet them with faith, love, and a calm resilience that came from knowing he was never truly alone.

Chapter 25

The Future Beckons

Mateo sat quietly outside *Tan* Chai's house, the old wooden chair beneath him creaking as he shifted his weight. The sky had begun its slow descent into darkness, streaked with fading orange and purple hues. The house and its surroundings seemed alive with sounds; the chirp of crickets, the rustling leaves swayed by the gentle breeze, and the faint hum of life in the garden *Tan* Chai had so lovingly cultivated.

This place had become his home, his sanctuary. It was where he felt most connected to the spirits, to the land, and to the people he was called to serve. Sitting there, surrounded by the quiet hum of nature, Mateo allowed his mind to wander.

He thought back to everything that had brought him to this moment: the trials, the losses, and the triumphs. He remembered Annie's kindness, her tragic passing, and how her love had planted the seed of faith within him. He thought of *Tan* Chai's wisdom, her tireless work as a healer, and the lessons she had imparted to him. And of course, there was Anufat, the malevolent spirit who had tested his resolve and nearly cost him his life.

Mateo also thought of the people who had supported him throughout his journey. Jesse, his closest friend, had been a constant source of humor and strength. *Tun* Kiko, with his vast knowledge and quiet courage, had become a mentor. The priests, Father Tony and Father Rogelio, had shared their spiritual insight and never wavered in their belief in him. Even the spirits, those who guided him, protected him, and sometimes challenged him, had played a role in shaping who he had become.

He let out a deep breath, a small smile tugging at the corners of his mouth. "I wouldn't have made it this far without them," he murmured to himself.

The man Mateo was now, felt worlds apart from the man he had been when this journey began. Back then, he had been full of doubt - doubt about his abilities, his purpose, and his place in the world. But those doubts had been replaced with a quiet confidence, born not from arrogance but from a deep sense of faith and understanding.

He had fully embraced his role as a *suruhånu*. While the weight of that responsibility was great, it no longer scared him. Instead, it gave him a sense of purpose. He had learned to balance tradition with his unique gifts, blending the old ways with the spiritual abilities he had come to accept.

Above all, Mateo had come to understand the importance of faith and love. They were the foundation of everything he did. Whether he was preparing a healing remedy, saying a prayer for someone in need, or facing a malevolent spirit, it was his faith and love that guided him.

He revisited some of the key lessons he had learned along the way.

First was the intertwining of the physical and spiritual worlds. By then, Mateo knew that the two were not separate but fused. A physical illness could have spiritual roots, and a spiritual problem could manifest in the physical body. Healing required addressing both sides of the equation.

Second was the importance of surrendering to divine will and trusting the unseen. There had been moments when Mateo felt completely powerless, but those moments taught him to let go of fear and trust in God's plan. Even when he didn't understand why something was happening, he learned to have faith that it was for a reason.

Lastly, Mateo had come to understand the necessity of intention in all acts of healing. It wasn't just about the plants he used or the prayers he said, it was about the love and faith behind them. Healing wasn't magic; it was an act of connection, a bridge between the healer, the person being healed, and the divine.

As Mateo reflected on these lessons, he felt a subtle shift in the air around him. The breeze seemed to carry a different energy now, as though someone unseen had joined him on the porch. He wasn't startled; by now, he was used to the presence of spirits.

"Thank you," he whispered softly. He didn't know exactly who or what was there, but he felt a sense of warmth and reassurance. It was a reminder that he was never truly alone.

The presence lingered for a moment before fading, leaving Mateo feeling both comforted and humbled. He knew this work wasn't about him, it was about serving others, being a bridge between the physical and spiritual worlds.

As peaceful as this moment was, Mateo knew his work was far from over. He had come a long way, but there was still much to learn and do.

For one, he needed to continue honing his healing practices. While he had learned a great deal from *Tan* Chai and *Tun* Kiko, there was still a lifetime's worth of knowledge to master. He also wanted to help others recognize their own spiritual potential. Mateo believed that everyone had the capacity for faith, love, and healing; they just needed guidance to unlock it.

And then there were the challenges he couldn't

predict, new threats, perhaps from other malevolent entities like Anufat. Mateo didn't know what form those challenges might take, but he was determined to face them with courage and faith.

His eyes drifted to the journal sitting on the small table beside him. Jesse had been helping him compile it, filling its pages with notes on traditional remedies, spiritual encounters, and lessons learned. It was a labor of love, and Mateo felt a deep sense of pride every time he flipped through it.

This journal wasn't just for him; it was for future generations. Mateo wanted the knowledge to live on, to inspire others to continue the work of healing and connection. He hoped that one day, this journal would help someone else find their path as a *suruhånu*.

The sound of footsteps pulled Mateo from his thoughts. He looked up to see Jesse walking up the path, carrying a plastic bag that looked like it was filled with food.

"Hey, Matt!" Jesse called out, his usual grin plastered across his face. "I brought some snacks. You can't just live on plants and prayers, you know."

Mateo laughed, shaking his head. "Thanks, Jess. You always know how to ruin a perfectly serene moment."

"Hey, that's what I'm here for," Jesse said, plopping down in the chair next to Mateo. He handed over a container of chicken *kelaguen* and corn *titiyas*, and Mateo's stomach growled in appreciation.

As they ate, the conversation turned to the future.

Jesse, as always, was full of ideas. "So, I've been thinking," he suggested between bites. "We should start teaching other people about this stuff. Like workshops or something. Maybe even write a guidebook; something simple that explains the basics of traditional healing."

Mateo considered the idea. "That's not a bad plan," he agreed. "People need to know that healing isn't just about one person. It's about the whole community coming together with faith and love."

Jesse nodded. "Exactly. And we can make it fun, too. You know, so people don't get scared off by all the serious stuff."

Mateo laughed again. "Leave it to you to turn spiritual healing into a party."

As night fell, Mateo stood up and walked to the small altar inside the house. He lit a fresh candle for *Tan* Chai, bowing his head in silent prayer.

"Thank you for everything," he whispered. "For teaching me, for guiding me, and for believing in me. I'll do my best to carry on your work."

The candle's flame flickered, casting shifting shadows on the wall. For a moment, Mateo thought he saw something in the corner of his eye - a faint outline of a figure. But when he turned, it was gone.

Stepping back outside, Mateo felt the wind pick up. This time, it carried something different. It was colder now, sharper, and there was an edge to it that made the hairs on his arms stand on end.

"Did you feel that?" Mateo asked, glancing at Jesse.

Jesse looked up from his container of food, confused. "Feel what?"

Before Mateo could answer, a faint sound carried on the wind, a low whisper. It was barely audible, but Mateo's sharp senses picked it up.

It wasn't comforting like the spirits who usually visited him. This was something else. Something darker.

"Matt?" Jesse said, his tone more serious now.

Mateo held up a hand, signaling for silence. He listened closely, trying to make out the whispering words. They were unclear, distorted, like a voice trying to speak through water. But one word stood out, unmistakable.

Beware.

The wind died down abruptly, leaving an eerie stillness in its wake. Mateo's heart raced, but he steadied himself with a deep breath.

"Matt... what was that?" Jesse asked, his voice barely above a whisper.

"I don't know," Mateo admitted, his eyes scanning the darkened garden. "But it's not over."

Mateo looked down at the journal in his hands, running his fingers over the cover. The sense of peace he'd felt earlier was gone, replaced by a simmering tension. The spirits had warned him before when danger was near, and he couldn't shake the feeling that something was coming.

He glanced back at Jesse, who was watching him with concern. Mateo managed a small, reassuring smile.

"We'll be ready," he said firmly.

But deep down, he knew the road ahead would not be easy.

As the wind picked up again, carrying the faint sound of distant whispers, Mateo felt the weight of his responsibility settle on his shoulders once more. He stood tall, his resolve unshaken. Whatever lay ahead, he would face it, with faith, with love, and with the knowledge that he was never alone.

The flickering candlelight from the altar caught his eye, and for a moment, Mateo thought he saw a shadow pass across the flame. He blinked, and it was gone.

The wind carried a final whisper, just loud enough for Mateo to hear.

We're watching.

A chill ran down his spine, but Mateo didn't falter.

He smiled faintly, whispering back to the unseen presence, "So am I."

As the night deepened, Mateo sat back down on the porch, the journal resting in his lap. The future beckoned, full of uncertainty and challenges. But Mateo was ready.

This was only the beginning.

From the Author

Hi there, reader!

First and foremost, *un dångkulu na si yu'us ma'ase!* (Thank you very much!) I write my stories as a way to share my CHamoru culture and heritage with the world. I truly appreciate that you have taken interest in this novel. I hope that you enjoyed this story.

There is so much about Guam and the CHamoru culture that most of the world knows little about. For this reason, I have provided a glossary at the end of this book with terms and phrases used in this story.

To take things a step further, I have also decided to provide additional background information on my website to help you better understand the world, culture, and traditions portrayed in this book. I hope you will take the time to visit my website to learn more.

Visit me online at mkaleja.com.

I humbly ask that you also post a review of this book online wherever you buy books. I would love to know what you think. Plus, even just a few words from you could influence other readers to give my book a chance.

Glossary

The following CHamoru phrases are organized based on
the chapters in which they first appear: Please
understand that some spellings may differ between
CHamoru speakers. After centuries of suppression by
colonial forces, efforts to revitalize the CHamoru
language are still ongoing.

Prologue

Phrase	Pronunciation	Translation
makåna	ma-kaw-na	A traditional CHamoru shaman.

Chapter 1

Phrase	Pronunciation	Translation
donne' ti'au	doe-nee tee au	This is a favorite local hot pepper.
Agat	a-gat	This is a village in southern Guam.
Dededo	de-de-doe	This is a village in northern Guam and has the largest population.
Chalan Pågo	cha-lan paw-go	This is a village in central Guam.
Sinajaña	sin-nah-han-nya	This is a village in central Guam.

Chapter 2

Phrase	Pronunciation	Translation
Taotaomo'na	tau-tau-moe-nah	People from before - ancestors.
Ti siña hao humånao	tee see-nya hao hoo-maw-nao	You cannot leave.

Chapter 4

Phrase	Pronunciation	Translation
Hafa adai	ha-fa a-day	Hello

Chapter 5

Phrase	Pronunciation	Translation
Suruhåna	soo-roo-haw-na	A traditional healer. A *suruhåna* is a female healer. A *suruhånu* is a male healer. Typically, the plural form would be *suruhånos*.
nginge'	ngee-ngee	This is a traditional gesture for greeting elders.
Dioste ayudi	dzyos-tee ah-dzoo-dee	God bless you. This is a traditional response by an elder who is greeted with *nginge'*.
nene	neh-nee	This is a term of endearment similar to "sweetie".
Umatac	you-ma-tak	This is one of the southern-most villages in Guam.
Ga'an	Ga-an	This is the name of a river in the village of Agat.

Sumay	soo-maee	This is a former village in southern Guam.
Asan	a-san	This is a village in central Guam.
Piti	pee-tee	This is a village in central Guam.
kakahna	ka-kah-na	A malevolent version of a CHamoru shaman (*makåna*).

Chapter 7

Phrase	Pronunciation	Translation
palai	pa-laee	A topical medicinal ointment often made with a coconut oil base.
Espiritu, påtgon Yu'us este. Sotta put fabot.	es-spee-ree-too, pawt-goon dzoo-oos es-tee. sot-tah put fa-bot.	Spirit, this is a child of God. Please leave her.
Iyo-ku hao på'go.	Ee-dzo-koo hao paw gu.	You are mine, now.

Chapter 9

Phrase	Pronunciation	Translation
Maolek... maolek kannai-ña!	Mao-leck... mao-leck can-naee-nya!	Good... good hands!
Håle' tinanom katso	haw-lee tee-na-nom kaht-soo	This is the root of a medicinal plant used to make *åmot tininu*.
åmot tininu	aw-mut tee-nee-noo	A popular traditional medicine, often in the form of tea.

kalachucha	ka-la-choo-cha	Plumeria flower or plant.
Sigi mågge'	see-gee maw-gee	Come here
Tåya' guaha. *Man familia hit.*	Taw-dza gwa-ha. Man fa-mee-lya hit.	It's okay. We are your family.
Guella yan guello, dångkulu na si Yu'us ma'åse'!	gwe-la dzan gwe-loo, dawng-koo-loo na see dzoo-oos ma-aw-see!	Ancestors, thank you very much!
Guella yan guello, kao sina yu' manule' tinanoum-mu ya yanggen matto hao gi tano'-hu fanule' ha' sin mamaisen.	gwe-la dzan gwe-loo, kao see-nya dzoo ma-noo-li tee-na-no-mu dza dzang-gen mah-too hao gee tan-oo fa-noo-lee ha sin ma-mai-sen.	Ancestors, may I take some of your plants and if you come to my land, just take without asking.

Chapter 10

Phrase	Pronunciation	Translation
Gålak fedda'	gaw-lak fet-da	This is the CHamoru name for the bird's nest fern.
hågon pi'ao	haw-gun pee-ao	bamboo leaves

Chapter 11

Phrase	Pronunciation	Translation
Hagatña	Ha-gat-nya	This is the capital village of Guam.

Chapter 12

Phrase	Pronunciation	Translation
Suha, sigi humånao.	soo-ha, see-gee hoo-maw-nao	Stay away
Adahi. Sa guaha un ya'u.	Sa gwa-ha oon dza-oo	Beware. You have awakened something.
Ti siña hao umiscapa.	Tee see-nya hao oo-mee-sca-pa	You cannot escape.
Hu tungu i fuetsa mu, ya ti atman iyo-ku.	Hoo too-ngoo ee fwet-sa moo, dza tee at-man ee-dzo-koo	I know your power and it will soon be mine.

Chapter 13

Phrase	Pronunciation	Translation
ga'lågu	Ga-law-goo	A *taotaomo'na* that takes the form of a dog.
Iyo-ku hao på'go.	Ee-dzo-koo hao paw goo.	You are mine, now.

Chapter 17

Phrase	Pronunciation	Translation
minaipen chalan	min-aee-pen cha-lan	This is a *taotaomo'na* disease where a *taotaomo'na* can attach to an unknowing carrier who enters a house. Once that carrier makes contact with a child or pregnant woman inside the house, that *taotaomo'na* can make that child or woman

		sick. It is said that the *taotaomo'na* can only cling to the carrier for about 10–15 minutes after they enter the house.

Chapter 18

Phrase	Pronunciation	Translation
rosketti	ro-sket-tee	This is a kind of CHamoru cookie.

Chapter 21

Phrase	Pronunciation	Translation
Guella yan guello, pot fabot dispensa ham. In espipiha y påtgon palaoan ni makoni. Dispensa ham pot fabot ben fan maloffan gi tano' mu.	Gwe-la dzan gwe-lo, put fa-bot dis-pen-sa ham. In es-pee-pee-ha ee pawt-gun pa-la-wan nee ma-ko-nee. Dis-pen-sa ham put fa-bot ben fan ma-lo-fan gee ta-no moo.	Ancestors, please excuse us. We are searching for the little girl who was taken. Please excuse our trespass on your land.

Chapter 22

Phrase	Pronunciation	Translation
Kao makåna hao. Kao un tungo hayi yu?	Kao ma-kaw-na hao. Kao oon too-ngoo ha-dzee dzu?	So you are a *makåna*. Do you know who I am?

Mudoru hao!	Moo-do-roo hao!	You are stupid!
Iyo-ku hao på'go.	Ee-dzo-koo hao paw gu.	You are mine, now.

Chapter 25

Phrase	Pronunciation	Translation
kelaguen	ke-la-gwen	This is a dish where the meat is usually soaked in a lemon mixture with onions, similar to ceviche.
titiyas	tee-tee-dzas	This is the CHamoru word for "tortillas".

Don't miss M. K. Aleja's World War II Paranormal Thriller

Awarded 5 Stars by The Historical Fiction Company, Readers' Favorite, and Literary Titan.

Available Now!
Visit mkaleja.com for more information.